I0579350

HOLLYWOOD ENDINGS

LIZA MALLOY

Copyright © 2020 by Liza Malloy

All rights reserved.

ISBN- 978-1-950478-10-1 (Paperback edition)

ISBN- 978-1-950478-11-8 (Ebook edition)

This copy is intended for the original purchaser of the book. No part of this book may be reproduced in any form or by any electronic or mechanical means, including information storage and retrieval systems, without written permission from the author, except for the use of brief quotations in a book review.

This is a work of fiction. Names, places, characters and events are either products of the author's imagination or used fictitiously. All resemblance to actual events, locations, or persons, living or dead, is purely coincidental and not intended by the author.

To Kara, the girl who only looks sweet and innocent. Thank you for putting up with my antics for 30+ years now. I couldn't have asked for a better sidekick in all of my misadventures in celebrity stalking.

1

———

"You're up next," Ashley said, nudging Courtney with her elbow.

"Up for what?" Courtney delicately sipped her martini. She questioned her selection of a drink that was so easy to spill in a club with standing room only. Sure, it was tasty, but for what she'd paid, it had better be.

Ashley groaned. "It's your turn to get the autograph of the next celebrity we see."

"I wouldn't recognize most celebrities if they stepped on my foot," Courtney replied, eliciting a snort from her roommate, Erica.

"You guys, come on. It's spring break and we are at the coolest nightclub in L.A. Pull it together. Focus on the magazines I gave you to study during the drive."

Courtney cocked her head to the side. She hadn't realized the gossip magazines filling Ashley's car were actually dossiers for memorization. She slurped more of her drink and smiled, feeling the alcohol begin to lighten her mood. Just because she wasn't obsessed with the latest trendsetters in Hollywood didn't mean she wasn't here for a good time. In another week, she'd be back in law school, reading until her head felt like it would explode. So tonight, Courtney needed to let loose and dance.

She gazed around her, stunned by the authenticity of the club's atmosphere. Thick artificial fog streamed from the ceiling. The scarce, bright white tables and chairs glowed in contrast to the dark floors and walls. Silver lights lined the bar, where an excess of overdressed people barked out orders for overpriced drinks. The heavy bass beat of the music, growing louder by the minute, pulsed through Courtney's chest in an unsettling yet invigorating way. It was exactly what she expected from an L.A. nightclub, and she was determined to enjoy it.

She and her friends had anticipated spotting at least one or two celebrities at this Hollywood hotspot, but so far, they'd mostly just watched the monstrous line at the bar. Courtney was fine with that. She was here for the experience, not for snagging some socialite's autograph. For Ashley's sake though, she wouldn't mind a little more excitement.

"Oh my God! Oh my God! Oh my God!" Ashley squealed so loudly that Courtney had no trouble discerning her words over the thunderous music. "It's Justin Erikson!"

Courtney turned right as the strobe lights from the dance floor shifted, casting a clear view of the man. Her breath caught in her throat and she instantly understood the word 'starstruck.' He was talking with another guy, his head tilted so that Courtney could barely see his face under the shadow of his grey flat cap. But, there was not a doubt in Courtney's mind that she was staring at none other than Justin Erikson, the actor, model, and obvious hunk.

She watched, mesmerized, as his friend walked away. Justin glanced up briefly, looking right at Courtney without seeing her at all. He quickly focused back on his phone, his thumb darting rapidly back and forth across the screen. Courtney scraped her teeth across her bottom lip, still staring unabashedly.

"Quick! Go talk to him while he's alone," Ashley said.

Courtney snapped out of her trance. "You're not going to fight me for him?" she asked, only partially joking.

Ashley rolled her eyes. "I'm with Brian now, and it's your turn to get the autograph."

Courtney turned to Erica, who merely shrugged, nudging her thin-rimmed glasses up her nose.

Her heart already fluttered at the prospect of flirting with the cover model from the magazine she'd drooled over the day before. She hadn't seen most of his movies—probably couldn't even name half of them. She couldn't even remember which brand of boxer briefs he modeled, but none of that mattered. Justin Erikson met every component of Courtney's definition of "sexy" and for as tame as her normal life was, she owed it to herself to have some fun while she could.

Courtney started off towards Justin, swallowing nervously. Normally, she felt pretty confident around men, largely because she had nothing to lose if a guy didn't like her. Her focus was law school, not dating. Besides, she wasn't exactly undesirable. She was smart, with shiny hair and clear skin, and, thanks to all the running she did to keep sane during law school, a decent body.

Tonight, Courtney had pulled out all the stops. Between her short black skirt and slinky sleeveless top, Courtney was probably revealing more skin than she was covering up. She wore jewelry and makeup, two things she rarely bothered with in Berkeley, and she was sporting her sexiest lingerie. She had no intention of actually hooking up with a guy, but usually just knowing the caliber of fabric underneath her clothes gave her a little extra bounce in her step.

As she approached Justin, though, Courtney realized her respectable self-esteem only served her well for normal guys. With a man like Justin, all bets were off, and Courtney's nerves knew it. Her feet kept carrying her closer to him, but Courtney panicked, feeling herself transform into an incoherent, desperate fangirl.

Justin turned right as she reached him, making eye contact and grinning. She smiled back, pleased that his prominent dimples, chiseled jaw, and bright blue eyes were every bit as perfect in real life as they appeared in the magazine.

"Hey," he greeted her, his voice deeper than she'd expected.

She froze momentarily, realizing she had no idea what to say to him. "Could I get your autograph?" she finally stammered, her voice coming out like that of a schoolgirl begging for a better grade on an essay.

He laughed and shook his head, his dimples taunting her.

Heat surged to Courtney's face, but she still couldn't look away. Everything about him drew her closer, from his piercing eyes to his thick dirty blond hair peeking out from under the edges of his hat. Even the way he stood, with impeccably perfect posture, made her mouth water.

"How about I get you a drink instead?" he offered, raising his voice so she could hear over the music.

She hesitated. Was he mocking her? He looked sincere, but who was she to judge? Why would he offer to buy a drink for the dork who'd just accosted him in a night club?

He smiled again, raising just one eyebrow before nodding his head toward the bar. "I won't bite. Promise."

Courtney followed him to the bar, laughing at his joke, humorous since Justin was best known for his film portrayal of a zombie werewolf who frequently did bite cute young girls. She turned briefly to see her friends jumping giddily.

"What are you drinking?" he asked, his eyes scanning her body appreciatively.

"Vodka and Sprite," she said, certain she couldn't maneuver another martini to her lips now that her hands were trembling.

Justin held up two fingers to the bartender, who reappeared

with the drinks before she'd even had a chance to catch her breath. Justin grabbed both drinks and carried them over to a table in the corner, where the friend he'd spoken with earlier was seated. As they sat, the guy said something to Justin and left, his phone flush against his ear.

Justin turned to Courtney. "Hi. I'm Justin Erikson."

"I know," she replied with an embarrassed smile, trying to push half-naked magazine images of him out of her mind and focus on the moment. "I'm Courtney Robbins."

He grinned, flashing those dimples again. "Nice to meet you." He removed the stirrer from his drink and tossed it on the table before raising the glass to his lips. Courtney's eyes were drawn to his mouth as he drank. His lips were full and smooth, surrounded by a light layer of impeccably manicured stubble. It was obvious how he'd become so successful in Hollywood—everything about him was hypnotizing. Courtney forced herself to blink, overzealously sipping her drink instead of ogling him.

"So are you from L.A.?" Justin asked, gazing around the room.

Courtney hesitated, panicked that he was already growing bored with her company. "No. I'm from the Midwest, but I'm in law school in Berkeley now."

Justin leaned back in his chair, crossing his arms in a way that made his already prominent biceps bulge even more. "Then what are you doing here?"

"I'm involved with a lot of charity work through the law school, and we had a charity auction a few weeks ago. One of the prizes was a night here." She paused, tucking her hair behind her ear. "I bid on it with some friends."

His eyebrows dipped. "How much is it to get in here?"

"Twenty bucks, but that wasn't the main thing we were auctioning. It's normally really hard to get in here, unless," her voice trailed off.

"Unless what?"

She laughed. "Well, unless you're someone famous."

Now he blushed, which made him even more endearing. "I guess I have noticed that line around the front."

Courtney shrugged. She watched his eyes scan down her body and back up. She wondered what he was thinking, why he was even talking to her. Courtney had seen photos of his last girlfriend, an actress, and knew that even on her best day, she couldn't compete.

"What charity?"

"Huh?"

"The auction. What charity was it for?"

"A women's shelter in Oakland."

"How'd you get involved with that?"

Courtney settled into her chair, finally feeling herself start to relax. Justin had stopped surveying the club, his liquid eyes like an ocean as they stared back at her. "Berkeley has a lot of opportunities for pro bono legal work and other social justice programs. That's really why I wanted to go to law school, to help people."

Justin frowned skeptically. "Pro bono, that's where you do legal work for free, right?" He paused long enough for her to nod. "So you're telling me that you're studying your ass off in law school so you can do work for free?"

Courtney laughed. She sounded like such a dork, and yet somehow, he hadn't left yet.

A waitress stopped by and Courtney glanced at her empty glass. Apparently, she had already emptied her drink. Justin ordered a beer she hadn't heard of, then turned to her. "Another of the same, or you want to switch it up?"

"I'll get what you're having," she replied.

He asked her more about the auction and charity, so she kept talking. Courtney suspected she'd look back on this moment and be horrified that she wasted the one hour of her life she spent with a celebrity yammering on about herself, but she was way too nervous to come up with a cooler topic.

They'd just begun the second round of drinks when Justin made a face. "It's fucking loud in here!"

Courtney nodded in agreement, letting her hair fall across her face.

Justin's friend returned, leaned down to whisper something, then straightened, his hand planted on the back of Justin's chair. Courtney eyed the guy suspiciously, trying to decide if he was an actor too. He was tall and slender, with dark curly hair, and not by any means unattractive. She didn't recognize him from any movies, but Courtney hadn't exactly kept up with any aspect of the entertainment industry since starting law school.

Justin turned to Courtney. "Keith, meet Courtney. Courtney, Keith."

Keith nodded politely but couldn't conceal his boredom. As he leaned in again, Justin scooted his chair to face Keith, and they continued talking. Though less than three feet away, Courtney couldn't hear what they were discussing and got the impression she wasn't intended to hear. But just as she considered excusing herself to give them privacy, Keith stood.

"Later," he called, exiting the club.

Justin turned back to Courtney. "Sorry. What were you saying?"

Honestly, she had no clue. But she was now feeling comfortably tipsy and knew she shouldn't waste what was likely to be her only celebrity encounter. "You want to dance?"

His smile widened, his dauntingly blue eyes lighting up. "I'd love to, but I should get going." He paused just long enough for Courtney to realize she was actually disappointed. "Want to come with me?"

Her stomach lurched. Courtney had never been so thankful

to be seated before, as she was certain her knees would've buckled and dumped her onto the floor if she'd been standing. "Where to?"

"The Retreat," he replied. "I'm staying there for a few nights."

Courtney wasn't familiar with the name, but she assumed it was a hotel. The rational part of her knew it was a terrible idea to leave with a man she'd just met, but she couldn't bring herself to turn him down. She braced herself on the table as she stood slowly. "I, um, I just need to check in with my friends. Do you have a minute?"

He grinned again, clearly pleased by her response, and she hurried over to her friends, peeking behind her every few steps to make sure he hadn't started to leave without her.

"Oh my God!" Ashley squealed as she approached.

Courtney pulled Ashley and Erica in closer. "He wants me to go back to his hotel with him. What do I do?"

Ashley appeared horrified at this question. "You stop talking to us and go with him!"

Courtney turned to Erica, the most rational one of the group.

"Can I seriously hook up with Justin Erikson? I mean, isn't that the sluttiest thing ever?" Courtney asked.

Now Erica smiled. "Well, yeah, but that doesn't mean you shouldn't go for it. When are you ever again going to have the chance to see someone that hot naked? Use protection though... I can't imagine you're the first girl he's dragged home from a club."

Courtney grimaced. What was she thinking? She wasn't the girl who went home from a club with some guy, famous or not. "It's rude to ditch you guys," she said.

Erica pulled her close. "If you don't want to go, don't. But you are not using us as an excuse to miss out on your chance for a wild and crazy night."

"You need a wild and crazy night," Ashley chimed in. "This night might be all you have to keep you going through countless hours of Land Use treatises when we return to school."

Courtney giggled at that thought. "I want to go," she admitted. "I've never gone home with some guy I just met though."

Erica glanced past her. "Stop stalling and go. He's not going to wait forever."

Courtney turned to see Justin gazing in her direction. He was smiling, but it was a bored, practiced smile, not the genuine grin from earlier. She took a deep breath, and returned to him.

A car waiting outside took them to the hotel. It was a short drive, but Courtney was too nervous to stop herself from chattering.

"Do you like living in L.A.?" she asked, regretting the question as soon as the words left her mouth. While she hadn't technically left a bar with a guy she'd just met before, Courtney suspected the traditional protocol involved making out on the ride to the hotel, not discussing real estate.

"Yeah. I think I'd enjoy living New York too, but this is definitely where I need to be for work now." He typed a quick text on his phone. "So you're from the Midwest?"

"Indiana." She inhaled deeply through her nose, now acutely aware of the tantalizing scent of his cologne that had been undetectable in the crowded club.

He set down his phone and glanced over at her. "I'm from Indiana."

"I know," she said with a blush, wishing she had the tact to pretend to be surprised instead. She didn't want to creep him out by letting him think she was a stalker. She normally didn't memorize celebrity hometowns, but she'd read the article about him in Ashley's magazine just the day before, so it was still fresh in her mind.

"What brought you to Berkeley?"

"I heard one of the faculty members give a talk on the economics of environmentalism a few years back and it intrigued me. Plus it's a good program."

The car slowed to a stop. Justin thanked the driver and slipped sunglasses on before stepping out of the car. Courtney wasn't sure the sunglasses were the best disguise, as they did nothing to hide his famous 6'1 perfectly muscled physique. He led her through the lobby and straight up to the fifteenth floor, Courtney pinching the inside of her wrist to make sure she wasn't dreaming.

~

JUSTIN FLICKED on the light switch as they entered the suite. It was noticeably tidier than he had left it; a sizable perk of hotel life. "Make yourself at home," he offered, gesturing to the couch.

Courtney's lips curved upwards. There was something so innocent in her smile, it was contagious. Even her eyes, bright blue and sparkling, seemed to lack that jaded skepticism that he'd come to expect from women.

"How old are you?" he asked, in a sudden panic. Out of habit, he had already begun unbuttoning his shirt. Once he was in for the night, he couldn't stand to remain in the clothes he'd had on earlier.

"Twenty-four," she replied, not bothering to ask his age. He wondered if she already knew that he had just turned twenty-six.

"Sorry, I need to change," he mumbled, pulling his tee shirt over his head and throwing it onto the armchair with his other shirt and then heading into the bedroom to grab a new shirt. He returned quickly, eager to see Courtney's reaction to his little striptease.

Courtney smiled, but not the aroused smile he was anticipating—it was more of a bemused smirk, like she was trying not to laugh at him.

"What's so funny?"

"Do you own any other brand of clothes?"

Justin glanced down. He knew what his undershirt and boxer briefs were, but as it happened, his jeans were the same brand tonight too. "I'm contractually obligated to wear the shirts and boxers. The rest I just like." He paused, then added, "Plus it's free."

"Wait, they actually wrote in your contract what kind of underwear you have to wear?"

He laughed. It did seem odd when she said it aloud, but after all, he was a representative of the company. "I guess it's only required in public."

"You're not in public now," she reminded him.

"I could take it all off if it bothers you," he joked, reaching his hand towards his waistband as though he were about to strip.

She stepped back, suddenly seeming uncomfortable. "Could I use your bathroom?"

He nodded, pointing the way. He was starting to regret inviting her back there. Their entire encounter since leaving the club had been awkward.

Usually, Justin could read women. He could tell if they wanted him, and in what way. He had plenty of fans who liked to flirt with him, and nothing else, but usually those were the unavailable ones. Single girls who flirted with him generally expected sex, probably just for the experience of fucking a celebrity, but whatever. So far, he didn't mind being used, and he knew he should consider himself lucky that most women he hooked up with didn't expect anything from him afterwards.

With Courtney, though, he wasn't sure what she was up to. She was clearly a fan—she had asked for his autograph, and why else would she come back to his hotel if not for sex? But now, Justin couldn't tell if she was just nervous or playing hard to get.

Justin made his way to the bar. He opened the fridge and, after contemplating the options, pulled out a beer. He considered mixing another vodka and soda for Courtney but didn't, unsure if she'd want another. She popped out of the bathroom then, looking more nervous than before, but with her long dark hair brushed smooth and a fresh layer of makeup.

"Can I fix you a drink?" he offered, his glance darting down to her chest.

She stepped closer, then stopped. "Look, I'm sorry, but I can't sleep with you," she blurted out.

Justin heard the chuckling before he realized it was his own. At least she'd answered his question.

Courtney appeared flustered at this reaction, but continued. "It's not that I don't want to, it's just that I never sleep with guys I've just met, and I can't make an exception just because you're you and I have a huge crush on you."

Justin ran his tongue over his teeth. *Women are so strange*, he thought. "Boyfriend?"

"No."

"Well, fine, I wasn't going to sleep with you anyway." He plopped down onto the couch and slung his feet up onto the coffee table. He kicked his shoes off and waited for her to make the next move.

She paused awkwardly. "Why not?"

He laughed, loving that she had the nerve to sound offended when he'd merely said the same thing she had. "Look, I know what you may think of me, but I don't know you. And I don't want my private life ending up in a tabloid. How do I know you wouldn't run straight to Twitter if we slept together?"

"I could do that anyway," she said.

"But you'd be lying," he replied, gauging her expression. "And besides, you wouldn't."

"Then why did you invite me back here?"

He opened his beer. "To talk. It was noisy at the club, and my agent would kill me if I stayed out late again."

"Why would your agent care?"

"I have a photo shoot Tuesday morning. Apparently I looked tired at my last one."

She nodded. "So you need to sleep now?"

He shook his head. "Not tired. But I'm also not interested in a lecture from my agent. If I'm not out in public, he can't monitor my bedtime."

She relaxed noticeably. "May I?" she asked, gesturing to the bar.

He nodded, standing to mix her a drink. "So why did you agree to come back here with me?"

She laughed. "You mean if I wasn't going to have sex with you?"

He grinned.

"Maybe I considered it initially," she finally admitted.

"Ouch!" he replied. "What did I do to make you change your mind?"

Her bold blue eyes widened. "Nothing! I just, I don't know. I don't normally do that anyway, and if I'd done it, it would've been just because you're famous, and you deserve better than that."

Justin wasn't sure how to respond to a hot girl telling him he "deserved better" than casual sex. He wasn't accustomed to that level of honesty in L.A. He returned to his spot on the couch. Courtney followed and tentatively sat beside him. Justin glanced at the fleshy part of her thigh peeking out from beneath her skirt, wondering if the fact that she claimed she wouldn't have sex with him would make him want her more.

After a long pause, she spoke again. "Is it weird that I told you I have a crush on you?"

"A little."

"Sorry. I'd think you'd be used to that by now."

He didn't want to admit that no one over the age of fifteen had ever admitted to having a crush on him, at least not to his face anyway. "It's mostly just strange when someone else knows stuff about me and I don't know anything about them," he said finally.

"Well, what do you want to know?"

He shrugged.

"Okay, well, I'm in my second year of law school, and I'm focusing on public interest law. I'd love to do some work for a women's shelter, or if that doesn't work out then maybe a legal aid clinic or housing department. I love running, hate that there aren't any real sports teams in Berkeley, and I drive a Camry but really want a new car for graduation. I'm oddly obsessed with BMWs but I'm absolutely going to buy something more practical."

She paused, but then continued when he didn't speak. "I can't stand red wine or horror movies and my favorite thing about California is the ocean. I don't know how anyone gets any work done in L.A. ever—it's so beautiful I'd think you'd all just wander along the boardwalk day and night."

He smiled sleepily. "Tell me more about law school."

She obeyed, but Justin found himself tuning out her words and simply watching her as she spoke. There was something intriguing about the way she absentmindedly twirled her dark hair around her finger, scrunched her toes together every few minutes, and drew miniature circles in the air with her feet. He could tell she wasn't from L.A., and even that she hadn't been in California long. There was still something fresh, innocent about her. He just couldn't quite put his finger on what that was.

"I'm boring you," she suddenly exclaimed, starting to look tired herself. "And you said you had to get to bed, right?"

He glanced down at his phone. It was well after one o'clock in the morning, but he didn't feel like sleeping yet. Aside from Keith, Justin didn't have any real friends in L.A. who weren't also actors, and he couldn't remember the last time he talked with someone who wasn't preoccupied by the entertainment industry. Justin found this girl so refreshing that he just wanted to keep listening to her melodic voice. Besides, he knew if she left now, he'd be disappointed. After watching her lips move for the last hour, he at least needed to kiss her, just to see what it was like.

He'd been mostly telling the truth earlier, when he'd said he didn't plan to have sex with her when he invited her back to the hotel. Sure, he had realized it was a possibility, and he knew himself well enough to admit that if she had insisted, or, hell, even offered, he wouldn't have refused. But in all honesty, he really had just wanted someone to talk to. Someone who wasn't blathering on about her own modeling career or her new highlights or some crap like that.

As she stood, Justin realized he hadn't answered her. Instinctively, he reached his hand out and grabbed hers, pulling her back onto the couch. Thankfully, she sat a little closer this time.

"Stay," he commanded. "So is there anything else you wanted to know about me?"

She considered this briefly before speaking. "Is that your real eye color and how many pushups can you do at one time?"

He licked his lips, trying to tame the smile spreading across his face. "Yes. When they're brown, red, yellow or black in movies, it's contacts. The blue is all natural. And as for the pushups, I don't know. I could try, if you care to count?"

She giggled. "Why are you staying in a hotel?" She settled

back onto the couch, letting his arm graze the side of her shoulder.

"I'm having the house painted and I didn't want to mess with the fumes."

"What color?"

"Stone Harbor."

She raised an eyebrow.

"It's like a slate grey, with a hint of green. The whole house was beige before."

"Do you live alone?"

He shook his head. "Na, my entourage is there, too." He laughed. "I'm just kidding. I have no entourage. Did you watch that show? I loved it."

She shrugged. "I've seen it some. I honestly don't have a lot of time to watch TV. And I don't even have a TV at the moment."

He couldn't imagine a person not owning a television, but decided not to comment on that. "I have one roommate, Keith. You met him earlier, at the club. He's been my best friend since high school, and he moved out here a few years ago. Now he's my manager."

She nodded, then grew quiet. He gazed down at her, eying her slinky tank top that drooped pleasantly low in the front and nearly to the top of her tight low-rise skirt in the back. He guessed she didn't wear that type of outfit frequently, but she pulled off the look perfectly. She was thin, but not unnaturally so like most of the girls he'd been around lately, and she was curvy and muscular in all the right places, in all the right amounts.

"Are you cold?" he asked, realizing she was running her hands up and down her arms. He was always too warm, so he tended to overdo it on the A/C. He didn't wait for her to answer, instead offering his arm and scooting closer. Courtney started to say something, but he wasn't listening anymore. Her neck was only inches from his face. Her skin smelled deliciously of vanilla and her throat pulsed gently as her heart sped up. Before he realized what he was doing, his lips were on her neck.

She turned slightly, and his mouth found hers immediately. Her kiss was stronger than he had expected —more needy, more passionate, and much less reserved. He tasted her fruity lip balm and then a hint of alcohol on her tongue as it brushed against his own. He shifted, pulling her with him until her body was stretched out across his, lengthwise on the couch. She acquiesced easily to his touch and he relaxed, no longer as uncertain about her attraction to him. Justin let his hands wander down to her thighs, squeezing the firm length of her leg, and allowed his fingers to inch slowly back up her thighs, past the hem of her skirt, before he pulled them back.

He felt her hands on his shoulders and biceps and was thankful, yet again, that he spent two hours in the gym most days. Justin sensed that she was rethinking her earlier insistence on not sleeping with him, and while he loved that she was second guessing that decision, he didn't want her to change her mind. If they hooked up now, he suspected he'd never see her again.

She moaned quietly and he instinctively plunged his hands up her shirt, caressing her back and sides, struggling to reach anything else while her body was pinned against his. Justin grabbed her thigh, lifted her up to a seated position, and reached for her shirt again, but she stopped him, her hand subtly squeezing his. He kissed her one more time, then let his head drop, his forehead beside her lips.

Courtney didn't speak. Justin took this as a sign she was still debating. His body told him to forge onward, but instead he paused, focused on his breathing, and leaned back. She scooted back to her position beside him, tugging her skirt back down over her thighs. He glanced furtively in her direction and saw her biting her lip anxiously.

"Sorry," he mumbled.

She blushed. "No, don't be. Really."

He grinned and patted her thigh. She stood slowly. "I should probably go, though."

She said it so tentatively that Justin knew she didn't want to.

"It's late," he said. "You could just stay."

She turned and made eye contact. He realized her eyes were bright, bright blue, almost a mirror image of his own, but hers contrasted seductively with her dark brown hair.

"I can call you a cab if you want. But you're welcome to stick around." He flashed his most charming grin, the one he used to reserve for sales pitches in the linens department of his home-town department store, and added, "I promise I'll keep my hands to myself."

"But you need your sleep."

He shrugged. "I'm a night owl anyway. But if it'll make you feel any better, I'll sleep." He stood, motioned for her to follow, then made his way to the adjacent bedroom. A single bedside lamp cast a soft, dim glow across the room. He unbuckled his belt and tossed it across the room. Then he lifted his shirt up over his head, slowly like he did in the ad campaigns, and stepped out of his jeans. When he turned back to face her, wearing nothing but his boxer briefs, she was visibly flushed. She opened her mouth to speak, but no words came out.

He flashed his most playful smile, then climbed onto the bed, slipping his legs under the thin sheet. She didn't move. "I can't sleep with you standing there," he teased. "Come on, get in."

She smiled and stepped closer. "I can't sleep in this," she insisted.

"Then don't," he said, leaning forward until he could reach

her hand and pulling her to the side of the bed. She sat beside him, tentatively, and he switched off the lamp before slowly lifting her shirt up over her head. It was dark enough that he couldn't see her expression, but she didn't protest, so he reached around, and unzipped the skirt. She stood, shimmied out of the skirt, then walked around the bed, climbing in on the other side.

"You are bad," she chastised him playfully.

"So is that why you're so far away?"

"I don't trust myself to get any closer," she admitted.

He groaned. Hearing that only made him want her more. He started to inch his way closer when a pillow suddenly appeared directly between them. He paused, momentarily confused. "Oh, so it's going to be like that, huh?"

"Hey, I'm just trying to protect your public reputation," she said, her voice sexy in a way he sensed she hadn't intended. She was quiet for a moment before resuming the friendly banter. "How did you end up in L.A. if you grew up in the Midwest?"

Justin rolled onto his back. He knew the answer to this one in his sleep. The how-did-you-get-your-start-question was a frequent favorite of the interviewers, except for the late night hosts, who tended to stick to the raunchier topics. The truth was that he'd been blessed with athleticism, charm, and dimples; a triple threat he used to get everything from the highest sales commissions at his after-school job to a full ride at U.C.L.A. (which he promptly turned down). He'd gotten a minor role in the first film he'd ever auditioned for. There wasn't much acting involved in his part, less than five pages of actual lines, but a lot of athleticism. It wasn't a high budget film, so the producers couldn't pay a stunt man to do the gymnastics, hockey, soccer, and football tricks required for his role.

Next, Justin had snagged a role in an independent flick, filmed entirely overseas, which was, so far, his favorite movie he'd been in. While filming that in Indonesia, he'd been asked to start modeling men's underwear. His instinct had been to say no, he had never dreamed of being that kind of a model, but his agent had persuaded him. Within a year, he was modeling everything from jeans and undershirts to boxers and briefs. He filled in the gaps in his schedule with small temporary roles on TV shows, commercials, or music videos.

And then he filmed *Days' End*, the movie that would change his life.

He hadn't predicted the popularity of the film series, not even having bothered to read for the lead role even though he'd been asked. In truth, Justin was satisfied with the supporting role, but he regretted not even having tried for the lead. *Days End* was a success overnight, and was followed by three more in the series. His role grew larger in each, as did his fan base. By the time the second movie of the series came out, Justin couldn't go in public without being blinded by the lights of cameras or groped by random women.

Of course, one could learn all of that from a basic internet search, something he'd gradually grown less accustomed to doing after his publicist took the reins. What fewer people knew was that he had read for more than twenty films that he didn't subsequently get an offer from, or that the first agent he'd approached had told him his ears were crooked and suggested he look into professional wrestling instead.

Justin realized he hadn't answered her question and wondered how much of the truth she wanted, or how much she already knew anyway. He opted to provide the short answer. "I was always interested in acting, and my mom let me get involved with modeling in high school. I was big into sports, so I figured I'd go to college on athletic scholarship, but I deferred a year to try out acting and decided that was a better fit for me than college."

"What sports did you play?"

He laughed. "Almost all of them. Football, rugby, lacrosse, basketball, wrestling. I did some gymnastics, swimming, skateboarding and snowboarding too, but not at school."

"Do you still do all that?"

"I wish. I don't have a lot of time now, and I'm not supposed to risk any injuries with my current filming schedule."

"You obviously still work out."

"I have a trainer," he admitted. "Lots of weight lifting and boxing. Some running. Nothing too exciting."

"Were your parents supportive when you started acting?"

He pictured the expression on his mom's face when he first told her his plans to move to L.A. He had honestly wondered at the time if she would lock him in the house just to keep him from going. "They wanted me to follow my dream, and I could tell they were really proud, but my mom especially wasn't thrilled about me moving away. My older brothers had all gone to college or the military and everyone assumed I'd follow the same path."

Courtney laughed. "Both of my older brothers moved away for grad school and my parents were fine with it, but when I said I planned to go to Berkeley, they were crushed. It was like they didn't care if my brothers left, but for me to go was some sort of personal attack."

Justin tried to picture Courtney's brothers, envisioning male versions of her. "Do you have any sisters?"

"No. You?"

"No. So are both of your brothers lawyers?"

"Nope. My oldest brother got his MBA and lives in New York doing investment banking stuff now and my other one is in med school in Chicago. He still has a while till he graduates."

"Are you close with your brothers?"

"I don't know. We were, growing up, but now I don't see them very often. Eric, the one in med school, is only a year older and we both went to the same undergrad, but we haven't kept in touch as much since he started med school." She exhaled, and Justin again wished he could see her more clearly in the dark room. "What about your brothers? Are you still close?"

Justin laughed. "I have five of them, but yeah, we're still pretty tight. We've got very different lives now, but it still works."

"Are they still in Indiana?"

"Well, the two in the military move around a lot. My youngest brother is in college now at IU, the oldest lives in South Bend and Rob is in Indianapolis at med school." He paused, wondering how best to explain how little he had in common with his brothers now. "They all wanted to stay pretty close and help out my mom. And three of them are married already, so, I don't know. It's just different."

"I had no idea you were such a fascinating guy," Courtney replied, her fingers casually tickling his forearm. He grinned, and slowly inched his arm up until her hand rested atop his own.

They kept talking, mostly about their respective pilgrimages to L.A., with the pauses in their discussion growing longer and longer as they both grew drowsy. At some point, Justin realized he was no longer distracted by the fact that a hot girl was in bed with him and that they were literally just talking. Eventually, they both slept.

2
___

When Courtney first opened her eyes, she saw traces of light streaming in through the gap in the curtains. For the briefest of moments, she forgot whose hotel room she was in. She startled when it came back to her, not fully trusting her memory until she turned slowly to her side.

As her eyes focused, Courtney inhaled sharply. There beside her, sprawled out on his stomach, was Justin Erikson. The sheets were pushed down to his waist, revealing the top band of his boxers, the precise logo that had made him famous and undoubtedly rich. Even as he lay there motionless, Courtney could see each distinct muscle in his hips, back, and shoulders. His left arm was stretched over his head, blocking her view of his face. She had an overwhelming urge to run her fingers along his smooth, tanned skin or to touch his wispy dark blond hair.

"Oh my God," she mouthed silently, forcing herself to exhale and then breathe normally so she wouldn't pass out before he awoke. Just then, his arm twitched, and his eyes popped open.

Justin grinned, pushing himself up on his elbows. "Morning, sunshine."

"Morning," she mumbled back, embarrassed at how breathless she sounded.

He climbed out of bed and went into the bathroom. Courtney sat up and glanced around for her clothes, debating whether she even had time to get dressed before he returned. She started to lean over the bed to grab her skirt when she heard the toilet flush. Panicked, she lay back down, and a minute later, Justin reappeared from the bathroom. He disappeared momentarily into the main room of the suite, and returned carrying two bottles of water. He tossed one to her, drank from the other, and playfully tumbled back onto the bed.

"How'd you sleep?"

She smiled and sipped the water. "Terrible," she confessed.

He laughed, seemingly appreciating her honesty.

She nodded and brushed her hair out of her face, certain she was the first woman he'd slept with that hadn't had the sense to reapply makeup and brush her hair and teeth before he awoke. "You make me nervous."

"I do?" His expression was so innocent, so surprised. It reminded her of a puppy dog.

Courtney tilted her head in disbelief. He had to know, didn't he? "How am I supposed to relax enough to sleep when I'm inches away from this..." she gestured at his body. Now he was stretched out on his side, his head propped up on his hand. His chest muscles popped out even more with his weight on his elbow, and she was fairly certain she'd seen an ad where he was in that precise position. "I mean, you look like a statue of a Greek god."

She glanced back up to his face, and saw that he was blushing. She wondered where her comment ranked on the list of Top 100 Things Not to Say to a Celebrity.

Justin apparently didn't mind, though, because as soon as

she finished taking another nervous sip of water, he inched closer. "You look cold," he commented, his voice a mere whisper.

Courtney realized she'd pulled the sheet and blanket up to her neck, more out of modesty than anything else. Still, she didn't want him to think she was a nun, so she lied. "A little."

Thankfully, that was the right response. He climbed over on top of her and gently lowered himself down onto his forearms, his face maybe an inch from hers. Courtney felt her heart racing the second his body began to press against hers. She wanted to panic, to freak out that she hadn't brushed her teeth and that she was still sporting the same panties she'd worn to a dance club the night before. But this morning, Courtney couldn't even focus on that. Instead, the only thought running through her head over and over was "Oh my God."

He relaxed onto her further, bringing his mouth to hers for a kiss, and Courtney suddenly felt her body temperature rocket up. She wanted to savor the moment, to forever remember the sensations of the weight of his perfect body sinking into her. But then, she heard a buzzing, and Justin pulled his mouth back, groaned, and climbed off of her.

He grabbed his phone from its spot on the nightstand. "What?" he growled.

Courtney wondered if he answered all of his calls that way.

She could hear a woman's voice on the other line. Courtney considered whether it could be a girlfriend, realizing with shame that she hadn't even asked if he had one. She watched Justin's expression for clues, but he just looked irritated.

"I don't fucking remember," he finally said, flinging his hand in the air as though the caller could see him. "Why does it even matter what I wear when I walk my own damn dog?"

The voice on the other line grew louder, more agitated. Finally, he interrupted. "Fine. Send me the photo. I wanna see." He clicked off the phone and rolled his eyes. Then he stared at the phone for a minute until it beeped and quickly pulled a photo on the screen. Courtney peered over his shoulder. It was a picture of him wearing sweatpants and a white tee shirt, jogging with a large German Shepherd. He ran his fingers along the screen until the photo zoomed in on his crotch. He squinted at it before tilting the phone to Courtney.

"What do you think?" he asked. "Can you tell if I'm wearing anything under the sweats?"

Courtney burst into laughter, not in a million years having expected that to be his crisis. His expression remained serious though, so she stifled her laughs and peered closer at the photo. "I don't know," she said. "It's hard to say." With the photo zoomed, Courtney's best guess was that no, he wasn't wearing anything under the sweats, but she sensed that wasn't the right answer.

He tossed his phone back to the nightstand and sighed. "I was totally wearing boxers. Their fucking boxers," he insisted. "Why would I go commando on a jog? No one does that."

She wasn't sure what to say. Courtney had never considered how annoying it would be to have someone secretly photographing you at any given moment, only to have another group of people openly critiquing and questioning you based on what the photo may or may not show.

"Was that your agent?"

He shook his head. "Publicist. She saw the photo and the internet comments first. My agent will get it later today, and I'm sure I'll get to sign some delightful statement assuring the company I'll never go for a jog without wearing their briefs under my clothes."

"I'm sorry," she mumbled. "That sucks."

He nodded, seemingly focusing on maintaining the serious expression on his face. Then, he shook his head. "I need to eat," he announced, reaching for the hotel phone. "What do you want?"

She panicked, momentarily forgetting what she normally did eat for breakfast. "Um, toast, fruit?"

Justin was already ordering food—lots of it, it seemed, and then he hung up and turned to face her. "You eat carbs?"

She tried to ignore his expression of disbelief and simply nodded instead. "Yeah, I'm out of place in L.A."

He smiled, then his expression turned serious. "Where was I?" he asked, his voice suddenly deep.

Courtney's heart fluttered as she let him push her flat onto her back and climb back on top of her. She had just started to lose herself in the kissing again, when his phone rang. Justin pulled back, thrust his head onto her shoulder, kissed it, and tried unsuccessfully to reach the phone without rolling off of her. Determined, he lifted her, and they both rolled onto their sides. He grabbed his phone, glanced at the screen, then set it on the bed beside him.

"They can wait," he mumbled, going in for another kiss.

She felt him tugging at the sheets she'd wrapped around herself like a robe. Unable to think rationally, or to stop herself, she helped him. As soon as his bare stomach touched hers, Courtney heard a quiet moan escape her throat. She tried to get control of herself, but she couldn't, and instead of pushing him back like she thought she should, she reached her hand around him and pressed him closer to her, nervously groping the ass he'd made a career out of.

Just as Courtney was shifting to let Justin's eager hand reach between them, another noise interrupted them. Courtney initially thought it was his phone again, but then realized it was a knocking at the door.

Justin laughed. "Perfect timing, huh." He stood up, grabbed a robe from the bathroom, then started out. He paused and turned to her. "If you could stay in here until they're gone," he began. She nodded, unsure if she should be offended that he didn't want to risk anyone seeing her.

She took the opportunity to sneak into the bathroom and assess herself. She grabbed the second robe hanging on the door, brushed her hair, washed her face, and swished some mouthwash. She left the bathroom right as she heard a man say, "Thank you Mr. Danes. Have a good day."

Courtney waited until she heard the lock on the door click, and then she poked her head around the corner. She immediately noticed her shoes had been hidden behind the bar. She had to wonder how often Justin did this, to have become so adept at pretending to be alone in his room. "Who's Mr. Danes?"

He laughed, uncovering the various platters. "It's my undercover name."

Courtney laughed, wondering what the point was when everyone recognized you anyway.

"I've got a few others," he added.

"How did you come up with them?"

He shrugged and motioned for her to sit. "Well, Chris Danes is a combination of my older brother's first name with his wife's maiden name."

She smiled. "That's sweet."

"Most of them are combinations of my brother's names, used as last names. I can be Mr. Michaels, Mr. Lucas, Mr. Scott, you know. Makes it easier to keep track of."

He scooted a plate of dry toast towards her, following with a massive plate of fruit, some of which were so exotic she couldn't even identify them with certainty. Courtney tentatively spread blackberry preserves on the toast while watching Justin begin to eat. He approached his food hungrily, and ate quickly. There were two large plates containing egg white omelets, a smaller plate of turkey sausage, a small pitcher of milk, and two mini boxes of frosted flakes.

"Do you eat that much every day?" she asked, not realizing until the words had been spoken that they might be offensive.

"Most days," he admitted. "I'm on a high protein diet." He scooted one omelet plate, already emptied, under the other before gesturing to the cereals. "Don't tell my trainer about that, though."

Courtney considered this, envying that he could—no had to—consume that much food and still maintain the perfect physique.

"When do you head back to Berkeley?" he asked, interrupting her thoughts.

"Later this week sometime. We're on spring break now, so there's no real rush. We just planned on sticking around until we got bored," she replied, suddenly realizing her friends were probably wondering what happened to her. "When do you go back to your house?"

He considered this. "Well, assuming the painting is done, probably tomorrow. But they were supposed to finish while I was gone anyway, so who knows if they'll get it done this time." He grimaced. "I came straight here from New York, haven't been home in two weeks."

"You travel a lot?"

He wolfed down the rest of the sausage, stacked the three empty plates back on the room service tray, and turned to his cereal. "Yeah. The modeling work is mostly local. The interviews and press junkets are about fifty-fifty, L.A. or New York, and if I'm doing a movie, we shoot wherever. I've spent less than a hundred nights at my house since I bought it nearly a year ago, and my schedule for the next six months is even worse."

He said it so matter-of-factly that it quickly dispelled some of the glam. For a moment, Courtney forgot that she was sitting there, wearing virtually nothing but the plushest bath robe she'd ever touched, with an underwear model-turned-movie star. It was almost like an ordinary day, between two equals.

"I love traveling, though. I pick a lot of movies based on where they're filming." He wiped his lips with a crisp white napkin. "What do you and your friends have planned for the rest of your trip?"

"I don't know. Any recommendations?"

He went over his list of favorite L.A. spots while they finished eating. When they were done, he glanced obviously at the clock. Courtney assumed this was her cue to leave.

"Do you mind if I make a quick call? I just want to check in with my friends."

He nodded and headed into the bathroom while she dialed.

Ashley answered immediately.

"Hey," Courtney greeted her, as though nothing out of the ordinary was going on, "I can't talk long, but I just wanted to check in and tell you I'd be back to the hotel probably in a little while." She covered the phone's tiny speaker as Ashley shrieked. "I gotta go, Ashley. See you soon," she mumbled, hanging up as Justin returned wearing athletic shorts and socks. His shorts, she noted, were deliberately placed on his hips so the brand name and logo was clearly visible.

"I have to meet my trainer at 2," he explained.

Courtney panicked, realizing she had no idea what time it was. She glanced at the clock, surprised that it was nearly 11. "Right, well, I can get out of your hair. Thanks for breakfast."

He nodded, expressionless, and she hurried into the bedroom to gather her clothes. She dressed in the bathroom, cringing as she put her stretchy tank top back on, the distinct odors of alcohol and sweat permeating the thin fabric. When she left the bathroom, Justin was seated on the bed, facing her. He was holding a black tee shirt.

"Here," he said, tossing the shirt to her. "That has to be better than wearing your shirt again," he guessed, as though he'd been reading her mind.

She nodded, relieved, and quickly debated returning to the bathroom to avoid changing in front of him. But before she could move, Justin popped up and was at her side. "I'll help," he whispered, lifting the shirt over her head and moving in for a kiss before she could get the other one on. Courtney felt the tee shirt slip out of her hands and onto the floor, all of her body's muscles weakening at his magnetic touch. They kissed slowly, Courtney's lips eagerly pressing into his as her body relaxed further and further into his arms. She couldn't remember ever enjoying a simple kiss this much and couldn't imagine ever breaking her lips away from his.

But then, there was a knock at the door. Courtney prayed he hadn't heard it, that he'd just keep kissing her, but instead, he groaned.

"No idea who that could be," he mumbled, heading to the door. Courtney quickly pulled his tee shirt on, lamenting that he'd offered her a clean one instead of one that bore any hint of his scent.

"Crap," Justin muttered. He turned to Courtney right before opening the door. "Sorry," he told her. The moment the door swung open, a waifish woman with long, wavy hair sauntered into the room.

"I heard you were staying here," she began, removing the oversized blue sunglasses shielding her face. "Were you not going to call me?"

"Wasn't planning on it," Justin replied.

Courtney remained frozen where she stood, but closely eyed the woman. She immediately recognized her from a weeknight network TV drama but couldn't recall the actress's name. She dressed just like her character, in a stretchy sleeveless dress that seemed oddly formal for the time of day. Her caramel-colored hair was perfectly coiffed, her nails impeccably manicured, and her heels added an extra three, maybe four, inches to her otherwise average height.

Most striking, though, was her weight, or lack thereof. Courtney had always heard the camera added ten pounds, but had never really bought that, given how skinny all the actresses appeared even on camera. But here, this woman was so slight that it seemed plausible. Her shoulders jutted out and even her cheekbones made her seem too thin.

Just then, Courtney realized the woman was looking at her. Actually, she was glaring.

"You have company," the woman deduced with a sigh. "Why shouldn't I be surprised?"

Justin turned to Courtney and smiled. "Kinzie, this is Courtney Robbins. Courtney, this is MacKinzie Martindale."

Courtney stepped forward. MacKinzie flashed an insincere smirk. "Delighted," she jeered.

"I should be going anyway," Courtney announced softly. Justin frowned and followed her to the corner of the room where she retrieved her shoes.

"You don't have to go on her account," he said. Courtney couldn't tell how sincere he was, but she knew she couldn't stand to be around that woman for much longer.

She slipped her shoes onto her feet in lieu of answering. She thought she caught a glimmer of disappointment on Justin's face. "Oh," she suddenly realized, "your shirt."

"Keep it," he instructed. "I've got plenty."

She nodded. "Thanks." Then she turned to MacKinzie. "Nice meeting you," she lied, heading to the door.

"Hang on," Justin called. Courtney paused at the door while he picked up the phone and spoke to someone about a car. Then, he jotted something down on a piece of the hotel paper beside the phone. He handed her the paper as she opened the door. "I called you a car. Go by the concierge desk and he'll show you where to find it."

"Thanks," she mumbled. "What's this?" She took the paper from him.

He grinned. "The autograph you wanted. And my cell phone number."

Courtney opened her mouth to speak but wasn't sure what to say. She wanted to know, was she supposed to call him? Did he want her to? But she couldn't bring herself to ask. Why else would he have given her his number?

Again, as though he could read her mind, Justin explained. "In case you're bored with your friends."

She smiled, praying he'd kiss her goodbye. When he didn't, she started on down the hall.

JUSTIN CLOSED the door behind Courtney and glared at Kinzie. "Why do you have to be such a bitch?"

She cackled. "Why do you have to be such a whore? Who was she? Some random fan you picked up at a bar?"

He grabbed his phone, scrolling through his texts from the morning instead of answering immediately. Finally, he looked up at her. "I didn't sleep with her. She's just a friend."

Kinzie laughed even harder. "Sure."

Justin had had about enough of her crap. Why did he always let her do this to him? Why had he even opened the door? "How's the new boyfriend, Kinzie?"

She grimaced smugly. "Oh, you heard about that?"

Justin rolled his eyes. Obviously he'd heard about it. He had read about it in *US Weekly* along with the rest of the country, and then, when his publicist had asked about it, he'd had to pretend he'd broken up with her before she'd hooked up with Jackson. Of course, Justin had suspected as much long before then, assuming she'd been dating—or at least screwing—Jackson since she'd met him six months prior on the set of their crappy movie. Not that she'd had the decency to ever tell Justin.

"Why are you here?"

"I thought we could have lunch, you know, catch up," she replied, scanning the bedroom for God knows what. "I missed you," she added. "And you are in my neighborhood."

"You could've called."

She smiled. "I like surprising you." She paused, then turned suddenly. "You really didn't fuck her?"

He shook his head staunchly, suspecting where this was headed. He was right. Within moments, Kinzie had taken off her dress and was standing in front of the chaise lounge by the bar, wearing nothing but a heavily padded black bra and matching lacy panties. She sat down slowly, stretched back over the chaise, then motioned for him to join her. Justin briefly toyed with the idea of refusing her, but knew he never would.

It was ironic, really. After they'd met on the set of a TV show and hung out with friends a few times, Kinzie still wouldn't sleep with him until their fourth real date. And even after that first time, they'd never been one of those couples that was constantly doing it. But now that they were broken up, Kinzie had been calling him for sex pretty regularly. It didn't bother him, and in a strange way, Justin felt vindicated every time he was with Kinzie knowing that she was now cheating on the very guy she'd dumped him for.

He'd told Keith about the hookups, and, aside from some concern that Jackson would find out and kick Justin's ass, Keith had been supportive. Of course, Keith also insisted Justin and Kinzie were going to get back together for real at some point, and Justin knew that wasn't true.

Kinzie left her bra on the entire time they had sex. She always did that, and it drove Justin crazy. The entire eighteen months or so that they'd dated, on and off again, Justin figured he'd maybe seen her breasts twice. And, thanks to a topless scene in her movie, the rest of the country thought they'd seen her breasts exactly that many times too. Justin knew those breasts—the ones in the movie—weren't really hers. He'd never mentioned it to her, certain that accusing a woman of hiring a tit-double for a film wasn't a compliment, but he was positive, beyond a doubt, that she had done precisely that. Justin knew that once that bra came off, Kinzie had nothing left, just the kind of breasts you'd expect to find on a scrawny preteen, two tiny nipples poking slightly out of an otherwise flat surface. He could never pretend she wasn't beautiful, or even sexy, but the old attraction just wasn't there anymore.

"Shall we grab lunch?" she suggested, smoothing the front of her dress when they were done. There was no cuddling, not even the most perfunctory of post-sex kissing—just Kinzie popping up and redressing.

He shrugged. "Why not?"

They walked down the street to one of their old favorite cafes. Justin knew it had to drive her crazy that he was wearing his workout gear in public, especially when she was clearly glammed up, but he didn't care. It amused him to piss her off. "So where is your old man today?"

Kinzie was confused for a moment before she figured it out. "Now, Justin, be nice. He's really not that much older."

"Isn't he like fifty?"

"He's forty-two," she snapped. Justin knew that, but he wanted to make sure she knew how ridiculous it was for her—a twenty-three year old—to be involved with someone old enough to be her father. "And he's in Panama for another week," she added. The tone of her voice irritated him, since it sounded like she sincerely missed her new beau.

They were quickly seated in one of the corner seats, where they were a little less likely to be bothered by paparazzi. Justin wondered how Jackson would react when he found out Kinzie had gone to lunch with him. He figured Kinzie would have to mention it to Jackson, just in case there was a photo taken that showed up somewhere later.

An older waitress came to take their order. Kinzie spoke first. "I'd like a green salad, no dressing, no meat, no cheese, no croutons, no carrots, no bread. And an iced tea with lemon. No sugar," she added. The waitress turned to Justin, alarmingly unfazed by Kinzie's order.

He smiled pleasantly. "Could I get a cheeseburger, medium, with your grilled chicken salad and a Coke?" He started to hand her the menus they hadn't even glanced at, then added, "Oh, and could you bring me a hardboiled egg, too?"

Kinzie grimaced, but the waitress just nodded and left.

Kinzie began prattling on about some issue with her new hairdresser and Justin let his mind wander, betting whether or not Courtney would have the nerve to call him. When their food came, he focused on that, and tried to ignore the way Kinzie nervously fidgeted with her fork and took obnoxiously small bites of the lettuce.

When they finished eating, he paid, then quickly stood. Kinzie smiled, a seemingly sincere gesture. "Well, Kinzie, it's been good catching up, but I've got an appointment with my trainer. Tell your new man I said hello," Justin said. And he sauntered off without awaiting her response.

3

Eager to keep the juicy details to herself, Courtney offered only the briefest recap of her night to Erica and Ashley. Both girls were persistent in urging Courtney to call him before they left town.

On the one hand, he had given her his number. But on the other hand, he was a movie star. He couldn't seriously be interested in her, could he?

It was Tuesday before Courtney finally got up the nerve to call. She shooed her friends away as she dialed, stepping into the bathroom of their shared hotel room for privacy. She perched on the edge of the tub, worried that her already wobbling knees would give out if she called while standing.

After three long rings, it went to voice mail. It was a generic voice mail, giving no indication she'd even called the right number, but she resisted the urge to hang up. She'd never work up the nerve to call again later. "Hey there, it's Courtney. I'm still in town and don't have plans for the evening, so if you want to meet up later, give me a call."

She peered out of the bathroom. Erica and Ashley stared back anxiously.

"Voice mail," she murmured, eliciting disappointed groans from them both.

"Well, we can't just wait around here for him to call. Let's get out and explore. Maybe do some shopping." Erica suggested.

Courtney nodded in agreement. Erica was the most practical one of their group and always had a solution for every contingency.

A half an hour into their shopping spree, Courtney's phone rang, nearly stopping her heart. To her dismay, it was her mother.

Nearly two hours after that, her phone rang again. The number had been blocked, so Courtney couldn't be sure, but something told her this was him. She dropped her bags and scurried out of the store, motioning to Erica.

"Hello?" She hoped her voice didn't sound as uncertain to the caller as it did to her.

"Hey, Courtney? It's Justin Erikson."

She smiled, amused that he felt it necessary to add his last name. "Hey there. How's the photo shoot?"

"Almost done," he replied. "So no plans for tonight, huh?"

"Nope, none at all," she replied coyly. She heard someone ask him a question in the background, then heard him whispering a muffled answer.

"Sorry," he said, returning to the phone. "I was thinking about going to another club tonight. Would you meet up there?"

"Yeah, that sounds great," she replied. "Um, but I don't know if I'd be able to get in."

He was quiet for a moment, and she nearly regretted having said it.

When he did speak again, it was to give her an address. She quickly fumbled through her purse for a pen, scribbling on the back of a Victoria's Secret receipt. "I'll meet you at that corner, um, let's say at 9. It's right across from the club. And bring your friends if they want to come. It shouldn't be too crowded on a Tuesday."

"Sounds good."

"I better go. I've got so much Vaseline on me now I'm afraid I might drop the phone."

Courtney laughed. "Did you just say what I think you said?"

He laughed along with her. "Yeah. I'm covered in the stuff. It makes me all shimmery, you know, in case my real sweat doesn't look authentic enough." He paused while she giggled again. "Don't worry, I'll shower before tonight."

"I don't know if I want you to now. Maybe I want to see the shimmer-version of you," she teased.

"Well, too bad. You'll have to wait till the ads come out. See you tonight, cool?"

He hung up before she could reply. She glanced down at her watch. It was nearly five o'clock. This was going to be the longest four hours of her life.

"You'll introduce us tonight, right?" Ashley asked, tossing her bags onto the bed as they returned to their hotel room.

"Yes, as long as you promise not to turn in to a rabid fangirl again."

She dug through her suitcase and bags of new clothes to put together the perfect ensemble: a short, fitted, navy blue strapless dress and silver heels with a thin strap that wrapped up her calf. She'd already purchased new, sexier lingerie when they were out that day, so she wore that, wedging a second pair of sexy panties, a toothbrush, and makeup into her purse, just in case she stayed the night again.

They went out for dinner before heading over to the club, but Courtney was too nervous to eat much. As soon as they arrived at the corner Justin had directed them to, the excitement started to overcome her nerves. But by ten after nine, there was still no sign of him.

"Maybe we should just get in line," Erica suggested, warily eying the line of people already winding down the block, well past the security rope.

"Or you could try calling him," Ashley repeated anxiously, as she'd been doing for the past ten minutes.

Courtney turned around, starting to panic, but found herself face to face with the man Justin had introduced as his roommate. "Hi," she greeted him, relieved. "Keith, right?"

"So you must be Courtney." He paused, making her wonder if he just didn't remember meeting her or couldn't tell her apart from her friends. "Justin went in the back to avoid the crowd. He wanted me to come get you guys."

They followed Keith across the street and to the front of the line at the club, where he leaned in and spoke to the bouncer briefly. The bouncer unclipped the rope blocking off the door and the girls rushed in. Keith followed them through the door, then stepped around to show them to the opposite side of the club where Justin was seated with four other guys and two women. Courtney felt the familiar frantic thumping in her chest.

Justin stood as he saw Courtney approach. To his relief, she was just as he remembered her. Actually, she was hotter. He greeted her with a friendly hug, casually running his hands over her bare shoulders.

"Ladies," he nodded to her friends. They breezed through all the introductions, then Justin dragged a chair around to where he had been seated and motioned for Courtney to join him. He flipped his chair around and straddled it, resting his chin on the back of it. Man, he hadn't realized how tired he was.

"Sorry I had to send Keith out for you," he shouted over the music. "Just didn't feel like messing with photographers tonight."

She nodded, but he wondered if she really had any idea what it was like for him. She looked nervous, which was a bummer since he'd enjoyed how chatty and normal she'd acted the last time. Just then, a waitress appeared with a tray of shots. Hopefully, Courtney would relax after a couple of drinks. After tossing back the shots, Courtney's friends went to dance. Justin was excited that her full attention would now be on him.

"I like the dress," he confessed.

She smiled. "I'd hoped you might."

Justin beamed. That was more like it. "This was the first club I got into without waiting in line," he told her.

"Really? What was it like?"

"The club?"

She shook her head. "No, realizing you were officially cool enough to jump the line."

He laughed. "Well, I think I was always cool enough, but it was pretty fucking great when the bouncers started to think so too." He paused, taking another drink, then regretting it, knowing he should be getting her to drink more and slowing down himself. "It wasn't that long ago, really. I'd already done two movies and hundreds of modeling gigs before anyone knew who I was."

"What were you like as a kid?"

The question caught him off guard. No one ever asked him that, especially when he was talking about becoming famous. "I was kind of a punk," he said.

She gazed back in disbelief. "No, I bet you were a mama's boy."

He laughed, motioning for the waitress to bring Courtney another drink. "Yeah, maybe I was a little of both. I'd pull some crazy stunt, like trying to sell my mom's antique bells to the neighbors, then I'd flash my little dimples at my mom when I got caught. And if that didn't get me off the hook, I'd cry."

She laughed again, those blue eyes of hers reflecting the lights off the floor. She scooted closer, sneakily resting her hand on his leg. He tried not to think about it, just to ignore her fingers casually draped mere inches away from his groin. He wanted to take her hand in his and inch it up higher, just a little, to see what she'd do. Instead, he clasped both hands tightly around his glass.

"How has your week been so far?" he asked, lamenting how lame he sounded.

"Excellent. Yours?"

Justin raised an eyebrow and tilted his head back and forth. "Kind of shitty, honestly."

She seemed genuinely concerned. "Why? What happened?"

He shrugged. "Nothing. Just the job."

"I thought you said you liked modeling."

"I do," he insisted, glancing back down at her hand, still firmly planted at its post. "But I like being in front of the camera, playing around, posing, just having fun. I'm not such a big fan of spending two hours in a makeup chair or being coated from the neck down in Vaseline. It's hotter than hell in the studio anyway, and then they grease you up and bitch at you if you sweat it off. Oh, and they squirt you with cold water until your nipples are hard as rocks."

Keith looked up from his phone, laughing. "Come on, tell her about the best part," he urged, before turning to Courtney and whispering, "First few times he had it done, he cried like a baby."

Justin rolled his eyes, but Courtney gazed back, intrigued. "I have to get waxed regularly for the photo shoots," he explained.

She bit her lip, probably to quash a laugh, but it was a pretty sexy look anyway. "So, um, where, exactly do they do this? I mean, are you completely hairless um, everywhere?" She waved her hand in the general vicinity of his midsection.

Justin leaned forward. "Guess you'll have to find that out for yourself."

Keith stood, letting out a disgusted groan. "I'm going to go hurl in the men's room. Text if you need me."

Courtney laughed at his exit.

"His girlfriend's out of town," Justin explained. "Makes him cranky."

She nodded, quietly, then glanced out to the dance floor where her friends were. He could tell she wanted to go join them. Hell, he felt like dancing too. He missed being able to flirt, just grinding up against a girl without knowing if he'd ever get to follow through later. He glanced around the club, deciding it really wasn't crowded.

"You want to dance?"

"I thought you don't dance in public," she countered.

He stood, grabbing her hand. "I'll make an exception."

As soon as her body pressed in to his, swaying to the beat of the music, Justin felt his body temperature rising. Courtney was so sexy, and it didn't even seem like she was trying to turn him on.

They hadn't been dancing for long when Courtney's friends came and hauled her away for a few minutes. When Courtney returned, she was alone.

"Friends went home," she explained, shouting over the music.

He hoped his smile wasn't too obvious. "So, looks like you're stuck here, huh."

"I could take a cab," she said, sauntering back to their table.

The waitress came back, and he switched to Coke, not wanting to be too tired when things got really interesting. Courtney was still nursing her last drink anyway.

"Hey, so I figured I should probably apologize about Sunday, you know, that girl who showed up at the hotel, Kinzie? She's my ex," he heard himself say.

"I know," she replied.

Justin immediately felt stupid. Of course she knew that. Everyone knew that. His relationship with Kinzie—and its messy downfall—had been way too public.

"I didn't know she was coming over or anything," he added. "Do you keep in touch with any of your exes?"

She shook her head.

Justin quickly regretted saying anything at all. It wasn't like he owed her an explanation. But then he found himself talking again. "Kinzie and I had an on and off again type of thing. But it's definitely off for good now," he said, knowing that to be true, despite the little encounter Sunday. "It was always a love-hate type of relationship. Without the love, I guess."

Courtney laughed. "Sounds great," she joked uncomfortably. "So who ended it?"

Justin sipped the last of his beer before starting on his soda, not really certain of the accurate answer to this seemingly basic question. "I guess she did." He laughed. "I called her some names, and then we didn't speak to each other for a couple weeks. But then she was the first one to publicly say we weren't an item anymore. We'd never officially confirmed we were a couple, so I don't know why she needed to say that, except maybe to make herself seem less slutty when she hooked up with someone new."

Courtney grimaced. "But you're still friends with her," she finally reminded him.

He shrugged, wondering if there was any way he could possibly explain it so she would understand. "We have a lot in common," he finally explained. "It's not, I don't know. Most people can't really relate to what life is like for her, always having to look perfect any time she leaves her house, spending two hours getting her makeup and hair done just so she can go to the gym, never eating, never really knowing what anyone honestly thinks about her. And she gets what it's like for me." He paused. "It's sometimes just easier to date someone else with a fan base."

"I could see that," she replied.

A long silence ensued. Justin shook his head and laughed. "God, I'm terrible."

"What do you mean?"

"You finally call me, and I invite you out here so we can start up where we left off, and instead I end up rambling on about my stupid ex and how I never date people who aren't famous."

To his relief, Courtney smiled. "Where did we leave off, exactly?"

He didn't wait for the opportunity to pass. He pulled her in for a kiss without even checking who might be watching. He leaned forward, wrapped his arms around her waist, and lifted until she was sitting sideways on his lap. She draped her arms around his neck and kissed him back, at first, but then he sensed her pulling back. He tilted his head away, ending the kiss, but kept his firm hold on her lower back.

"You up for another sleepover tonight?" he whispered.

She shrugged coyly, giggling a little as his lips brushed the edge of her ear. "That depends. There was a lot of talking last time. Is there a chance things might get a little more, I don't know, interesting, if I stay tonight?"

Justin exhaled slowly through pursed lips. He was so hard right now that he wished he was the kind of guy who could just take her back to the men's room and fuck her there. Instead, he played the game. "Yeah, I think maybe we could shake things up a little. If you're up for it."

She nodded and scooted back to her own chair, reaching for

her purse. He stood quickly and reached for her hand, but she hesitated. He turned to see what the holdup was.

"Am I going to hear from you again after tomorrow?" she spoke quietly.

The question was so simple, so straightforward that it caught him off guard. He sighed, wishing he could tell her what she wanted to hear and still look at himself in the mirror later, but he couldn't lie to her. "I don't know," he replied.

She gazed back at him for a minute, and he was sure he'd blown it. He'd already started debating whether he would just go home and catch up on sleep or see if any of his other friends were still out.

But then she took his hand, nodded, and they left.

He wasn't staying at the hotel anymore, a fact which made for a noticeably longer ride. They were quiet during the drive back to his place, kissing some, but mostly waiting patiently until they were alone. Once they arrived, Justin led Courtney into the kitchen. She immediately began fidgeting with her shoes.

"Hey Bella!" Justin crouched down to pet his German Shepherd, letting her lick his cheek eagerly before he stood back up.

Courtney smiled at Bella, offering her a token pat on the back. "She doesn't bark at strangers?"

"She's a great cuddler, but a shitty guard dog." he said, watching Bella wag her tail and retreat happily to her favorite armchair.

He grabbed two waters from the fridge, opened them, and drank from one. Courtney took hers and made her way back across the room. "Nice place," she observed, staring out at the darkened room, her back to him. Justin considered that this was maybe her way of slowing things down, or telling him she wasn't into it anymore anyway, but then he dismissed the idea. He didn't want to wait any longer, and if she felt differently, well, she'd have to say so.

He kicked off his shoes and stepped up behind her, wrapping his arms around her waist. Her body relaxed into his, and she tilted her head slightly to the side, exposing a small patch of her neck. He grinned, immediately planting his mouth on her soft, salty skin, tracing his tongue back and forth until he felt her tremble. He kissed her shoulders, and began to slowly unzip her dress. She turned right as the zipper reached her waist, as though it was a dance they'd rehearsed. Justin sighed breathlessly, letting her lift his shirt above his head.

Courtney gently ran her fingers over his chest, smiling. "Smooth," she cooed. She looked up, innocently, and kissed him on the lips, gently, just once. Then she kissed his neck and chest, and pressed her hands down his back, over his ass, and back up in the front, rubbing the length of his already hard dick through his jeans. Justin felt his breath speed up and he clutched at her hands, knowing he'd never last long if she kept touching him like that.

Justin kissed her again, her hands still pinned within his own, then stopped. He picked her up, her dress still draped around her waist, and carried her up the stairs to the bedroom, settling her gently onto the bed.

He flipped on a single light and turned on some music. When Justin looked up again, Courtney was standing beside the bed, her dress around her ankles. Her hair fell in loose tendrils across her chest, casting a sexy silhouette in the dimly lit room, and her hands were poised on her hips, drawing his eyes immediately in to her red lace panties. For someone who didn't do one-night stands, she sure knew how to get a guy all worked up.

He smiled and she reciprocated. Justin stepped closer and then froze as she reached her hands behind her back and unfastened her bra. He watched with wonder as her breasts tumbled out of the bra—full, perky, and noticeably paler than the rest of her body. He reached for her until his mouth met hers, pulling away only long enough to whisper, "You're beautiful."

He meant it too, and not just because her hands were already unbuckling his belt and eagerly tugging at his pants. He helped her undress him, then guided her back onto the bed, climbing on top of her smooth, nearly naked body.

They kissed again, their mouths frantically searching for each other. He grinned, wondering if he could actually make love to her in this position, pressed on top of her, or if she'd shift around until they were on their sides and eventually take the top herself, like Kinzie always did, claiming he was crushing her.

Justin startled as Courtney's cool hands slipped past the band of his boxer briefs. He loved that she wanted him so badly. He toyed with the idea of pulling away now, teasing her and saying they shouldn't go any further, but he couldn't bring himself to stop kissing her, couldn't stop his fingers from pushing down her panties.

In that first moment, when their bodies pressed together with no barriers between them, Courtney breath stilled, and Justin realized she was anxious. He rolled over, glad her nervousness had prompted him to pause long enough to grab a condom from the nightstand. Justin couldn't tell if she was still holding her breath or not, but he knew she was still ready to go when she snatched the condom out of his hands and slid it over him herself.

He nibbled the side of her ear, then gently pushed into her. Justin felt her breath against his shoulder, her rapid breathing mimicking his own. He groaned as Courtney's hands roamed his back, her nails lightly scratching against his hips as she pulled him into her harder. He placed his mouth over hers again, desperate to feel her tongue pressing into his own, and tried to remember if sex always felt this good. He dropped one knee to the side of her, balancing himself so he could grab her hands, pinning them above her head with his other hand. He opened his eyes, watched her breasts sway back and forth with the movement, then pressed his chest against hers until her hardened nipples tickled the skin on his own chest.

Courtney moaned slightly, the corners of her mouth turning up, as her eyes stared back at him drunkenly. He released her hands, immediately reaching for her breasts as she dug her fingers into his waist. He groped and squeezed, hoping he wasn't being too rough, too overly excited at having this amazing set to play with after being with Kinzie for so long, moving his hand only long enough to lick his finger before reaching back for her nipples. She cried out, louder now, and he pressed his mouth against hers, shushing them both as they rocked back and forth.

When the euphoria wore off, Justin shifted his hips and rested beside her. His leg still covered hers, his hand still rested on her firm, trembling stomach. Neither of them spoke, both of them too breathless for words.

THE ROOM SPUN around Courtney as she struggled to catch her breath. She turned to face Justin, the weight of his broad arm still over her waist. His eyes were open, but he was quiet. Just when she started to panic that he hadn't found that as amazing as she had, his lips parted in a smile.

"You are awesome," he finally whispered.

Courtney smiled, wondering how she'd never known sex could be that perfect. "I was just thinking the same thing about you," she replied, nestling her head into the crook of his arm.

"Why didn't we do this on Saturday?"

She laughed, refreshed by his candor, surprised at how comfortable she felt with him.

He sighed, positioning his deep blue eyes directly in front of her own. "Why'd you come back here with me?"

She frowned. "Isn't it obvious?"

He grinned. "I mean, when you asked if you'd see me again. I sort of figured you'd change your mind then."

Courtney considered this. She wasn't even sure why she had asked him, really. She hadn't exactly experienced a one-night stand before, but it wasn't like she was morally opposed to the concept or anything. It just hadn't felt right before. "I guess I liked your honesty."

He closed his eyes, making her wonder if he was falling asleep. But then he replied, "that's exactly what I like about you."

Courtney smiled, then gradually rolled onto her back, Justin's arm still draped across her growing heavy. She felt him shift slightly after a few minutes, then pop his head up. "Sorry," he mumbled, "Didn't sleep much the past few days."

"It's late, sleeping probably isn't a bad idea," she said.

He shook his head. "It's a terrible idea. The night is young, you're here, I'm here, we can't just waste it." He moved his hand up to cover her breast. "I mean, Berkeley is really far away, isn't it?"

"About six hours from here," Courtney replied.

He perked his head up. "Really?"

She expected him to lie back down, but instead, he reached his tongue out and firmly licked the length of her breast. She inhaled sharply, a warm twinge shooting through her, and he did it again, tracing imaginary patterns around her nipple with his tongue. Then she felt his hand slip between her legs, his fingers exploring the dampness remaining from earlier then rubbing back and forth, gently at first, then more firmly.

She moaned quietly, then bit her lip, embarrassed. "I thought you were tired," she finally murmured.

He lifted his mouth away from her breast and raised his eyes to hers. "Oh, so you want me to stop?"

She pulled his head closer, covering his mouth with hers, then shifting her thighs against his hand, forcing his fingers against her harder. "No," she mumbled between kisses.

"No what?" he teased, his mouth hovering just above her breast.

"Don't stop," Courtney pleaded. She felt like a completely different person, so desperate for him to pleasure her. She'd never been like that before, with any guy. Courtney felt herself squirming at his touch, nearly quivering with excitement as he inched himself lower until his tongue met his fingers, flicking across her most sensitive parts until she felt like she was about to melt into the bed. She nudged him away, grabbing his firm length in her hand and kissing his muscled chest.

Courtney pushed him onto his back, working her way down his body with wet kisses, smiling contentedly as she reached her goal. She traced the length of him with her tongue before taking the tip in her mouth, moving her lips up and down, savoring every groan and passionate exhale escaping his lips until he finally pulled her back with a mischievous smile. He fumbled with the second condom wrapper and leaned back, lifting her on top of him.

She watched his eyes, staring into hers at first, then rolling back in his head as his breath quickened. She placed her hands on his massive chest, squeezing muscles she didn't know existed, then let her head tilt backwards as his own hands grasped at her breasts, hips, and butt.

After the orgasm she'd just had, Courtney didn't expect another, but within moments, she felt her body tensing as a familiar pressure grew, deep in her core. The closer she got, the less control Courtney had over her movements, but Justin took over for her, thrusting harder and faster into her until she felt her body explode into a million fragments of pleasure. Justin found his release a moment later, groaning loudly and clutching her hips tightly.

Courtney collapsed over him, laying her head on his chest. After several minutes, Justin scooted her head off his chest, kissing it, then reached for his boxers. He pulled them on before standing, and made his way to the bathroom. She heard the toilet flush, heard the water run, then he reemerged, holding a robe, which he tossed to her.

"I seriously need a shower," he said with a laugh.

"Me too," she mumbled, wrapping herself in the robe.

"Ladies first," he offered, and she went into the bathroom.

She'd only been showering for a minute or two when she saw the bathroom door open, then close again. Courtney had just rubbed shampoo in her hair and was rinsing it out, her arms raised so she could massage her head with her hands. She saw him watching her and immediately felt self-conscious, but he didn't seem to mind.

She slid the door open slightly and flashed him her best seductive look. "Care to join me?"

He grinned but shook his head. "I don't know. I got nothing left," he insisted.

She laughed, and motioned with her finger for him to get in, so he did.

As soon as the water began beading off his firm rounded shoulders and dripping down from his short, blond hair, Courtney felt like the wind had been knocked out of her. Luckily, Justin placed his arm on her back then, both holding her up and pulling her closer, and they kissed. Now that the tension was gone, or at least temporarily at bay, he kissed differently. His kisses were less hungry, less demanding, and more tender and nurturing.

Neither of them tried to take it past the kissing, and they

both collapsed into bed, exhausted, shortly after the shower. "So now are we sleeping?" she asked, almost hopeful he'd want to talk more.

"Actually, I'm starving," he admitted. "Do you want some pizza?"

She laughed. "It's two-thirty in the morning."

"Suit yourself," he replied, picking up the phone and ordering a pepperoni pizza. "You're not a vegetarian, are you?" he asked after hanging up.

Courtney shook her head. "Nope. Pepperoni pizza sounds pretty good."

He settled back into the bed, pulling her onto his chest. "Now we just have to stay awake till it gets here." He paused. "So what's it like being a lawyer?"

She laughed. "That's a terrible discussion to have if you're tired. Two minutes of me talking about law school and you'll be out like a light."

"What would you have done if you weren't going to be a lawyer?"

Courtney knew the answer to this without thinking. It had been a tough call for her, actually, deciding between the two paths. "Social worker."

"I could see that about you," he said.

"So what about you? What if you weren't an actor?"

Justin chuckled. "Well, since I blew off college and an athletic scholarship to go into acting, I guess I'd be pretty screwed if it hadn't worked out."

Courtney smiled. "Was there ever anything else you wanted to do?"

He took a few quiet breaths. "I always wanted to be an actor. But I guess for a while, when I was thinking more rationally and knew the chances of the acting gig paying off were slim, I thought about joining the military. That would've been even harder on my mom than acting though, I think."

"Are you and your parents still close?"

"My dad passed away three years ago. Lung cancer."

"I'm sorry to hear that."

He appeared uncomfortable. "My mom and I are pretty close. I mean, she lives out in Indiana, so I don't see the family too often, but we talk a lot. My mom is still a worrier, though."

"But you're doing amazing, what could she possibly be worried about?"

"I don't know. The modeling thing can't last forever, and the acting isn't a regular paycheck."

Courtney lifted her head off his chest to stare in disbelief at him.

He grinned. "Okay, yeah, I'm not going broke anytime soon. I guess mostly she just worries about my personal life. Three of my brothers are married already, and she just wants me to settle down like them."

"And what do you want?"

There was a long pause. "I'd like that too. Someday," he added. "But for now, I'm having fun." He turned to the clock. "I don't think we'll hear the door up here. Why don't we head downstairs and watch a movie while we wait for the pizza?"

He stepped into a pair of boxers and jeans and tossed one of his longer shirts to her. Courtney followed him down the stairs, still buttoning the shirt. Justin had a massive collection of movies, many of which she'd never seen.

"Wow," she mumbled.

"I really like movies," he explained.

She laughed. "That's probably a good thing."

"What sounds good?"

"You're the expert. You pick."

He grinned, then made his selection. He gestured for her to

follow him to the oversized massive sofa across the room. She sat beside him, pulling an Xbox controller out from under her, then snuggled against him as he pulled a fuzzy turquoise blanket over their laps. They were only a few minutes into the movie when there was a loud buzz. Justin hopped up and pushed a button to let the delivery guy past the gate.

They finished the movie and ate pizza before slowly climbing back up the stairs. By that point, Courtney was so tired she knew she'd have no trouble sleeping. "I like the color, the walls," she mumbled, just before her eyes closed. He laughed, pressing the length of his nearly-nude body against her, and she fell asleep, her face so close to his that she felt his breath tickling her eyelids.

When she awoke, Justin was in the bathroom. She climbed out of bed and wrapped the robe back around her, waiting for him to emerge from the bathroom. He smiled when he saw that she was up, and quickly invited her downstairs for breakfast.

"I should get dressed first," she began, but he shook his head.

"Just wear my shirt again. You look cute in it."

She smiled and followed him down the stairs. The house seemed even more beautiful in the daytime, with sunlight pouring in the abundance of windows. It was nothing like the bachelor pad she'd expected to find two young guys living in.

"How long have you lived here?" Courtney asked.

"Just over a year."

"It really is gorgeous. Did you use a decorator?"

He cleared his throat awkwardly.

Courtney heard a laugh from across the large room and turned to see Keith sitting on an armchair in the corner with his feet propped on the coffee table, a laptop perched on his thighs. She immediately regretted asking, certain his hesitation indicated Kinzie, or some other past girlfriend, had decorated the place.

"We had an awesome decorator," Keith chimed in. "And she was free."

Justin rolled his eyes, blushing. "My mom flew out and decorated the place for us."

Courtney smiled, understanding his embarrassment now. "I think that's sweet," she said, gently caressing his bicep.

Justin headed on to the kitchen and poured two giant mugs of coffee. "Morning," he greeted an older woman who was folding a basket of laundry. Courtney suddenly felt very vulnerable, wearing nothing but his shirt that barely covered her butt. "Courtney, this is Cathy, our housekeeper."

Courtney opened her mouth to greet the woman, but Cathy spoke first. "Good morning. You like eggs?"

"She makes the best eggs," Justin said.

Courtney nodded hesitantly. "Okay, thanks."

They sat at the table and Justin began flipping through a large stack of paper. "Wanna help me with lines?"

She smiled eagerly and grabbed the papers from him. She read through two scenes of his new movie with him, and then he drove her back to her hotel after breakfast. When he finally dropped her off, offering her a reserved kiss on the cheek, he said he'd call her sometime. And somehow, she believed him.

4

———————

The next two weeks were a blur. Justin met with his agent and publicist, reviewed ten new scripts to see if he was interested in the roles, and suffered through a studio reading with the female lead of an edgy romantic comedy whose director was considering casting him. He appeared on a TV talk show, met with the designer of a new clothing line that wanted him for TV and print ads, and he practiced his lines for the movie he was filming over the summer. And of course, Justin hit the gym.

For the most part, he didn't really think about women during those times, when his work occupied nearly every waking moment. He had a brief make-out session in the back of his Escalade with a girl he met at a bar after the last game of the Final Four, but that was it.

Then, Courtney called.

She was casual on the phone, saying she'd just seen one of his movies and loved it. He suspected that was just an excuse to call, but he was glad. He wasn't sure how exactly they'd left off. Courtney was easy to talk to and good in bed, so he had wanted to see her again, but the fact that she lived on the other end of the state complicated things.

"Do you like baseball?" he asked her.

"Everyone likes baseball," she replied sassily.

"If you're free this Saturday, we've got a suite at the Angels game and then some friends are coming by the house for a party."

There was a pause. He wondered if she was checking her calendar or just debating whether he was worth the drive.

"Should I meet you at your place?"

"Yeah. I'll be hanging at the pool that day, so come by early if you can."

They hung up, and Justin grabbed his skateboard and headed out with Bella.

ON SATURDAY, Courtney arrived at Justin's early in the afternoon. After a nerve-racking delay, Keith answered the door.

"Justin's by the pool," he said, his forehead wrinkled in confusion. Courtney followed him through the house and onto back deck.

Justin was stretched out on a lounge chair, broad sunglasses covering his eyes and a stack of papers firmly grasped in his hands. As she approached, she realized he probably couldn't see or hear her, thanks to headphones in his ears and a script blocking his face. She paused, admiring his perfect physique, wondering how it was even possible to look that amazing in a simple pair of athletic shorts. She inched closer, still unsure if he saw her.

Suddenly, his hand reached out and grabbed at her leg. She giggled as he sat up, his legs straddling the chair. He tossed the ear buds behind him and placed the script on a table next to what appeared to be a glass of iced tea.

"Well, hello there, Courtney Robbins," he purred, flashing those pesky dimples.

"Hi, yourself. Were you working?"

"Not anymore." He patted the section of the chair in front of him. She perched gingerly on the chair.

She exhaled sharply. God, she was nervous. More nervous, perhaps, then the last time she'd seen him, thanks to the absence of alcohol in her system.

"Oh, so that's how it's going to be?" Justin teased.

She slipped off her sandals and swung one leg over his, allowing him to pull her closer. She expected him to kiss her now, but instead, he spoke.

"How was the drive?"

"Not bad. I finished the audiobook of *Water for Elephants*."

For some reason, this amused him.

"Why is that funny? It's a long drive!"

He shook his head. "I don't know. I think listening to someone read me a book out loud would make the drive feel even longer. Or I'd fall asleep."

"Have you read it?"

"I'm not a big fan of books," he confessed.

Courtney paused, certain she'd never before heard someone say they didn't like books. She frowned. "But, you're an actor. You read all the time."

He shrugged. "That's different. Scripts are mostly just dialogue, none of the boring descriptive crap books have. And I don't have a choice. It's not my favorite part of the job, though."

Courtney jumped as the door to the house slammed.

"Everybody decent?" Keith called.

"No, dude," Justin shouted back, "I'm trying to get rid of the tan lines around my balls."

Keith correctly interpreted his sarcasm and joined them by the pool. "Dickhead," he mumbled to Justin. "Phone's for you."

Justin wrinkled his nose.

"She said she tried your cell phone already."

Justin glanced down at his phone, grimacing. "I couldn't hear it," he insisted, shimmying out from under Courtney's leg and standing. "Did you bring a suit?"

She nodded.

"Why don't you go inside and change and I'll meet you back out here in a few," Justin suggested, taking off towards the house.

When she returned to the pool, feeling naked in her solid black string bikini—a boring, but flattering suit, Justin was already there, waist-deep in the water. He stepped out of the pool as she approached, water beading down his chiseled torso. Courtney was immediately breathless, and certain he could hear her heart thumping as he finally reached her and placed his damp hands on her biceps.

He leaned close, then whispered "Nice suit," in a deep, heady voice, nearly making her legs give out beneath her. His mouth lingered beside her ear, his warm breath falling evenly across the side of her neck, making Courtney wish he would just kiss her already.

But he didn't. Instead, he pulled back and guided her to the pool. She stepped in timidly, cringing as the cool water hit her bare stomach.

"You'll get used to it," he promised, lifting her so she would wrap her legs around him, her groin pressed firmly into his stomach.

She shivered again, but this time, it wasn't from the water. Justin backed up, still carrying her, until they were in deeper water. "You ever been to an Angels game before?"

She shook her head. "I used to go to a few Indians games

each summer growing up, but that's just the minor leagues. I'm excited."

He smirked. "You're excited?"

"About the game," she clarified, watching his mischievous smile widen. "They're primed for a great season."

"So you really do like baseball, you weren't just saying that?"

"I would've been even more excited if we were headed to a Lakers game, but yeah, I'm looking forward to tonight."

Justin set her down, the water sloshing up towards her bikini top. "Seriously?"

Courtney nodded, unsure of why this was so surprising.

"You like basketball and baseball?"

She nodded again, laughing. "And football, although I'm not a huge Raiders fan."

The bemused grin remained plastered on his face.

"What? I have two brothers. I grew up watching sports. It's not that strange," she insisted.

"But it's kind of sexy," he replied, stepping closer. He wrapped his arms tightly around her waist, nearly lifting her off her toes, and she reciprocated, looping her arms around his neck. He stared at her, silently, his breathing soft and even.

"Are you ever going to kiss me?" she finally asked.

As his lips pressed into hers, she felt him smiling. Their kiss intensified, their tongues seeking out each other as his lips pulled her deeper and deeper into him. Courtney soon forgot where she was, focusing all her attention on the sensation of his mouth against her own. His hands migrated downward, resting on the back of her bikini bottoms for a moment before playfully darting between the strings on the side of the suit.

Courtney ran her hands down the length of his firm arms, feeling the burning deep inside her grow with each muscular ridge she stroked. Suddenly, Justin picked her up, carrying her to shallower water and placing her on the side of the pool so effortlessly that she felt like she was flying out of the water. She tilted her head to keep kissing him, her legs wrapping tightly around his back so that she could feel his firm abdomen moving in and out with each breath he took.

Justin's hands grazed the sides of her breasts, gently at first, then with greater determination, pushing across the front of her breasts and pulling her nipples towards him. He quickly scooted the thin material to the side, revealing both breasts and groaned, his own joy at seeing her breasts distracting Courtney long enough for him to place his mouth on one before she remembered they were still outside, in broad daylight.

She glanced around. She didn't want him to stop, but knew that even in the secluded pool, they certainly weren't in private. She shimmied her suit back over her breasts, Justin's eyes quickly raising to meet hers, his confused daze visible through the dark sunglasses.

"We're outside," she panted.

"There's a brick wall and tons of trees. No one can see back here," he insisted, kissing her neck before tracing his tongue along her clavicle.

"But your house is right there, and it has a billion windows."

His lips moved to her stomach, which she quickly sucked in before placing her hands on his head and guiding him back up.

"No one's inside."

"Keith is," she reminded him. "What if he comes back outside? And what about your housekeeper?"

He sighed, seeming moderately irritated now. "Cathy isn't working today. And Keith would check before coming out, like he did earlier. Trust me, he is not into watching."

Courtney considered this for a moment, then slid back into the water, barely fitting between the wall and his toned body. She pushed her hands down the back of his suit and slowly worked them around to the front, figuring at least they were more hidden if they stayed in the water. She wanted him—badly, and while she'd already been much more forward with him than she'd ever before been in her life, she still couldn't bring herself to go topless with Keith right inside.

This seemed to appease Justin, as he pulled her in for another kiss, scooting the rest of his body a few inches further to give her hands room to work. She roamed her hands around his inner thighs before gently tracing her forefinger up the length of his erection. His breath quickened, and Courtney responded by wrapping her hand around him, rubbing up and down amid the splashing of the water. After a moment, his lips parted from hers, and he pulled her hand out of his suit, nodding for her to follow him.

He led her to a lounge chair, a few feet away from where she'd found him initially, this one shaded by a large tree which also mostly blocked the view of the house. Courtney sat tentatively, then held her arms out for him as he climbed on top of her and gently lowered her to her back. They kissed again, frantically now, their breath coming in faster and faster spurts.

He shifted his weight towards one side, first uncovering her breast just long enough to kiss it, sucking and biting at her nipple until the pressure in her groin was nearly unbearable. Then he pulled his hand downward, rubbing back and forth, first through the thin material of her suit, but then, finally slipping under the suit so his bare fingers stroked directly against her tingling, hot flesh.

Courtney was so distracted by the delicious sensations that she didn't even realize Justin had somehow moved both of their suits out of the way until he was bringing his mouth back to hers and gently pushed into her. As the sensation of him finally filling her alleviated some of the burning desire, Courtney moaned with relief and frantically pulled him harder into her. She was vaguely aware of her hips lifting to meet his, and she no longer cared if anyone could see them. Her hands wandered across his body, finding satisfaction with every inch of him that she could reach, grasping loosely at his hair, before resting on his stubbled cheek.

As Justin pulled her fingers into his mouth, sucking them one at a time before again searching out her lips, his tongue thrusting into her mouth, Courtney realized, with panic, that they'd forgotten the condom. She knew she should say something, but suddenly her whole body started to tingle, gently at first, but then it intensified, like a tidal wave working its way through her entire being. So instead of stopping or speaking up, she pressed her mouth into his shoulder, her teeth scratching along his muscled flesh. His hands squeezed her sides, and he pushed into her harder until she heard herself scream out. He moved his mouth over hers, muffling her cries, then rocked back and forth a few more times before settling, still, on top of her.

They both caught their breath and then Justin shifted to his side, pulling his suit up as she readjusted hers. He glanced down, then panicked. "Oh shit! I forgot..." he turned to her, gauging her expression.

Courtney felt drunk although she'd had nothing to drink, and too winded to form any coherent response. "I'm on the pill," she finally breathed, watching the relief wash over his face before his head plopped back down onto her chest.

They swam and hung out by the pool for a while longer and then showered and left for the game. Keith and his girlfriend Tara drove with them. If Keith had seen any of their activities by the pool, he certainly didn't let on. Courtney had to wonder how many other women he'd seen Justin "swim" with, cringing again at the whole condom mishap.

She glanced over at Justin, who was preoccupied with his phone. He had changed into an Angels jersey and jeans, with sunglasses, and a black baseball cap turned backwards.

Courtney stared at his chest, the muscles visible beneath the shirt, and decided he probably looked better in the jersey than most of the players did. They stopped at the valet, something Courtney had never known was even available at a sporting event, and Justin flipped his hat forward, pulling it down over his face before stepping out of the car.

They made their way into the stadium, then directly up to the suite, without anyone recognizing him. The suite was already crowded, and Courtney was instantly overwhelmed. Justin initially stayed close, introducing her to people she'd probably never see again, but eventually he was drawn into the group in the center of the room. Courtney grabbed a beer from the bar and made her way out to the seats in front of the suite. She had been watching for about fifteen minutes when Justin plopped down beside her, grinning.

"You're actually watching the game," he muttered, leaning forward in his seat, his knees spread wide so his thighs rested against hers.

"Don't act so surprised. I told you I like baseball," she retorted, sipping her beer.

He glanced sideways at her, smiled subtly, and turned back to the game.

BY THE TIME they got home from the game, people were already starting to arrive at the house. They'd stocked the outdoor bar earlier in the day, so Justin just needed to change his shirt and he was ready to party. Keith started up the music and switched the pool lights on and they both stood back to appreciate the setting, before it got trashed.

When he'd bought this house, the pool had been the main attraction. Well, that and the location. Justin hadn't cared about a beach view, but he wanted to be close to the beach. As soon as the realtor had shown Keith and him the place, they were sold. It had been way out of his price range at the time, since up to that point he'd managed to spend most of the profits of his work on the Escalade and general living expenses. But when he saw that pool, Justin had immediately pictured all the awesome parties they could have there. And really, even based solely on the events from earlier in the day, Justin had to admit the pool was worth every penny.

Keith poured some tequila shots, and Justin was in full party mode within minutes. He'd had a couple of beers at the game, but that was spread out over a few hours. His trainer was always lecturing him about the alcohol, especially beer, but Justin didn't care. He was killing himself to look good for his job, and he had no intention of giving up his favorite vice.

Courtney emerged from the house in a stretchy tube top just in time for the second round of shots. Justin had no regrets about inviting her. She couldn't have been less clingy, and he loved that. Whenever he went off to talk with someone else, she just made herself at home, chatting up the other guests.

He went inside briefly, giving the tour of the house to another actor from his last movie, and then returned to the patio, scanning the area for Courtney. Instead, the first person Justin spotted when he headed back outside was Mari.

Justin knew he would never forget her name. Mari with an "i" she had said when they met, tracing the letters of her name into his lower abdomen with her fingernail—pushing so hard he'd initially panicked that she was using a pen—and drawing her hand lower and lower with each letter until the dot on the i about brought him to his knees. After that night, he hadn't called her again. Unfortunately, she was the stalker type, and while he was apparently too drunk to figure that out before he had slept with her, he would never make that mistake again.

Justin caught a glimpse of Keith out of the corner of his eye and made a beeline for him. "Dude, who invited the crazy?"

Keith followed his stare to where Mari stood, wearing a bikini that was skimpy even by Hollywood standards. He immediately broke into laughter.

Justin swatted his arm, maybe a little too hard.

Keith hit him back, then glared and rubbed his arm. "I think she's friends with Tara. Not good friends, but Tara probably mentioned the party." He paused, and glanced over to where Courtney was chatting with their friend David. "Is she why you're worried, or is it Jasmine?"

Justin frowned, confused, then saw that Keith was right, there was a third girl here that he'd technically hooked up with. But Jasmine he could handle. She was young—maybe twenty-one at most, but mature. Justin had met Jasmine at an afterparty for a runway show. She was a high-end underwear model, of course. Justin had been immediately smitten, but after, while they were still lying naked in bed, she'd lit up a cigarette, and he couldn't refrain from lecturing her about it. After that, he realized he considered Jasmine to be more like a sister than a girlfriend. Not that he'd ever bang his sister if he had one, but just that he felt compelled to take care of her, or at least to steer her away from the crap a lot of the younger models got into when they became famous overnight.

Since that initial night, he'd kept in touch with Jasmine, mostly through social media where she posted some hilarious shit about her work, but he also ran into her occasionally at various fashion events. She was always friendly, always flirty, and always fun, not a bad combination.

"Hello? Justin?"

Justin snapped back to the present when he heard Keith's voice. He sighed and glanced back over at Courtney, who was now stroking the arm of David's leather jacket. He laughed, knowing David was probably just bragging about the material, but finding the whole scenario hilarious nonetheless. He turned back to Keith. "I'll take care of both of them," he said, nodding towards Mari and Jasmine. "She's the one I'm keeping tonight," he gestured to Courtney. "And tell Tara to keep her mouth shut next time!"

He took a deep breath, then casually walked by Mari, pausing as though he just noticed her. "Hi, there, how are you?" he said, avoiding eye contact and doing his best to act disinterested.

She didn't take the hint. Her hands immediately found his ass, pulling him close so fast that he nearly tripped, and then she planted her mouth on his. The scent of tequila on her breath was overpowering, and her hands clung fiercely to him as he pried her fingers off his jeans one at a time. His hand instinctively rose to his lip as he finally broke free, wiping away the lipstick-saliva blend she'd smeared across his mouth.

"I've got to get a drink, but uh, have a good time, alright?" He backed away quickly, hoping she'd take the hint. After another quick glance at Courtney, he did head to the bar, grabbing a Jack and Coke, more for the caffeine than anything else. He made small talk with a few people that found him at the bar, then made his way right over to Jasmine, hoping he could speak with her while Courtney was still distracted so he could avoid any awkward moments later.

"Jas," he greeted her warmly as he approached her from behind.

She spun around gracefully and smiled. "Hi, Justin."

He leaned in and offered her a quick hug and polite kiss on the cheek, lingering just a moment too long with his face right beside hers, where he could smell the floral infusions in her perfume. "You get more beautiful each time I see you," he said, cursing himself as soon as the words came out. So much for not flirting.

She clicked her tongue to her top lip, flashing that "come hither look" that she was famous for. With her long blonde hair trailing across her shoulders, a few wisps blocking her eye, those high cheekbones and her thick rosy lips, it was hard to look away.

He shook his head and grinned. "Don't give me that look, Jas. You know I can't resist you."

She swatted him playfully, offering a sultry pout in response.

Justin turned, determined not to be sucked in.

"Keith said you have a girlfriend now," she finally said, as though she'd been testing him.

He glanced over at Keith, silently thanking him, grateful his friend knew him well enough to predict he'd struggle at turning down Jasmine. "I wouldn't say that, but I'm..." his voice trailed off as he realized he couldn't actually tell a girl she wasn't the one he planned on fucking that night.

"Give me a call the next time you're in New York. We'll go shopping or something innocent," she promised, the look in her eyes anything but innocent.

"Sounds good, Jasmine." He hugged her one last time, giving her another kiss on the cheek, then returned to Keith, who was now seated near the pool with Tara draped across his lap.

"You owe me big time," Justin snarled at Tara, who simply laughed drunkenly and stole another slurp of Keith's drink.

He felt a soft hand on his back and turned quickly. Courtney was beside him, her bright eyes gazing up at him expectantly.

"You need a drink," he deduced, guiding her by the hand toward the bar. "You having a good time?"

She nodded.

"You seemed to be hitting it off well with David." For some reason, it amused him that in a party filled with several actors, models, and musicians, a girl who had no apparent interest in fashion gravitated towards David instead.

"Well, yeah. Did you know he designs clothes?" she said with fascination.

Justin couldn't contain his smile as he nodded and turned the collar of his shirt out so she could read the label. "He's one of my best friends. He makes great stuff. Keep on flirting with him and he might just start a new women's line."

She blushed. "*I* wasn't flirting. But you on the other hand, you certainly do have your hands full with the ladies tonight."

He hesitated, running his tongue over his smooth teeth, trying to gauge her tone and determine which girl she'd seen him with. "I have a lot of friends," he finally replied, as nonchalantly as he could muster.

Courtney bit her lip, but he could tell she was smiling a little. "I have friends, too, but they don't greet me like that."

He knew then that she was talking about Mari. But apparently, she hadn't been too bothered by what she saw. Man, that was a turn on. Kinzie would have slapped him if he'd even spoken to someone like Mari. "Oh, her. She is a crazy person I, uh, sort of went out with once."

Courtney raised an eyebrow doubtfully.

"Seriously, it was one night, and she is definitely insane, and now, well, now she's at my house for some reason. She's probably inside sniffing my boxers or something."

She giggled then. "And your other friend?" She nodded towards Jasmine.

Justin's eyes narrowed as he thought through this one. He didn't want to lie, but even he could sense that no girl, even one as confident and sexy as Courtney, would eagerly hop into bed with a guy who'd recently slept with a prestigious lingerie model. "She really is a friend," he finally insisted. "She's pretty cool if you want me to introduce you."

Courtney seemed to consider this, then shook her head. "Maybe later. I was thinking I might sit down for a minute," she replied, a hint of mischief in her voice. She led him to a chair on the side of the pool and stretched back, a devilish grin spreading across her face.

Justin didn't get the gesture at first, but as he realized she was in the chair they'd been in earlier, blurred visions of the afternoon came flashing back to him. He leaned over and pulled her up by her hands. "You are a bad, bad girl," he whispered in her ear, letting the tip of his tongue graze her neck before he pulled away. She smiled and raised her eyebrows. "Dance with me?" he asked.

She glanced across the pool, where Mari was now flirting with some other poor schmuck. "I don't know, will your stalker get jealous and beat me up?"

"I'll protect you," he promised, prying her drink from her hand and then pressing his body against hers to the beat of the music. This was Justin's favorite thing about having friends over to their house—he could get the club atmosphere, sort of, without feeling the same level of scrutiny. At home, well, he could just be himself.

He reached his hand to Courtney's back and squeezed her firm flesh through the back pocket of her jeans, his eyes focusing in on her chest, bobbing vibrantly with the music. Justin instantly wished the party were over, or at least that he could just head on up to bed with Courtney. And then, he realized he could.

He stared at her for a moment, unsuccessfully trying to gauge whether she was in the mood, and then opted for the direct approach. "What would you think about meeting me up in my room in a few minutes?"

She frowned. "The party's not over."

He couldn't decipher her tone. "We could come right back

out," he insisted.

Courtney dropped his hand and started back to the house. "See you in a few," she called over her shoulder.

Justin exhaled hard, his eyes glued to her ass as she walked off, then went to find Keith and tell him he'd be back out in a little while. When he got into the house, he half expected to find Courtney downstairs, waiting on him. He could tell she was drunk, and he still wasn't sure if she'd picked up on what he wanted to do. He didn't see her anywhere, so he went on into his bedroom.

He opened his door and there she was, stretched out on his bed, stark naked, her hands stretched above her head, crossed at the wrists like she was tied up. Justin laughed with nervous excitement, locking the door behind him. Courtney stood and slowly approached him, casually brushing her hair off her bare shoulder as she walked. He opened his mouth to speak, but she quickly pressed her finger against his lips, chastising him with a shake of her head.

He smiled, the anticipation building as she lifted his shirt over his head and slowly unzipped his jeans. When Justin's jeans were at his ankles, she stepped back, as though admiring her work. He reached for her, eager for a kiss, but she pulled back, dropping to her knees and taking his boxer briefs with her.

He inhaled sharply as her lips touched his skin, her tongue surprisingly cool against his warm, hard flesh. Justin reached his hand behind her head, feeling the softness of her hair as it sifted between his fingers. As his breathing became more frantic, she pulled her mouth away in one quick, titillating motion. He was tempted to nudge her back in place, to beg her to finish what she started, but she had already turned and grabbed something from atop his nightstand. She tossed the small object to him and he caught it, realizing immediately it was a wrapped condom. He slipped it on quickly and turned back to Courtney.

Justin grabbed hold of her tightly and pushed her back against the wall. He saw a smile escape her lips as he bent in to kiss her, working his hand down her body until his fingers reached the damp area between her legs. His finger pushed into her briefly, but it was all too much for him. He couldn't wait any longer. He grabbed her firm thigh, lifted her leg slightly and entered her, a loud moan immediately escaping her throat. They were quick, both of them coming within minutes.

He kissed her neck hungrily as he pulled out. Courtney ducked beneath his arm, which was still planted against the wall behind her, and she bent to retrieve his clothes, tossing them to him one article at a time.

"You should probably get back out there, seeing as how it is your house and all."

He ran his fingers through his hair and began dressing, clumsily. Courtney went into the bathroom, returning just as he finished. "I'll be out in a minute," she assured him.

He nodded, leaning in for a final kiss, savoring the hint of tequila on her tongue before making his way back to the pool.

Keith eyed him knowingly as soon as he walked out. Justin blushed and shrugged, silently admitting it all. "Seriously?" Keith asked with disbelief. "How are you so fucking lucky? I'm the one with an actual girlfriend and you're the one sneaking off for quickies."

"Go give Tara some more of that tequila," Justin suggested with a laugh, and then he turned and talked with David for a while.

It was late when the party finally died down, and Courtney and Justin were both drunk. They stripped down to their underpants and passed out on his bed, sleeping until late the next morning.

When he finally pried his eyes open, Courtney was already dressing.

"Do you have to leave soon?" he asked, groggily.

"No, but I don't want to get back too late." She paused, leaning in to run her fingers through his hair. "I was going to go for a jog. You could join me."

He winced. "I hate running."

"Really?"

She seemed genuinely surprised. He assumed she'd seen one of the countless photos of him jogging. For some reason, the paparazzi found his shirtless runs along the boardwalk fascinating.

He nodded.

"Well, okay. I'll go by myself. I just figured it'd be pretty along the coast."

Justin smiled, agreeing with that sentiment. "I didn't say I wouldn't go with you, just that I hate running. I've still got to do it."

They ate breakfast and hung out by the pool for a few minutes before heading out for their run. Justin started out a little slower than his normal pace, unsure of Courtney's comfort-level, but she kept speeding up until he was the winded one. He remembered the times he'd run with Kinzie, how she'd trot along at an obnoxiously slow speed, sipping her water like she was in the Iron Man competition. It surprised him a little that Courtney was seemingly in better shape than him.

When they got back to the house, they showered together, but even he was too exhausted for more sex. She dressed, he kissed her goodbye, and that was it.

5

———

The drive home from Justin's was unbearably long. Courtney was tired, hungover, and thoroughly irritated with herself that she hadn't made plans to see Justin again. With finals coming up, Courtney didn't have time to obsess over Justin. She'd never been the type to get preoccupied by a guy, and now was not the time to start. She'd always taken a cavalier approach- if he called, he called. If he didn't, well... She'd never been one to sit around and wait for that call. If the guy was truly "the one," Courtney figured it would work out whether or not she fixated on it.

Somehow though, she'd let Justin consume her. Well, maybe not so much Justin as thoughts of him. No matter how much she tried, Courtney couldn't stop replaying each and every moment of their encounter by the pool, along with all of the moments she remembered from later that night. The whole thing was surreal. Courtney had initially hoped only for his autograph, then for a quick fling. And now it was, well, she didn't know what exactly.

The chemistry was undeniable, and they seemed to have a lot of other things in common, too, but based on the lengthy gaps in communication, Courtney wasn't even sure they were actually dating. She wasn't naïve enough to think she'd ever be his girlfriend, that he'd suddenly forgo all his other girls for her, but she also found herself eagerly hoping to see him again. It was pathetic, pining for a guy who probably had more partners in a month than she would her whole life, but she also couldn't shake the urge to see him.

It didn't help that she kept seeing Justin everywhere. She wasn't actively searching him out, but everywhere she turned, there he was. In a matter of days, she spotted Justin on a talk show, an ad, and even a billboard. Courtney was determined to push him out of her mind for the time being, at least until finals were over. After that, if she saw him again in the flesh, at least it wouldn't be at the expense of her GPA.

After her second final, with several days to study before the next one, Courtney and Erica went to a local coffee shop to study. They were both desperate to get out of the apartment, having divided their time the last few weeks pretty evenly between the law school library and the living room of their crappy apartment. They staked out a table in the corner of the coffee shop and started towards the counter to order.

They'd only made it a few feet when they passed an empty table with a discarded fashion magazine on top, a photo of Justin on the cover. Erica quickly grabbed it, probably hoping Courtney hadn't already spotted it, but Courtney snatched it back and stared at the photo. Justin wore a long sleeve shirt, unbuttoned, and low-rise jeans. His hair had been dyed a dark brownish shade which made his blue eyes pop even more than usual. And the expression on his face, well, Courtney had definitely seen that look in the bedroom before.

She slumped into a chair and groaned.

"Still no call from him?"

Courtney shook her head.

"Have you called him?"

"I called him last time."

"Look, we're not thirteen. If you want to see him, call him and tell him." Erica said. "But if it's hard being apart from him now, you have to figure it'll be even harder if you hook up again."

"I know, but I just can't stop thinking about him. He's just so hot." She angled the magazine so Erica could see it better, sure she'd agree.

Erica shrugged. "I guess I can see the appeal, but he's about as far from my type as you could possibly get."

"Really? I mean, if you were into men, you still don't think you'd be attracted to him?"

"Who knows? All I'm saying is that he looks about as manly as you can get. All those muscles, that jawline, he even manages to make jewelry look masculine. I bet he smells like a man, too." Erica laughed.

"He smells amazing," Courtney mused, closing her eyes so she could better recall the exact aroma of his aftershave. "And you wouldn't believe how good he is in bed."

"Well, I bet he's had a lot of practice." She paused. "Just call him now so we can get back to studying."

Courtney sighed and handed Erica money for her coffee. She briefly considered her options, then sent him a text. "Just saw your magazine cover—smoking hot!" She clicked send, then immediately filled with regret, certain It sounded too pathetic. She didn't have too long to worry, though. Her phone buzzed just as Erica returned with their lattes.

Courtney bounced in her chair. "It's from him!" she squealed. Then, she read the message aloud.

"Thanks," was all it said.

She frowned, but before she could sip her coffee, let alone bitch about the brevity or coldness of his text, her phone buzzed again. This message was better, reading "Why haven't you called me?"

She quickly typed back her retort: "Why haven't you called me?"

There was a delay of a few minutes before the response. Courtney giggled as she read it: "Kidnapped by flying monkeys. Home safe now. Will call sometime."

Erica rolled her eyes. "At least he's okay," she joked, pulling out a book.

Courtney opened her laptop to her outline for Criminal Justice, then grimaced.

"What?" The gruffness of Erica's voice made it clear she'd had enough of Courtney's drama, but Courtney couldn't help it. No one other than Ashley or Erica even knew she'd slept with Justin Erikson, and Ashley certainly wasn't going to give her sound advice on the situation.

"Do you think I'm like a groupie to him?" Courtney asked, averting her eyes to avoid Erica's scowl.

"Groupies are for musicians."

Courtney tilted her head to the side. "We've never even gone on an actual date, so we can't be dating."

"The baseball game doesn't count as a date?"

"There were lots of other people with us. Don't we have to be alone for it to count?"

Erica sighed. "I don't know. I'm not good at this game. I've never even dated a man, so I have no idea to interpret how a man might view you."

Now Courtney rolled her eyes. Erica played the lesbian card whenever she wanted to dodge a question. "People are people and you've dated plenty. I'm begging you to share your wisdom."

There was a long pause before Erica relented. "You were the only woman at his house before the game, and the only one who spent the night with him, so I'd say he likes you. But from what little I know of him from reading the tabloids you keep forcing on me, it doesn't seem like he's a one-woman type of guy. And based on the fact that you go days without talking or texting, I don't think he wants to be exclusive."

Courtney frowned. "So I'm not a groupie, but not his girlfriend either."

Erica wrinkled her nose. "Right, but none of that matters if you don't know what you want. Do you want to be his girlfriend? Or are you okay with casual sex? Lots of people have someone they hook up with on occasion but never get serious with. And if you're looking for a friends-with-benefits arrangement, you definitely could do worse. I mean, he's got an amazing pool and can get tickets to every sporting event there is."

"Yeah," Courtney said. Erica definitely had a point. Sure, she'd never before had casual sex. In the past, she'd only slept with guys she considered her boyfriend. But she had to admit she enjoyed the sex with Justin, and besides, her life wasn't exactly conducive to a relationship right then. "Thanks," she said, happily sipping her coffee.

Erica's eyebrow shot up but she simply nodded and turned the page in her book.

A FEW DAYS after the text from Courtney, Justin was lounging around with David and Keith, discussing the party David was planning to celebrate his new line. Justin wanted to support his friend, but he was already dreading the harassment he was sure to endure at the party. David was cool, but his parties always included a lot of newer designers and others just starting out in the fashion industry. Justin knew he'd spend the entire night fielding requests for favors from random wannabes.

"Look, just bring a date," David said, well aware of the cause for Justin's reservations.

"But then he can't hook up with all the models," Keith pointed out.

Justin chuckled, but had to wonder whether Keith really just wanted to live vicariously through his escapades.

"What about that model, Anna, from a while back? She was hot," David said.

"Amber, not Anna, and there's no way I could handle a whole night of her babbling about her hair products." Justin grimaced at the thought. "I'll ask Courtney."

Keith raised an eyebrow. "You don't think she'll get the wrong idea? You've spent a lot of time with her lately."

Keith was right, but so far, Courtney had shown no signs of being the clingy, possessive type. Surely one more weekend together wouldn't make her think they were soul mates. Justin dialed her number and she answered quickly, her voice sounding breathless.

Justin smiled. "It's Justin," he said, hoping she already knew that. "How have you been?"

There was a long pause. "Good. And you?"

"Great. So, when are you done with school for the year?"

"Finals started Monday. My last one is next Thursday."

"Perfect." He motioned for Keith and David to stop following him as he paced around the room. "So listen, there's a party next weekend. My friend David is launching a new line—remember him?" He paused, but not long enough for her to confirm she did. "The official show is Friday night, then there will be an afterparty, and then his private party is Saturday night."

She was quiet.

"Courtney?"

She laughed. "Yeah, sorry, I'm still here. I, um, was just in the middle of a run, so I'm not..." her voice trailed off. "This is next Friday?"

"Yeah. I mean, you'd basically be stuck with me the whole weekend."

"I think I could handle that," she replied with a breathy laugh.

"So..."

"Yeah, that sounds great."

"Good. So have you found any more magazines with me on them?"

She laughed, comfortably, and they talked until Justin had lost track of time. He realized, suddenly, that it was getting dark outside, and he still needed to read over some scripts before he met with his agent in the morning.

"I better get going," he said, his voice quiet so he wouldn't offend her.

"Yeah," she agreed, "I need to study."

He paused. "I thought you were running."

Courtney laughed. "I was, an hour ago. I walked back while we talked."

"Sorry. I didn't mean to interrupt your workout."

"No, it was really nice talking to someone who isn't in law school. I am so ready to be out of this place and away from everything school-related for a while."

"So I might be a good distraction."

"That's what I was thinking," she agreed.

Justin hesitated, but knew he'd regret it later if he didn't speak his mind. "Hey, Courtney, I don't want you to get the wrong impression. I'm not looking for anything serious. I mean, I'm going to be out of the state for a good part of next year."

"I understand," she replied.

They hung up, and Justin went back downstairs, where David and Keith were eating pizza and gaming. Keith paused the game when he saw Justin.

"Tell me you were not on the phone that entire time," he groaned.

Justin shrugged, lifting a slice of pizza from the box.

"Were you at least having phone sex?" David teased.

Justin swiped David's controller and unpaused the game, watching on the screen and cackling as David's car crashed into a bridge, and then handed the controller back to him with a smirk.

The fashion show went seamlessly. Justin had booked a room in the hotel hosting the afterparty, certain he wouldn't want to drive home in between the runway show and the party. The moment David took his final bow, Justin tugged Courtney's hand out to lead her of the crowded room, and straight into the elevator across the hotel lobby, eager to be alone with her. As the elevator doors clanged shut, Justin turned.

His lips were on hers instantly, his hands reaching to her hips, almost accidentally slipping down to stroke the curve of her butt. Her tongue was warm, its wet length taunting his own tongue, pulling him deeper and deeper into the kiss. The elevator doors opened, and they separated, innocently, his mouth still tingling. They reached the door to the suite and paused, Justin so goal-oriented that he had temporarily forgotten the key was in his pocket. He opened the door, and they both fell into the room.

Courtney leaned closer to continue the kiss, but Justin shook his head, knowing once they started up again, he'd never be able to stop, and with Keith and Tara also staying in the suite, they at least needed to move beyond the shared main room. He pulled her back to their bedroom, nearly falling as he tripped over a suitcase that had been placed on the floor beside the bed. Courtney laughed, her breasts and shoulders jostling.

He nudged the door, which slammed loudly, eliciting another giggle from Courtney. She kicked her shoes off, one at a time, then fumbled with her dress before throwing it over the lamp by the bed.

He unbuttoned his own shirt right as Courtney's hands pressed into his chest, her fingers massaging his shoulders, chest, and stomach. She literally couldn't keep her hands off him, and Justin loved that. He lifted Courtney up, her legs wrapping around his waist, and fell on top of her on the bed. She squealed, then kissed him harder.

Justin sat up and slipped his fingers beneath the soft cotton of her panties, watching her hips rise towards him as he slowly removed her last article of clothing. He worked his way back up, his lips tracing the smooth skin of her warm thighs, her abdomen, and all the way up to her perfect breasts. He paused for a moment to admire her. As if she could read his mind, Courtney reached her hand to her breast, her slender fingers gently stroking the delicate pale skin, and Justin swore his heart skipped a beat. He stood quickly, pulled off his own clothes, grabbing a condom and rejoining her on the bed, kissing her eagerly.

Courtney pulled back, then nudged him over and climbed on top of him. "Enough foreplay," she mumbled, her breath coming in short, fast spurts as she guided him to her. Her eyelids fluttered shut as they began to shift together, finding the familiar back and forth he'd been aching for. But Justin kept his eyes on her, drawn to the pulsing in her neck as she tilted her head back, the rhythmic bobbing of her breasts, and the drunken smile on her face.

Eager to feel more of her skin against his own, Justin flipped Courtney onto her back, relaxing over her so her nipples rubbed against his chest. Courtney wrapped her legs around him, lifting her hips off the bed and squeezing his waist as they moved, until they both lost control.

"Mmmm," Courtney groaned. "You're good at that."

Justin laughed.

"Seriously, we should do that more often."

He smiled, and rolled over onto his back. Courtney scooted closer, swinging her thigh over his and resting her head on his chest, her bare stomach pressing into his own.

"I might need a nap first though."

Justin glanced down in time to see her eyes droop shut. She really was beautiful, he realized, but not in the way his past girlfriends had been. He grimaced as the word "girlfriend" fluttered through his brain. He knew this would be risky, spending yet another weekend with Courtney without intending for it to become anything serious, but he hadn't expected his own thoughts to get so complicated so quickly. He'd assume she would fall for him first, not the other way around.

"Courtney?" he whispered in case she was already asleep.

She laughed softly in response. "Don't worry, I won't pass out and trap you here."

"Oh. No, I just wanted to make sure you knew I, um, I'm not really looking for a relationship right now."

Courtney lifted her head and stared straight at him. "You have the worst possible timing," she said, her voice level and surprisingly sober.

Yeah, maybe he could've waited until that post-coital haze wore off.

She plopped her head back onto his chest. "You already told me that, but a little tip, girls like hearing something nice after sex."

"Alright, I know. My timing sucks. The sex was amazing and you are amazing and I just, well, whatever. I like you, and I don't want you to get hurt. I know normally if a guy invites a girl out for a bunch of stuff like this, there's some sort of expectation for something to continue after, and I just can't promise that. I have a really busy year coming up and I'm not going to be in town much."

He paused, wishing she'd say something to interrupt his rambling, but she didn't. "I really do like you, and I'm not saying I don't want to see you more, just that I'm going to be traveling a lot."

She sighed against his chest before sitting up. She reached out and ruffled his hair, a gesture which confused him even further.

"Justin, do you have any idea what that next year of my life is going to be like?" She paused, but only briefly.

He barely had time to shake his head.

"When I get back to Berkeley, I'll have another week off before my twelve-week internship where I'll work sixty hours a week for virtually no money. Then, school will start, and I'll spend every waking hour either in class or studying or working on the law review. I'll have finals, a few weeks off for the holidays, another semester of the same, then graduation. Then, I'll get to spend eight hours a day in classes studying for the bar exam only to go home each night and spend another four or five studying for the next day."

She wrinkled her nose. "What I'm trying to say is that I'm not looking for a relationship either. I don't have time for one now, and I don't really want to spend any energy I might have left at the end of the day dealing with someone else's issues instead of just focusing on myself. And no offense, but your life is complicated. Any sort of serious relationship with you would be full of drama and I'm just not up for that. I really enjoy hanging out with you, though, and I would like to get together again sometime after this trip."

She paused again, this time with her eyes gazing down obviously at his package. "And I definitely like having sex with you. I can totally make time for that whenever you have a lonely night."

Justin frowned, certain he misheard her. "I don't understand."

She giggled. "You like me, I like you, but neither of us is up for a commitment now, right? So let's not do that. Let's just have fun and keep it casual and then nobody gets hurt."

Her words seemed simple and straightforward enough, but Justin was still baffled. As a guy who'd either been in a serious relationship or strictly into one-night stands, Courtney's proposed arrangement was definitely unfamiliar territory.

"So let me get this straight. You're saying you don't want to be my girlfriend, you're not going to fall in love with me, and you're not going to go apeshit if I date someone else, but you want to keep sleeping with me whenever it's convenient?"

Courtney brought her hand to her forehead. "Geez, when you say it like that, I sound like a total slut."

He shook his head. "No, you sound like a dude."

She laughed. "Seriously, though, if I had met you two years ago or two years from today, I'd probably take a different stance on all this, but I just can't get into anything right now. My school and my job have to be my priority, not dating. If the timing were different, I would totally be possessive, because you are without a doubt the sexiest man I will ever see naked." She sighed wistfully.

Justin chuckled again. This was all so strange to him. He needed to clear his mind for a while, but of course now they were due at the after-party. He excused himself to the bathroom, giving her privacy to get dressed and fix her hair and makeup, then they headed back down to the party together.

He didn't have time to overthink things anyway. In another week, he was headed to Thailand to shoot a film with his favorite Days End costar, Andrea Taylor.

6

Courtney glanced down at her phone when she heard it vibrating against the thick wooden table. Seeing the caller ID, she jumped up from the table and scrambled out of the study room, ignoring the glares from the student across the table from her.

Not wanting to miss the call, she answered on the second ring, her voice barely a whisper, "Hi, hang on just a second." She scurried all the way out of the library before raising the phone to her ear.

"Sorry about that. I was in the study room in the back of the library," she explained.

"No prob. Do you want to call me back later?" Justin's voice was clear, but she heard jumbled noise in the background.

"No, I'm free now. Where are you anyway?"

He laughed. "Just outside my trailer. They're shooting a fight scene about two blocks away."

She heard a click, and then it was quieter. She guessed he had gone into the trailer. "You're about done filming though, right?" she asked. Thanks to his regular social media updates, Courtney had remained apprised of his activities even though she'd only seen him once since the night of the fashion show. He'd left for Thailand after that, sending a random text here and there while he was gone, and then called her from the airport when he first set foot on U.S. soil. They'd caught up and spent a weekend together, and then he'd resumed ignoring her.

Courtney knew he was busy shooting another movie, but since this one was local, she struggled to not read into the fact that he contacted her even less now than when he'd been in Southeast Asia. He'd told her he was too busy for a relationship, and she'd said the same. Courtney desperately wanted to be that girl she'd claimed to be, the one who could handle hooking up whenever it suited him and not forming attachments, but she wasn't exactly sure how to be that girl and not lose her mind.

"Yup. We should finish up this week. They got off schedule by two weeks, though, which totally screws up everything since I'm supposed to be leaving to film *Days End* in three weeks, and we're filming a new commercial that will take at least three days next week."

Courtney smiled. Being prone to overworking herself, she understood completely how he could love his job enough to agree to do so much in a single year, even if it meant driving himself crazy. "Well, at least you don't have to gain or lose like fifty pounds for any of these parts."

She heard him breathe a chuckle.

"It gets really boring in the trailer all day. I can't even work out in between most takes because my costume is so damn hard to get off and on." He paused. "What are you wearing?"

Courtney glanced down, then around the room, noting dozens of other students in various parts of the atrium before deciding to just answer honestly. "Jeans and a tank top."

"Oh come on," he pleaded. "Didn't you hear me say how bored I am? That doesn't help. What's under it?"

She giggled. "Justin, I can't answer that. I'm in a crowded room."

"I'm sure no one is listening. Just tell me, is it lacy?"

She reached a hand up to her shoulder, trying to recall from the touch of the strap what bra she had worn. "Yes."

"Black?"

"How did you know?"

He sighed. "Just lucky, I guess. Don't you want to know what I'm wearing?"

"Definitely," she replied eagerly.

"A skirt. A mother fucking skirt."

Courtney snickered, having forgotten he was in costume. "I don't think that's the official wardrobe title."

"Yeah, well, it should be. I don't understand why men would ever fight a war wearing this shit. I feel like a girl, and the damn thing weighs a billion pounds. Oh, and it jingles whenever I run. Plus, I have this huge belt that they stick a bunch of other props in, so I can't sit down without spending ten minutes emptying all my belt loops. And don't get me started on these ridiculous sandals that wrap up my ankle."

"Ooh, those are actually in style now, for girls, of course," Courtney teased.

"You know the best part? They spend fifteen minutes every morning using makeup to cover up the scar I got the second week of filming and then another fifteen painting on a nearly identical fake scar an inch away."

"You're almost done, though. Just keep reminding yourself of that. And then, in the future, meet with the costume designer before accepting a part."

"Yeah, next week when I'm parading around in my underwear with a bunch of other dudes I'll probably miss this stupid skirt." He laughed. "How are classes going so far?"

She paused before answering, letting her mind dwell on the

image of him in his underwear. "Good. Not quite as boring as the last two years. I'm finally taking some classes that interest me, and everyone is a little less competitive now."

"Nice. Well, uh, the reason I was calling was that we're having a little screening party at our place this weekend, Saturday night."

"Already? How will anything be ready to screen by then?"

"No, it's one we shot in the spring."

"Oh, right." She paused. "I don't know. I don't do horror."

"What? You won't even watch my movie?"

She giggled. "What if I watch it and then I'm terrified to ever be alone with you again? Sometimes, your acting is so convincing that I might not remember that you aren't actually a serial killer."

"I don't play the killer!" he objected, clearly offended that she'd forgotten his role.

"Will there be a million other girls there pawing at you?"

Justin hesitated. "It's possible we've invited a few other ladies. But you can call dibs on staying over," he added.

Courtney smiled. "Alright then. I'll see you Saturday."

"Sounds good. I better go now so I have time to put my belt back together before the next scene."

She wasn't ready to disconnect yet. She'd missed hearing his voice. "Hey Justin, if it's that hard to get in and out of the costume, what do you do if you have to go to the bathroom?"

He paused. "You don't even want to know."

Courtney laughed, then hung up. She closed her eyes and tried to picture him in that ridiculous costume.

That weekend, Courtney got to Justin's house hours before the party began. When she arrived, he was lounging by the pool with a few guys that she didn't recognize. Justin immediately hopped up when he saw her.

She greeted him with a hug and skeptically eyed his outfit—navy athletic shorts and a sleeveless top.

"Sorry, just finished working out," he explained. "I should shower anyway." He motioned for her to follow, grinning devilishly.

She followed him towards the bathroom, then paused, not particularly eager to get in since she'd already done her hair and makeup. "Why don't I just watch? I'm not particularly dirty."

He laughed, lifting his shirt off before turning on the water. "I dunno. I've seen you do some pretty dirty things."

Courtney felt her lips part in a smile and for the briefest of moments she reconsidered joining him. But then Justin darted his hand into the shower, testing the temperature, casually stepped out of his shorts and hopped into the steamy shower alone. She watched as he showered, a little jealous at his uncanny ability to go about what she presumed to be his normal routine, all with an audience. How nice it must be to have that confidence, she thought, right as Justin turned and flashed a dimpled smile.

She perched on the edge of the marbled countertop. Courtney tried not to stare, but she couldn't take her eyes off his smooth, defined chest, mesmerized by the way the water beaded off his rounded shoulders, down his ribbed stomach and over the curve of his perfect butt.

Quickly, before she could change her mind, Courtney lifted her own shirt over her head and shimmied out of her jeans. As she stood, she saw that Justin was watching.

"You gonna join me after all?"

She shook her head. "Nope. I'll wait right here."

He laughed, rinsed his hair furiously and hopped out of the shower. In an instant, Justin was inches away from her, and Courtney eagerly pressed her mouth into his, feeling his damp skin moisten her own as she lost herself in the kiss.

After what felt like mere minutes, but was apparently closer to an hour according to the clock, Courtney found herself sitting on the edge of Justin's bed, fully dressed, watching curiously as he slowly pieced together an outfit. She saw a magazine on the nightstand and quickly grabbed it, noticing Justin's name on the cover. "Hey, is this the photo shoot you did in Thailand?"

He turned to see and nodded. "Yeah, what do you think?"

Courtney opened the magazine, her eyes immediately zeroing in on a racy photo of Justin, wearing short swim shorts and an unbuttoned long sleeve shirt, the sleeves rolled up. The photo was perfect—completely capturing his breathtaking physique and sultry expression, not to mention the exotic location—*except* that his hands were on the biceps of a beautiful brunette, clad in the skimpiest of bikinis and staring back at him with the same come-hither pout.

She knew it was a photo shoot—that they had been posed, but still, that photo on its own was so intimate, so captivating, she had to wonder if the chemistry was entirely limited to on-camera. The next photo was of Justin alone, glancing out at the water. It was the type of photo she would've taped above her bed as a teen. The third photo showed him reaching for the same stunning woman, their fingertips barely making contact, as though they were about to run away together. The last picture showed Justin, his hand gingerly placed on an elephant that the brunette was riding.

Glancing at the captions, Courtney realized the woman was Andrea, Justin's costar for the movie. She hadn't realized Andrea was in this photo shoot and wouldn't have recognized her without the caption, since Andrea's hair had been short and blonde in the *Days End* films, not long, wavy, and brown like in the photos.

"So, tell me the story about the photo shoot," she said casually.

"The photos are pretty sweet, right? They originally wanted to shoot on the beach in L.A. with both of us, but when they found out we were filming in Thailand, they switched the location. I was skeptical, but the photos definitely turned out great. The elephant really makes the photos stand apart from other beach shoots."

"How long does it take to shoot something like this?"

"Just a day, and then they waited until we were back in L.A. to conduct the individual interviews." He draped a silver chain around his neck and pulled on socks. "I had my doubts that we were going to finish though. Andi went crazy when they told her they wanted her on the elephant. I mean, it's hard to tell in the other photos, but that was just paint on her there, not a real swimsuit, and then they were asking her to straddle an elephant," he laughed. "Anyway, they finally just gave her full bikini bottoms and a sarong for that shot and she was cool."

Courtney's breath caught in her throat. "Wait, Andi? That's the Andi that you were traveling with?"

Justin frowned, clearly unaware of the source of her confusion. "Yeah, Andi, Andrea, whatever."

"Andrea Taylor goes by Andi?"

He nodded.

Courtney was grateful that Justin turned to the mirror then so he couldn't see her expression. How had she not made the connection? She knew his costar was named Andrea. He told her he was filming in Thailand with Andi, doing a photo shoot there with Andi, eating dinner every night with Andi, staying at the same hotel as Andi, and, worst of all, sightseeing at exotic and romantic locations throughout Thailand with Andi. All along, Courtney had assumed he meant some male named Andy, not this breathtakingly sexy and overly feminine Andrea.

"Is Andi coming to the party tonight?"

Justin shook his head. "I haven't talked to her since we

finished shooting. I should definitely introduce you sometime though—she's awesome."

Courtney nodded meekly and folded the magazine back on his nightstand, breathing through her sudden nausea. She'd probably never know everything his relationship with Andrea—Andi—entailed, and she shouldn't care. Justin had never claimed they were exclusive, so it shouldn't matter whether the other women he was seeing were regular ladies like her or stunning actresses like Andi.

Except it did.

Courtney couldn't compete with a woman like Andi, at least not in the ways that probably mattered to Justin.

The party was fun, although Courtney drank more than she should've thanks to her insecurities brought on by the delayed revelation about Andi. That night, she had predictably good sex with Justin, but then stayed awake wondering whether his chemistry in the bedroom was as good with Andi as it was with her. The next day, she lounged around the house with Justin and his buddies until mid-afternoon, when she knew she had to leave if she wanted to have any time to study before bed.

She didn't mention anything else about Andi to Justin, but as soon as she was safely past his front gate, she called Erica. Courtney tried to be casual, telling Erica first about the party and the amazing sex on the bathroom counter, but then mentioned the magazine article and the fact that Justin's good friend and traveling companion was apparently a sultry Hollywood hottie.

Erica listened quietly before laughing hysterically, as though mockery was what Courtney needed.

Before she could chastise her for the inappropriate response, Erica spoke. "Why won't you just admit it?"

"Admit what?" Courtney demanded, accelerating to zoom through a yellow light.

"You like him."

Courtney sighed. "Of course I like him."

"No, you *really* like him." Erica laughed again. "Why does that bother you? He clearly likes you, too."

"Erica, our whole relationship is premised on neither of us getting too attached. I'm not going to mess that up, and besides, he's not exactly boyfriend material. He's leaving for Toronto to start filming again in another week, and then he has a magazine shoot and some press tour around the country. I probably won't even see him again for months. And he's going to be with Andi the whole time."

"You could call him."

"I do call him," Courtney insisted. "Erica, I can't just unilaterally decide we're dating and then force it on him."

"But you already are dating. It doesn't matter what you guys call it. You hang out and talk, you care about each other, and you have sex. That's a relationship. I know you're not seeing anyone else, and you clearly don't like him seeing anyone else, so you should probably just tell him that and stop freaking out whenever he leaves town."

"I can't ask him to stop seeing other people. I specifically agreed not to do that."

"You're going to make yourself miserable if you don't. It is time you accept that you are not built for a friends- with- benefits arrangement. Not everyone is, and that's okay. But if that's all he wants, you need to end it. Stop kidding yourself."

Courtney hated when Erica was so blunt, especially when she was also right. "I have to merge soon. I should go," she lied, hanging up the phone and turning up the music.

～

JUSTIN AWOKE hungover the day of his flight to Toronto. By the time he'd finished breakfast, the headache was gone but his mood was worse. He hadn't thought to ask Andi or Ryan when they were flying out, so he was doing the trip alone. Normally, Justin didn't mind flying solo, but he was so stressed out about the filming that a little conversation, at least during the longer leg of the flight from L.A. to New York, would have been nice.

He was excited to see the whole cast again. They'd spent so much time together filming the first two movies and then touring around doing press junkets that Justin anticipated the reunion-like atmosphere to resurface as soon as they were all together. But he didn't feel prepared for the actual filming part of it. He didn't have many lines, but he hadn't had a chance to work on them much since he finished his last project. Plus, he had a lot of fighting scenes and choreographed moves he'd have to master.

By the time Keith pulled into the unloading lane at LAX, the headache was back. Justin rubbed his middle finger and thumb against his forehead above his eyebrows. Keith turned to him and laughed.

"Dude, pull it together. We weren't up that late."

Justin rolled his eyes in response then heaved a sigh as he pushed open the passenger door of the black Escalade. He draped a large duffel bag across his chest, lugged a bigger suitcase out of the back seat and grabbed his carry-on bag before turning back to Keith.

"I'm buying the Audi when I get back," he said, feeling his lips tug upward at the thought.

Keith nodded and stuck out his hand for a quick fist bump. "Have fun with those Canadian chicks," he shouted.

By the time he was comfortably seated in first class, music blaring through his headphones, a chilled Coke in one hand and his phone in the other, Justin was ready to go.

The first few weeks of filming flew by. When he had free

time, which wasn't often, Justin hung out with the rest of the cast, or at least with Ryan and Andi. Typically, when he was filming on-site, he enjoyed exploring the local hotspots, but since he'd already been to Toronto twice, Justin didn't feel too compelled to get out and about the town.

He got a few texts from Courtney, and she even called once, but by the time they'd reached the midpoint of filming, her texts came further and further apart. Justin missed talking to her, but wasn't exactly sure what to say. He'd mentioned once that she could visit, but she'd quickly insisted that she had classes and then final exams. He knew it was a dumb idea anyway. She didn't want anything serious and having her come visit on set would definitely send the wrong message.

Keith came up to visit, with Tara in tow, of course. They all went out one night, and Justin met another girl. He had assumed being with someone else would take his mind off Courtney, but instead he just found himself comparing the two women and unable to relax and enjoy himself. Clearly, he sucked at dating, or whatever it was that he and Courtney were doing. Justin hadn't expected to miss a girl that wasn't even his girlfriend, or even to still be thinking about her while he was away. He was definitely in unfamiliar territory with Courtney.

Justin dedicated his entire first day back in L.A. to sleeping outside by the pool, since he'd been short on both sunshine and sleep for about three months by that point. On his second day home, as soon as he woke up he grabbed Keith and went straight to the Audi dealership. He bought the precise car he'd had his eye on since the newest model came out—the S5, in Monsoon Metallic Grey. And then, following a quick victory lap around town, he called Courtney.

After the requisite phone pleasantries, he invited her down to L.A., figuring that was what they were both planning anyway, but Courtney reminded him of his earlier offer to come to

Berkeley. Justin hesitated, having been away from home long enough already, but then agreed. It would be the perfect drive to break in the new car.

Courtney had said she'd be doing some job research at the law school, so he had planned to meet her there. He texted her when he arrived, then went on into the large modern-looking building.

He stepped inside the massive atrium and glanced around hesitantly. With all the windows and indoor trees and plants, it reminded him of a greenhouse, not a law school. He had thought he'd see a bunch of stressed out guys in suits pacing around, but instead there were just small groups of people, mostly in jeans, clumped around various tables or sitting areas. He saw a girl approaching and squinted, confirming it was Courtney before waving.

As he got closer, he couldn't help but smile. She looked hot, wearing tight-fitting black leggings, a long pink tank top, and a thin grey long sleeve shirt wrapped around it, almost like she was going to ballet class.

He held out his arms and she fell into them for a long hug. Justin breathed in the scent of her hair and grinned. He had forgotten how good she smelled. Suddenly, Courtney backed away, wincing.

"What happened? You look terrible!"

Justin knew what she meant, but he still pouted. "And here I was just thinking how beautiful you looked."

She blushed, reaching for his right arm, still wrapped tightly in bandages up to his elbow. He also had a busted lip, a cut by his eyebrow, another nick on his cheek, and bruised knuckles on his left hand. And his hair was different. They'd dyed it black for the movie, and when they dyed back to his natural color, it ended up a little oranger. "Were you in a fight?"

He felt his smile widen. The concern on her face was a real turn on. "Yeah, but you should see the other guy."

Courtney frowned. "You really were fighting?"

Justin laughed, then pulled her over to a bench on the side of the atrium. "For the movie, Courtney, not a real fight." He paused. "I mean, there was actual fighting, obviously, but you know, it's in the script. We shot all the fight scenes at the very end because, well," he gestured at his face and hands. "This shit doesn't exactly disappear overnight, and there's no point in making extra work for the makeup crew."

"Don't they have stunt men for that?"

"Lots of big ticket actors do their own fight scenes," he replied, dodging the question.

She frowned, lightly touching his face. "But they don't have your perfect cheekbones."

He squeezed her thigh then quickly pulled his hand back, not wanting to draw attention.

"So do I get the tour?"

Courtney stood up and grabbed his hand. He let her guide him for a moment before casually slipping his hand away and placing his hand in his pocket. The school wasn't busy by any means, but he still didn't want to show up on the internet holding hands. If the gesture offended her, she hid it well.

"Here's the library, where I spend an obscene amount of time," she said, opening the doors and starting in. She began giving him a brief explanation of the different sections, apparently under the misconception he really cared for a detailed tour.

"Won't we get kicked out for talking in here?" he asked with a grin.

She rolled her eyes but took the hint. They returned to the atrium, then headed down another long hallway, where she showed him a mock courtroom and a few classrooms. It was pretty much what he'd expected, but not having gone to any college, let alone grad school, he hadn't known how accurate his expectations would be.

Her tour ended by the cafeteria. Justin immediately perked up at the smell of food. "I'm hungry."

"You don't want to eat here."

It couldn't possibly be worse than some of the food he'd eaten on set. Besides, by the time they got to a restaurant, ordered, and got their food, it would be at least an hour from now, and he was already starving. "Yeah I do. We can go somewhere else after and I'll eat again."

Courtney reluctantly agreed, but didn't eat anything. She introduced him to a few of her friends and they made small talk, then he mentioned his new car and dragged her outside to see it.

"So was that what you pictured when I talked law school?"

"Yeah, more or less," he replied. "That guy, Mark, were you guys, um, an item?"

"No, who told you that? He's just a friend."

"No one. But you went out with him, right?"

She was flustered. "Once. Or twice, sort of."

He shook his head. "I just read people pretty well. Especially you."

Courtney rolled her eyes at him.

He laughed. "Did you sleep with him?"

"Of course not. I just said we only went out once or twice."

"You slept with me," he reminded her, glad she hadn't been offended at the question.

She smiled. "Yeah, but you're you. I'm not always that easy."

He couldn't resist any longer. He grabbed her hand, spun her around to face him, and pulled her in for a kiss, placing his hands on her cheeks. Her lips were warm, and he smiled at the familiar taste of her lip balm, wishing they had enough privacy to linger in the kiss.

"So, if I show you my new car, will you show me that apartment of yours?"

"The one they're tearing down and kicking me out of in a month?"

Justin laughed. "Yeah."

"I thought we were going out to eat."

"I need to work up more of an appetite first," he replied, winking.

A couple hours later, they went out to a fondue restaurant.The restaurant was dimly lit, and each of the tables was set off from the others. They ordered drinks, a Manhattan for him and an Asian Pear Martini for her. Justin sniffed Courtney's drink with a grimace, then laughed.

"That smells nothing like a real martini."

She smiled, her blue eyes sparkling in the candlelight. "Yeah, so says the guy with a cherry in his drink."

They ordered their food, and then Justin scooted closer to Courtney, resting his hand on the bare patch of skin on her thigh between where her knee-high boots ended and her blue skirt started. He kissed her on the cheek, and she blushed.

"You know," he began, in his deep seductive voice, "I think this technically might be our first real date."

"I agreed to dinner, not a date," she said.

He couldn't gauge her expression, so he took a long swig of his drink, trying to figure out the right response. Finally, he noticed the slightest of smiles on her face. "So you'll sleep with me but not date me," he clarified.

She shrugged playfully. "That was our arrangement, wasn't it?"

Justin glanced around. "You picked a pretty romantic restaurant for a non-date."

"Technically, you picked the restaurant," she said.

"From a list you gave me. And I bet they were all secluded and candlelit places where you could take advantage of me."

She smiled, reaching down and quickly squeezing the hand he'd left on her leg. "I still have a few weeks of school left, then the bar exam. It's not that I don't want to get more involved, it's just too complicated. I'm too busy now."

Justin watched her as she spoke, suspecting she didn't really mean what she was saying. "You weren't too busy to date Mike. Did you take him to eat here?"

Courtney laughed. "It's Mark, and no. But that's different. He's in law school too. You're always out of town."

"I'm here now."

"For how long?"

He winced. Technically, she had him there. In a few more weeks, he was headed back to Canada to film the final *Days End* film. The two movies were being released nine months apart, but they wanted to do the filming closer together. Justin wasn't sure why, but he suspected one of the bigger stars had something else going on later in the year.

Their waitress brought the salads and they began eating, quietly.

After a minute, Courtney set down her fork and turned to face him. Her long dark hair fell across her eyes, casting a shadow over her entire face. "I missed you when you were in Toronto. I mean, I really missed you." She paused, swallowing loudly, and tucked her hair back behind her ear. "I just don't want to make it any harder the next time you're gone."

Justin thought he understood what she meant, but then she kissed him, hard, and on the lips, and he realized he was just as confused as ever.

7

———

Exactly one year after meeting Justin, Courtney moved to L.A. Not because of him, of course, but she did notice the symbolic timing of the move—scheduled to occur over Spring Break, since that was the only time she and Erica had time off to actually do the move. With almost a full month remaining of school between classes and finals, Courtney and Erica decided to stay at their old apartment in Berkeley during the week, sleeping on air mattresses in the otherwise empty and about-to-be-leveled building.

Courtney hadn't seen Justin since the weekend he'd spent in Berkeley with her, but she realized they could spend more time together now that she was living in L.A. The rational part of her knew this probably wasn't a good thing. The more time she spent with Justin and the more attached she grew, the harder it was going to be for her when he was gone, again, and the less available she'd be for meeting someone that might actually have potential for a future with her.

But the emotional side of her, the part that melted when she heard his voice during what had become their daily phone call and that felt a twinge of jealousy when she saw his photo in a magazine and knew other girls were drooling over it just as she was... that part of her couldn't wait to see him again. Fortunately, he was coming over that afternoon to see the new place.

Courtney walked through the apartment, her eyes scanning the stacks of boxes, when she heard a noise at the door.

She smiled as she turned to see Justin in the entryway. "You're early," she said, kissing him.

"You should lock your door. L.A. isn't Berkeley."

She opened her mouth to protest, but Justin had already pulled her close.

"This outfit is hot," he whispered, his breath tickling her ear.

Courtney grinned. She was wearing a pleated skirt and thin v-neck sweater. She wanted to look professional for when she went to the courthouse to register for her licensing exam, but hadn't known if she'd have time to change before their date. "So, the naughty school-girl look works for you?"

Justin thrust his hand up her skirt and tugged her panties down. She delicately lifted her foot to step out of them as he grinned, tossing them onto the floor. "Now it does," he cooed, kissing her forcefully. "Is Erica home?"

"Not yet." Courtney slipped her hands under his shirt, pressing her fingers against his smooth skin. Without even thinking about it, she pulled his shirt up, breaking from the kiss only long enough to lift the material over his head. As their mouths pressed together again, Courtney ran her fingers across his waist, tracing each pronounced ridge along his stomach. She felt his tongue against her own and noticed the warmth growing deep within her.

"When will she be back? How long do we have?" he mumbled before kissing behind her ear then sucking the thin skin along the side of her neck.

"She went to the store, so maybe another twenty minutes," she replied, her voice hoarse.

"I can work with that," he replied, and before Courtney caught her breath, her shirt and bra were on the floor.

Justin lifted her effortlessly onto the counter, his lips reaching for her breast. Courtney tilted her head back, arching her back with delight as he ran his hands and mouth across her breasts, his tongue flicking her nipples back and forth until she felt like she might explode. He paused to grin at her, his smoldering blue eyes focused directly on her as he slid his hand down her body, nudging her legs apart, and tracing his finger gently along her slit, darting it in and out of her body as she gasped for air. Courtney shivered, her entire body tingling from his touch. When she knew she couldn't wait any longer, she pulled him closer, fumbling with the button on his jeans until he laughed, breathlessly, before helping her.

Courtney opened her eyes, desperate to feel his mouth on hers again. Her arms reached for him, eagerly caressing his smooth back and curved arms. She felt his hand wander down her stomach and between her thighs again. She groaned, the damp heat between her thighs growing almost unbearable.

"I want you now," she whispered, her teeth grazing the side of his ear.

Justin drew his hand back, and scooted her off the counter, delicately lifting her closer until their bodies were pressed together. Courtney wrapped her thighs around his waist and dug her teeth into the full flesh of his shoulder to keep from crying out as he entered her. Her thighs trembled, and Courtney was grateful that he was holding her up, knowing her own legs couldn't support her own weight when she was this breathless, this overwhelmed with desire.

She focused on Justin's breath, coming faster and faster against the back of her neck, and his hands, rhythmically squeezing her back with every movement. Courtney grasped his butt firmly in both hands, pushing him further and further into her until she could feel every ridge and every smooth inch of him filling her. She opened her eyes again and caught Justin staring back at her, a hazy look in his deep blue eyes. She jolted, her entire body tensing, then relaxing, with the overpowering sensation spreading through her like wildfire. She felt her own voice crying out, heard his own deeper groan, and he pulled her closer, his fingers scratching into her back, and then they rocked together until the scorching heat in their bodies dissipated.

Justin gently set her back on the counter, easing her to a lying position, then kissed her where his nails had cut into her skin. "Sorry," he whispered.

Courtney tried to smile in response, but was still too dizzy, too breathless. She felt her heart beat heavily, shaking her entire body with each pulse. Justin leaned over her, resting his head against her glistening chest, his labored breath tickling her hardened nipples.

When she caught her breath, Courtney kissed the top of his head. Justin stood up, then bent to pick up her shirt, bra, and panties, tossing them to her before making his way to the tiny bathroom right off the kitchen.

Courtney glanced at the clock, realizing it was later than she'd thought. She had just fastened her bra when she heard Erica's key in the door. She quickly pulled her shirt over her head and, knowing she was out of time, wedged her panties into her purse right as the door opened.

Erica tromped in and dropped her bags on the counter. "There's a car parked in my spot," she grumbled. "A really nice car."

Courtney tried to sound natural. "Sorry. It's probably Justin. I'll have him move it."

Erica shook her head. "Too late now. I already parked across the lot." She started unpacking the groceries. "I didn't know he had a BMW."

"I don't," Justin replied, emerging from the bathroom. His pants were buttoned, but he was still shirtless. Courtney glanced down and saw his shirt was still on the floor beside the counter. She tossed it to him, blushing, nervously avoiding Erica's knowing stare.

"Then who's parked in our spot?" Courtney asked.

Justin reached in his pocket. "You are." He grinned, tossing a keychain at her.

The keys hit Courtney's stomach and fell to the ground with a clank. She stared blankly at him, confused.

His smile widened as he walked closer, picking up the keys and pulling her in for a hug. "It's a belated birthday, graduation, and housewarming combo gift."

Courtney's eyes widened as she broke away from him and ran outside to see the car. It was a dark grey metallic sedan.

"Before you get too excited, I didn't actually buy it for you," Justin confessed. "Officially, it's just on a test drive now. But, I already got the sales guy negotiated down and they're just waiting on us to bring back your car for the trade in. You pay what you were planning on spending on the car and I'll cover the rest."

"Justin, my parents gave me five grand towards a car. That plus my own five would hardly pay for any of this," she replied, heading outside and circling the car.

He shrugged. "You're forgetting the value of your trade in."

Courtney rolled her eyes. She didn't know exactly what her car was worth, but the sticker on the BMW said $54,999. She was positive her 2010 Toyota Camry wasn't worth that.

"It doesn't really cost that," he assured her, leaning against the car so he was blocking the sticker.

"You can't buy me a car."

He shook his head. "I didn't. You're buying it."

She was skeptical. She recognized that determined look in his eyes and suspected nothing she said would change his mind, but it still seemed wrong to accept such a big gift. She leaned in to him, letting her head rest on his thick shoulder while his arms pressed around her.

"It's been a good year for me," he finally said. "You're always doing great things for other people. Let me do something nice for you."

Courtney looked up and smiled. She couldn't really turn down a BMW.

He grinned. "Come on, we better get back to the dealership. I parked my car there and took this one like two hours ago. I'll drive your car, and you follow me in this."

She shook her head. "I'm too nervous to drive this, plus I need a farewell drive with my own car." She raced inside to grab her purse, and they left.

The rest of the day was a blur. After the briefest of reminiscing about her initial drive to California, feeling that she was all alone headed to a new state, a new school, for an entirely new experience, Courtney gladly said goodbye to the Camry. A little over an hour later, she nervously drove away in the BMW, Justin following closely behind her...a little too closely, really, given that Courtney could tell he was playing with his phone instead of focusing on not slamming his ridiculously expensive still-new car into the bumper of her not-quite-as-ridiculously expensive brand new car.

When they got back to her place, they went out to celebrate. Courtney wasn't completely sure what they were celebrating, nor did she care. She had a new car...a more amazing car than she ever would've pictured herself owning, and Justin had bought it for her. That had to mean something.

Courtney awoke early the next morning in Justin's bed. She

knew she should get back to her apartment to help Erica with the unpacking, but she didn't want to sneak out before Justin was up. She'd hate to make him think she was using him for fancy cars and mind-blowing sex. Courtney laughed out loud at her thought, then froze as Justin shifted under the covers.

Since she'd clearly awakened him, she hopped out of bed and went into the bathroom to make herself look more appealing before he actually saw her. When she returned to the bed, he was sitting up, checking something on his phone.

"Morning," he greeted her cheerily, without looking up from his phone. It irritated Courtney that Justin was always chipper in the morning, no matter how little sleep he'd gotten or how much alcohol he'd consumed.

She climbed up on the bed and swung a leg over him so she was straddling him, her knees on either side of him. She carefully pulled the phone out of his hand and set it on the nightstand.

He immediately made eye contact. "Why do you do that?"

"Do what? Take your phone? Because you seemed distracted."

He shook his head. "No, why do you put on makeup right away?"

Courtney bit her lip. "Because I'm self-conscious around you in the mornings. And it wasn't really makeup, just some cover up, really."

"And you brushed your hair," he commented, leaning forward and sniffing her. "And your teeth."

She shrugged.

"Now I'm the only one with morning breath."

Courtney leaned in and kissed him. "Now we both have the same breath," she said.

"What do you have to feel self-conscious about?" Justin's

tone was so incredulous that it rather amused her. Could he really not get it?

She sighed. "It's hard to wake up next to an underwear model and not be a little bothered by the circles under my eyes or the weird matting my hair does overnight. And the fact that, as far as I know, all the other women you've ever woken up next to were super models or actresses doesn't really help."

He frowned. "You've always seemed like the confident type to me. I didn't realize you were so uncomfortable with me."

Courtney rolled her eyes. "Okay, let's not be overdramatic here. How about I apologize for brushing my teeth and reapplying deodorant and we make up before Erica kills me for not helping out?"

"Deodorant too? Man, now I really smell bad by comparison!"

Courtney giggled, then let him topple her over in a tight embrace.

He paused after the first kiss. "Wait, does that mean you think you're leaving soon?"

"It means I am leaving soon," she clarified. "I have to. There's so much unpacking to do, and we've got to finish it all this week before finals."

Justin shook his head. "The thing with boxes is that they'll still be there after finals. You don't really have to unpack this week. What you need to do is relax a little and unwind before you return to school."

"What exactly do you have in mind?"

"How about breakfast and a quick jog on the boardwalk? Oh, and something else, but I'll have to demonstrate that," he said, laughing and ducking under the covers, his head quickly landing between her thighs.

When they eventually made their way out of bed, Justin having successfully convinced her to blow off Erica and the unpacking for a few more hours, they grabbed some breakfast and then went for a jog along the boardwalk, just as he'd suggested. As they finished their jog and neared Justin's house, they stopped for coffee.

The coffee shop was crowded, so they got their drinks to go, walking slowly back towards his house. Courtney wasn't bothered by the four separate women that approached Justin for an autograph, but froze like a deer in headlights when she noticed a creepy looking guy photographing them.

"What?" Justin stopped and followed her panicked glance. "Oh, yeah. Just ignore him." He shook his head. "For some reason, they've taken a shine to my morning runs lately."

Courtney couldn't just ignore it, especially since she knew she couldn't look great. She'd just run three miles, and probably had rings of sweat around her armpits and crazed wisps of hair slipping out of her ponytail. But Justin didn't give her long to worry about it, because he kept right on talking. She wondered how long it had taken him to get to the point where he could just ignore the weirdos stalking him with oversized film equipment.

"Any job leads?"

She sighed. This was not her favorite point of conversation at the moment, and she knew it was one she was going to argue about again with her parents the next time she spoke with them, since they thought she was insane for getting an apartment in L.A. when she didn't have a job lined up or anything else, as far as they knew, tying her to L.A.

"Courtney?"

"Oh, sorry. Um, maybe, but nothing definite. There is another legal aid clinic in L.A. that has a possible lead for a position with a battered women's shelter. I don't want to jinx it, but I've got an interview on Friday before I go back to Berkeley."

"What does an attorney do at a shelter?"

"Oh, different things. For the most part, I think I'd be handling civil stuff, since a lot of the women might have custody issues with kids or even more basic legal problems like housing or landlord troubles. But it might also involve criminal work, like if the woman defends herself against an abuser, or gets dragged into some crime as an accomplice, or whatever. I won't know exactly what the job would entail until after I talk with them."

"But you'd get paid this time?"

She nodded. "Enough to cover rent and the bare necessities, I think."

He frowned. "Just to play the devil's advocate here, but why not look for a job with better pay? I know you've got good grades and everything. I mean, isn't that the point of law school, to get a high-paying lawyer job?"

Courtney smiled. "Not for me." She sipped the coffee, trying not to spill it down her shirt while walking, especially not until she could be sure the photographer had left the vicinity. "I wouldn't turn down the extra money if they offered it, but I'd rather have this job with shitty pay than a different job with better pay."

"And why the focus on domestic violence? Why not represent old people or stray animals? Or charities or something? I'm sure there's lots of low-paying do-gooder lawyer jobs out there if you broaden the search some."

She hesitated. "Domestic violence is the cause that prompted me to go to law school. It's more personal for me, I guess."

Justin turned to her uncomfortably. "Oh, sorry, I didn't mean to..." he stuttered, then slowed his pace till he was nearly stopped.

Courtney quickly realized why he was suddenly acting so

strange. "No, Justin, I don't mean that I was ever in that sort of relationship."

She paused, and waited for the relief to show on his face before continuing. "My aunt's first husband was abusive. She got married really young and we all thought she was happy, but it turned out he was hitting her. He made her quit her job, stop coming to family gatherings, and was just really horrible, but she never felt like she could leave him because she didn't know how, didn't have any money, and didn't want him to get custody of their child. It kept getting worse, though, so she finally left him. She told us later that there was a law student volunteering at the shelter she stayed at that first night, when she was too scared to even call my dad for help. The student apparently gave her so much advice that she was able to get out of the bad situation, and now she's happy and has a little boy with her second husband and full custody of the little girl she had with her first husband."

Justin winced, then rubbed her back with his spare hand.

Courtney sighed, making a mental note to call her Aunt Alice on her drive back to Berkeley over the weekend. "I really better go when we get back to your place. Erica can be really scary when she wants to be, and I know she wasn't eager about unpacking."

He laughed, but they picked up the pace regardless.

As USUAL, Justin was running late to his meeting with his agent, Marty. He accepted an energy drink from Marty's assistant as he walked into the office.

"You know that stuff isn't good for you," Marty said, gesturing for Keith and Justin to sit down.

"I'm headed to the gym next," Justin replied, retrieving a

protein bar from his sweatshirt pocket. He plopped a stack of papers down and leaned back on the couch. "That's the no pile. The last one is a maybe. You got anything new?"

Marty nodded and handed a thick stack of scripts to Keith. "Four more that sound decent. The one on top there is my favorite, and they've already said the role is yours if you want it."

"What is it?" Justin leaned forward to glance at the cover.

"High school football movie. You'd have the lead. A little drama, a little action, lots of cute girls to kiss. Right up your alley."

Justin laughed. "High school?"

"Yeah, that's the downside. They want you to look young enough to fit the part, so they're asking you to drop twenty pounds." He paused. "Actually, what do you weigh now?"

He shrugged. "205 maybe."

"Alright, then twenty-five pounds. We could maybe negotiate that some. You know, those dimples keep you youthful." Marty laughed. "The problem is that they want to film next winter, so you'd have to lose the weight and gain it all back pretty quickly to stick with existing film schedule."

Justin sighed. "Veto. I want this one," he insisted, pushing another action script forward.

Marty nodded. "You're in the final running. I'll push for it, and we'll see. Alright," he started to scroll down his notes. "Let me see what else I have before I turn it over to Jamie here. Oh, cologne. How would you feel about your own fragrance?"

"That might be cool," he replied, turning to Keith for a second opinion.

"Would it be under the same contract as the modeling?" Keith asked. Justin could always rely on Keith to find out the important details. Even before he'd technically become Justin's manager, when he was really more of a personal assistant, Keith was always the one who kept Justin grounded and reminded him not to jump on every opportunity that sounded fun without thinking it through.

"Same company yes, same contract no." Marty shook his head. "They develop the scent—you have very limited involvement in the process, but then they use your name and image to market it. You'd get an initial pay and then some royalties for the use of the name and photos, along with a separate paycheck for any actual ads you shoot." He handed a manila folder to Keith. "Here's the paperwork on that. Look it over and let me know. And get back to me within a couple weeks. I need to know about those scripts before you leave the country again."

Justin nodded and finished up the last bite of his protein bar. His phone vibrated in his pocket and he pulled it out. It was a text from Courtney. "Call me after your spa appt—I'll make you feel all better," it read. Justin couldn't help but smile at that. She knew how much he hated getting waxed, but since he had another photo shoot next week, he had to go today after the gym.

"Hey, you still there?" Marty asked Justin. He turned to Jamie. "This might be a good point for you to jump in," he said to her.

Justin glanced up. "Can you all give me a minute? I need to make a call. You could double-check the schedule or something."

He caught the look of irritation on Marty's face, but Keith nodded, so he left anyway. Organizational skills were not Justin's strong suit. He knew that, and that's why he brought Keith to his meetings. Keith could deal with all the scheduling, making sure he knew exactly when he was supposed to do everything and what all he needed to do to prepare. He stepped into a vacant corner of the lobby and dialed Courtney. She answered immediately.

"I'm going to need a few more details," he said in lieu of a greeting. "How exactly do you plan on making it all better?"

She laughed, a carefree laugh that immediately calmed him, so he moved on to the more pressing issue.

"How did the interview go?"

"I don't want to jinx it."

He could hear the excitement in her voice and figured that must mean it went well. "If it had gone really bad, you would tell me, right?"

Courtney laughed again. "Of course. Then there wouldn't be anything to jinx."

Justin smiled, and then noticed Keith in the hall motioning at him. Justin mouthed the word "what" to Keith, and Keith stepped closer.

"They need you back in there. I don't want to field these questions." Keith mumbled.

Justin frowned. "Sorry, Courtney. I guess I have to get back to my meeting. Glad the interview went well, and I'll call you after the waxing. I'm holding you to your promise!" He hung up and turned to Keith.

"They're asking about her," Keith explained unapologetically.

They both returned to the office. Jamie stared at Justin expectantly, a small collection of photos in front of her. "We were asking Keith about this person, but he wasn't too helpful. So can you tell us who this is?" Jamie asked, pointing to a photo of Courtney jogging along the boardwalk with Justin.

Keith cleared his throat. "I'm going to step out for a minute."

"Her name's Courtney," Justin replied. "Courtney Robbins."

Jamie sighed. "No, I mean, who is she? Why am I getting emails from multiple sources asking me to identify a girl seen with you?"

Justin sipped his drink, trying to decide what answer would

satiate Jamie. He still remembered what a nightmare it had been when Jamie caught wind of his first date with Kinzie and then attempted to micromanage every aspect of their relationship to best suit his PR needs. "I don't know," he finally mumbled.

"Well, what is this?" she demanded, pointing to a photo of Justin at the BMW dealership.

"That's a car."

Jamie rolled her eyes. "Did you buy that car?"

Justin licked his lips. "Technically I paid for most of it, but Courtney's name is on the title."

Marty shook his head with disbelief. "Is she pregnant?"

Justin sat up with a jolt. "No! I mean, why? Did someone tell you that?" He racked his brain to think of a recent time they might not have been careful, but even if there had been once or twice, surely Courtney would've told him before anyone else.

"Why else would you buy her a car?" Marty demanded.

"It was a graduation present."

Marty winced. "Please tell me college, not high school."

Justin sighed. Did everyone think so little of his integrity? "Law school."

"Justin, an appropriate gift for a friend graduating from law school would be Black's Law Dictionary, or maybe an Amazon gift card. You can't tell me you give cars to all recent grads you know, so why this Courtney?" Jamie persisted.

"I like her," Justin finally admitted. "We're friends."

"Friends," Jamie repeated, sifting through the stack of pictures.

"We're um, dating, I guess."

Jamie gazed down at one of the photos in her hands. Justin could tell it was from the baseball game. "Have you been dating her for a full year, since this picture was taken?"

Justin really didn't know how to answer that one. Even if he did, he suspected the truth might make Jamie violent. "I don't know. Maybe? I mean, not exclusively. Is that a problem?"

Jamie pursed her lips, then stacked the photos and handed them to Justin, as though he wanted a collection of creepy shots taken by weirdos hiding in the bushes. "Look, Justin, you know most of your fans are women, and you know sex sells. Since your last breakup with Kinzie, we've been marketing you as single, which helps, to a point. But if you're suddenly off the market, we need to know that so we can work that angle."

"Well I don't know the exact parameters of our relationship. Sorry."

"Is she an aspiring actress or a model or something?"

"No, I told you she's a lawyer. Or, almost. She's got to take that bar exam, this summer."

Jamie sighed. "People don't want to see you dating a lawyer. They want to see you with someone else famous. Or at least hooking up with some random fans so they can think they have a chance with you."

"What did you tell them? The people who asked about Courtney?" Justin wanted to know.

"I said she was your assistant," Jamie replied.

"That works, right?"

"Justin, it's been a while since you've been seen dating anyone. Every time you're photographed, you're either with Keith or Courtney. If we tell people she's your assistant, they're going to think he's your boyfriend. And if the female fans think you're totally off the market for women altogether, that ain't good."

"I'm not going to stop seeing Courtney," he replied. "Or Keith," he added with a grin.

"No one's asking you to," Marty insisted. "But Jamie can't do her job when you cut her out of the loop of your personal life."

Jamie glared at Marty. "So far no one has photographed

anything that indicates you two are romantically involved, so let's just keep it that way. You do whatever you want in private, but just don't flaunt it in public. Pretend she's your assistant."

Justin laughed. "She'll love that," he joked.

"But in terms of the problem of you not appearing publicly with a date for a while, I think we can fix that, too." Jamie scooted a new collection of photos to him. "You have a premiere in New York next week. Any of these ladies would be happy to escort you. They're all models."

"I don't need a fix up! I can get my own dates, thank you."

"It wouldn't be like that. It would be a professional arrangement. It would help their careers to appear with you, and it would definitely help your image to appear with them. Just share a limo and pose for some photos outside, and then you don't even have to sit together if you don't want."

Justin didn't even respond to this. It was all so strange. He suddenly missed his early days in L.A., when he didn't have to consult a whole team of people just to date someone, when he could date whoever he wanted for however long he wanted as publicly or not as he wanted, and when no one, aside from maybe his mother, cared about his dating life. Sure, he'd been dirt poor then, despite working his ass off around the clock, but even an Audi and a sweet Venice Beach house didn't really compensate for this crap.

"And then when you have the publicity tour for *Days End*, we thought you could see if Andrea Taylor would accompany you to the different formal affairs."

He frowned. "You want me to date Andi?"

"Fans love it when they think costars are romantically involved," Jamie explained.

"I'll think about it," he mumbled, figuring that at least wouldn't be as awkward. "We done here?"

They both nodded, so he stood to leave.

Justin met up with Keith in the lobby downstairs. "Hey, thanks for ditching me in there!" he shouted.

"I thought they could talk some sense into you," Keith replied nonchalantly.

Justin frowned. "What is that supposed to mean?"

Keith shrugged. "Nothing. But you need to figure out what you're doing with Courtney. You're way too busy for a serious girlfriend now, especially one who doesn't understand what it's like for you."

"She's not my girlfriend. We're just dating."

Keith laughed. "You don't date, Justin. You sleep around, or you have a girlfriend. And now, Courtney's your girlfriend."

"Not. My. Girlfriend," Justin repeated.

"You text her more than me. And you spend more time on the phone with her than you do at the gym."

"Not true," he quickly replied. Although as Justin thought about it, Keith might've been right. He loved talking to Courtney. But that alone didn't make her his girlfriend, especially when she adamantly protested the title. She had left little room for confusion about their arrangement.

"I'm just worried that you're setting yourself up for a rough patch by not dating someone who gets where you're coming from," Keith continued.

"Like Kinzie?" Justin rolled his eyes. "The first thing that attracted me to Courtney was that she is nothing like Kinzie."

"Oh, I thought it was her tits," Keith replied.

Justin punched him in the shoulder.

Keith rubbed his arm but kept talking. "Every actress isn't like Kinzie. You know, they're not all so, well, shallow and moody. You always say how you're just this normal guy who happens to be an actor, so why don't you find some normal girl who happens to be an actor?"

Justin stopped walking and turned. "Drop it, okay?" Keith

nodded, and they both started moving towards the car again. "I'm leaving town soon and it's going to be a moot point anyway."

Courtney drove down from Berkeley the day after her first final exam. Justin had anticipated her being excited and ready to celebrate. She was almost done with school, and the shelter that had interviewed her had already offered her the job.

But, as soon as Justin carried her bag upstairs, she collapsed on the bed. "I'm exhausted. I just keep telling myself that these are my last final exams ever and I just have to make it through the next two weeks, but all I want to do is sleep."

Justin laughed, but he couldn't really relate. His grades hadn't been bad in high school, but he recalled final exams then being more of a pain in the ass than anything else. Law school finals, apparently, were different. Not just harder, which he had assumed, but also, the final exam grade was the only grade for most classes. So, even if Courtney had been studying hard and doing well all semester, she could flunk the class if she blew the final.

He sat on the bed, pillows propped up against his back, and she climbed over to him, nestling her head into its usual spot between his chest and shoulder. Justin smoothed her hair back, subtly inhaling its fresh floral scent, then wrapped his arm around her back, running his finger up and down her delicate skin.

"So you've got two tests next week, two the week after, and then a week off before you start studying for the bar?"

She groaned. "Don't remind me."

"You could come up to Toronto during that week," he mentioned, regretting it as soon as he'd said it. He already knew her response.

"I'm going to see my parents then. You'll be working anyway and I'd just get bored. I'll come over the Fourth." She sighed, her breath pouring out onto his shirt. Justin lifted her head and pulled his shirt off, wanting to feel her against his bare skin.

"Tell me about your plans," she asked.

He told her about flying to Toronto in two days, then once filming began, how he'd be getting up at the crack of dawn, going through makeup and wardrobe for hours, then sitting on set or in his trailer between scenes, only to head straight to the gym at the end of the long, exhausting day.

"Why don't you do your workout during the day when you're in your trailer? Then you'd cut down on the downtime and have more time to relax in the evening."

He laughed. Courtney loved to multitask, and was always trying to inflict it on others. "Because if I get all sweaty between scenes, I'll have to go through makeup all over again." He paused. "Besides, I need to work on my lines and rehearse when we're filming, too."

"Sounds rough. So why are you so excited?"

"I can't wait to see everyone again," he admitted. He had gotten so close to that group of actors over the last few years, between filming the first three movies and then traveling to promote them. This one, their last, would be bittersweet, but he knew he'd still see the group a lot over the next year, until the film had been released. "You know you can meet the whole cast when you visit."

"That will be nice," she replied. "I'm sure I'll have fun hanging out with you in Toronto."

And he knew she meant it just as she said it. That was one of the things he liked most about Courtney. Most chicks between the ages of twelve and thirty-five would probably pay their life savings for the opportunity to hang out with this cast—especially the two stars—but Courtney was, at best, indifferent.

Justin knew she'd get along with everyone and figured she'd probably gush at least a little over the other stars, but that when it came down to it, she would be most excited about seeing him. That was flattering.

She was quiet for a long time, and Justin realized she had fallen asleep. He kissed her forehead, relaxing back into the pillows, thinking about the next day. After a while, Keith came by. The door wasn't closed, so he nudged it open then laughed.

"Dude, we're going to be late."

Justin raised a finger to his lips to shush Keith. "She's asleep."

"Yeah, I can see that. Wake her up so we can go now."

He hesitated. "I think she needs her rest."

Keith rolled his eyes. "Then scoot her over, put your shirt on, and let's go. It's your second to last night to live it up Cali style for the next two months!"

While that was true, it was also his second to last night with Courtney. Justin shook his head. "You go. I'm gonna hang here tonight."

Keith looked skeptical, but nodded.

"Hey, toss me the remote," Justin whispered.

His friend picked it up, looked at Justin, then placed it beside the TV, shaking his head. "It's for your own good, man. Cuddlers never prosper."

Justin laughed, not as annoyed as he wanted to be. He listened to Courtney's peaceful breathing, focusing on her breath falling in light, even waves on his chest, and then the next thing he knew, light was streaming in the room.

He had shifted in his sleep, and was now lying on his side, with his arm draped around Courtney, who was also on her side, the length of her body pressed firmly against his chest and stomach. Justin winced, his arm feeling like it was covered in spikes. Courtney groaned softly.

"Why am I still wearing clothes?" she asked, turning to face him while rubbing the sleep out of her eyes. When she saw him, still clad in jeans, her eyes grew wide.

"Oh God, I am so sorry! I made you miss the party, didn't I?"

Justin smiled, trying not to laugh at the frantic look in her eyes. He was going to miss waking up next to her over the next few months.

8

Over two months later, Courtney was due to arrive on set early on the last day of filming before the holiday. Security was lax that day, with a few guards positioned at each barricade across the field. A gaggle of teenage girls stood about a hundred yards away, squealing and shrieking excitedly from behind the security barricades, but Justin had given Courtney instructions to bypass security and the crowd so she could wait for him by his trailer.

Justin took a break around noon to check his trailer for Courtney. She wasn't there, so he called. She answered immediately, but it was so loud, he could hardly hear her.

"Are you still at the airport?" he guessed based on the background noise.

"No. I'm here, on set."

He frowned and looked around. There weren't any extras for the day's scenes, so it wasn't very crowded. "Where?"

"I don't know, with everyone else."

"Who else?"

"I don't know. There's a big crowd, some guards," her voice trailed off.

"Courtney, are you behind the big orange security barricades?"

"Yep."

He laughed. "I thought you were going to meet me at my trailer."

"Security wouldn't let the cab through."

Justin figured he shouldn't be too surprised at this, but he was. He knew if they filmed in the U.S. the crowds would be unmanageable, with the films having such a large, cult-like following. But in Canada, most people didn't give a crap about the filming. "I'll come get you," he promised. He told Andi where he was going then started off across the field.

As he got closer to the cluster of people, the sound of girls shrieking with excitement pierced his eardrums. He squinted and tried to spot Courtney. Eventually, he saw her, standing in the corner, smiling and waving sweetly. He nodded to her, then approached a security guard.

"Hey, um, that girl back there with the dark brown hair, blue jeans, green tank top, can you let her through?" Justin asked the taller of the guards close to him. "I'm in the movie," he added, instantly realizing that between the squealing of the crowd and his full wardrobe and makeup that the guards probably knew who he was. While he waited for Courtney, he smiled and waved at the crowd, stepping forward to sign a few autographs.

When the guard closed the gate behind Courtney, Justin turned, nodding casually for Courtney to follow. As soon as they were far enough away, just off to the side of the set, he reached for Courtney's bag, draping it over his own shoulder and taking her hand. They walked the rest of the way to his trailer, where he set down her bag. He turned and got a good look at her now, her refreshing blue eyes twinkling back at him.

Courtney looked perfect, like always, but in that easy casual way, as if she hadn't really bothered with her appearance. She wore jeans, a turquoise tank top with intricate gold beading on the chest, and sandals. Her hair was twisted into a loose knot on her head, and she wore only the subtlest of makeup. Only Courtney would come to a movie set dressed like it was any other day. And only Courtney could manage to look that amazing after a flight.

She rose to her toes and kissed him, nearly catching him off guard. When she pulled back, she laughed. "Those aren't your teeth. I hardly recognize you."

Now Justin laughed, realizing that in an ironic turn of events, his lipstick had rubbed off on her. He wiped her lips with his thumb, hoping she didn't take off.

She didn't run. Instead, Courtney stared intently.

"What?" he finally asked.

"It's just so different." She reached out and touched his hair, as though expecting it to be fake.

Justin ran his fingers through his hair, then realized how unfamiliar he probably looked to her. It wasn't just the faux teeth and blood-red lipstick. His hair was dyed black, his skin was coated in makeup, and fluorescent yellow contacts covered all traces of his naturally blue eyes.

"Sorry," she mumbled, and he wondered why she was apologizing when he was the one who clearly was disappointing her.

He turned and grabbed a bottle of water, offering it to her. She accepted, and he took another for himself. "How was the flight?"

Now Courtney smiled widely. "You flew me first class."

Justin laughed, always pleasantly surprised at her easy-to-please demeanor. "What did you expect?"

She shrugged. "How has filming been going?"

"Good. It's been fun," he replied, and he meant it. He liked most of the things he'd acted in, but this one was right up his alley. He didn't have many lines, and he got to do a lot of action sequences.

"It feels so un-American to fly to Canada over Independence Day," Courtney said.

"I didn't even think of that," Justin said. "I guess you're right, it's not even a holiday up here. But, we still get Monday off."

"Knock knock," Andi called from outside the trailer.

He turned to Courtney. "Come on, I want to introduce you."

They stepped out of the trailer, where Andi was waiting.

"You must be Courtney," Andi greeted her, smiling politely. "I'm Andi."

Courtney smiled back. "Nice to meet you. I've heard a lot about you."

"Likewise," Andi replied, turning to Justin. "You're needed back on set. And Courtney, we'll talk tonight," she promised as she walked away.

Justin kissed Courtney on the forehead, leaving another dark red smudge. They both laughed. "Sorry. Come with me, and you can watch from up close. If you need anything, you can head back to the trailer at any point. Mine's the one with my name on it," he joked.

She rolled her eyes, but followed him closely.

Cassie, one of the makeup artists, reapplied his lip color and sprayed some goo in his hair. He pointed to a chair for Courtney, then took his place on set.

They filmed for another few hours, but whenever Justin glanced up, Courtney was still in the chair.

WATCHING them film was nothing like she'd imagined. While Courtney knew everyone would be in costume and makeup, she hadn't expected this. On screen, it all looked so natural. In person it was, well, unsettling. She had met Andi already, briefly, but she looked nothing like Courtney had imagined either. Even Ryan, who she'd met only a month before, seemed like a completely different person. And the two leads both looked older in person.

Still, the most startling change was definitely Justin. Even from a distance, Courtney noticed how much bigger he'd gotten, like he'd literally spent every spare moment doing pushups. And up close, she couldn't get past the eyes. She'd never realized it before, but Justin's pale blue eyes had always been her window into his thoughts. With the colored lenses in, she couldn't even see a trace of the real Justin.

She couldn't deny that he was in his element, though. Watching Justin act was just so easy. Not that Courtney had expected him to suck; only that she had anticipated being nervous for him. But he was so calm, so relaxed, so natural about it all, that Courtney kept forgetting he was technically working.

The other surprising thing was how long it took. They did dozens of identical takes for what probably ended up being a two-minute scene of the film. Courtney had never understood how much actually went into a film before and realized she now had a newfound appreciation for Justin's work.

Finally, Justin trudged over to her. "Done!" he announced proudly.

Courtney smiled and stood slowly, her legs aching from sitting so long.

He flashed his fake teeth at her quickly, then laughed. "Come on, I'm going to wash this off and change, and then I'll introduce you to some of the cast at dinner."

As soon as they reached the trailer, he stepped into the bathroom, scrubbed his face and lips, tugged out the bonus teeth, and removed the contacts. Courtney watched expectantly, instantly relieved when he turned around.

"Oh thank God," she mumbled, jumping up and wrapping her arms around his neck. "It is you in there."

He kissed her, this time with an eagerness that felt much more familiar to her. She roamed her hands across his chest and down his arms while they kissed. "Geez you're huge," she commented between kisses.

He pulled back, confused.

"Your arms, chest," she clarified.

He grinned, clearly having thought she meant something else. "You like?"

"Umm. Maybe it's the hair, but you're just a little too intimidating for me now. I keep expecting you to try to eat me."

"I still need to wash up and change," he reminded her. "We're heading out to an early dinner with everyone at six. Julie and Brad have a flight to catch later tonight. They're going away for the weekend."

Courtney glimpsed at her watch. It was already after five. She groaned. "Can't I meet them another time?"

Justin laughed, probably thinking she was a total freak for wanting more time in a crappy trailer with him instead of going to dinner with one of their generation's most famous couples in Hollywood. He kissed the tip of her nose before starting to undress. "I swear it'll just be us at the hotel later."

"So what should I wear tonight?"

"You look amazing in what you've got on."

Courtney snorted at the thought of wearing cheap faded jeans to a dinner with a bunch of movie stars. "If you don't give me some input, I'm going to just strip naked and wait until you dig through my bag and pick something out."

He poked his head around the corner out of the small bathroom, grinning. Courtney's heart thudded at the sight of him without his shirt. "If we weren't in a hurry, I might take you up on that threat," he teased. "How about a casual dress or a skirt?"

Courtney changed into a clingy black skirt, threw on a necklace, redid her makeup, and then was in the process of brushing her hair when Justin emerged from the bathroom, the towel draped around his hips. He stepped quickly up behind her, brushed her hair out of the way, and lightly pressed his lips into her neck, sending shivers down her back. "You smell good," he mumbled.

She smiled, and there was a tap at the door.

"Hang on," Justin called. He quickly dressed, pulling on grey slacks and a short sleeved black shirt he'd set out earlier, then he opened the door.

Brad Powell and Julie Huffman stood there. "You ready?" Brad asked.

Courtney suddenly felt nervous. Personally, she'd never been that impressed by either one of them, either their acting or their appearance, but they were the stars. Everyone knew who they were. Brad's arm was slung tightly around Julie, something she'd never seen before in photos. The two consistently pretended they were only friends in public, even though the whole world knew they'd been dating for almost two years.

Justin wrapped his watch around his wrist, then glanced at it pointedly. "You're early."

Brad shrugged. "This way we can hang at the restaurant longer." He eyed Courtney. "Or you can get back to your hotel sooner."

Justin smiled. "Brad, Julie, this is Courtney."

Brad politely offered his hand. Julie just smiled warmly. Courtney suddenly recalled reading somewhere that Julie was a total germaphobe.

"We'll be out in two minutes," Justin promised.

He spritzed on cologne, ran some gel through his hair, and rinsed his hands. "Ready?"

Courtney nodded.

Seven of them piled into a single limousine, with the driver and solo security guard in the front seat. Justin informed Courtney that Brad and Julie never went anywhere without security.

The restaurant was crowded, but they were seated immediately in a dimly lit private room towards the back. Justin squeezed Courtney's hand as they ordered the first round of drinks, signaling that she wasn't hiding her nervousness as well as she'd thought.

If she tuned out the conversation, they all seemed like normal people, just a regular group of friends or coworkers going out for dinner after a long day. But when she listened closer, their stories of crazed fans, overzealous paparazzi and constantly-hovering bodyguards reminded Courtney that there was nothing average about them. And if she looked at them, well, it was obvious they were all movie stars. It wasn't just that they were all stunningly gorgeous people wearing expensive clothes. Something about the way they carried themselves just oozed talent.

"Court," Justin nudged her.

She realized someone had spoken to her while she was daydreaming.

"Justin says you're a lawyer?" Julie repeated.

"Almost, hopefully," Courtney answered. "I just finished law school but haven't gotten my California license yet."

"If you're so smart, what are you doing with him?" Brad asked with a grin.

Courtney laughed, gently patting Justin's thigh.

"Seriously, we all think you're out of his league," Melissa, Justin's on-camera love interest, chimed in.

Courtney smiled again, turning to face Justin. "I'm sure you say that to all the ladies he flies up here."

"Oh, you mean his mother?" Brad laughed.

"Yes, she's out of his league too," Ryan added.

The conversation flowed freely, especially as the next round of drinks was consumed. By the time they'd enjoyed a ridiculously succulent dinner, Courtney was finally feeling more comfortable with the group. No one ordered dessert, not surprisingly, and then two large men in dark jeans came in and motioned to Brad.

He stood quickly, helping Julie up. "Well, it's been fun, but we've got to head out to catch our flight."

Justin stood. "Are you guys taking the limo? I left Courtney's bag in it."

Brad shook his head. "Nope, you guys take that back to the hotel. We're going in a less obvious ride to the airport." And they walked out, separately, each one with their own bodyguard.

Courtney anxiously waited for everyone else to stand so they could get back to the hotel already.

THAT NIGHT with Courtney everything was just as Justin remembered it. Since it had been so long since they'd been together, Justin had started to worry that maybe he'd built it up too much in his head, that he'd only imagined the chemistry. But from the moment they entered the hotel room, when her arms wrapped around his waist before he even finished locking the door, he knew it was real. He felt her smiling as her lips pressed into his, and it was clear she sensed it too.

They'd barely been back to the room for five minutes by the time they fell into bed together. A half hour after that, Justin was up, showering. Courtney was on the phone with someone by the time he got out of the shower, and then she went straight to the shower. He regretted not just asking her to join him so they could be back in bed by now, but instead he used the time to catch up on emails and social media.

She emerged from the shower minutes later wearing a barely-there lacy black negligee, her long, dark hair falling across her shoulders, still wet. She approached him slowly, playfully peering over his shoulder as he closed the computer. "You working?"

Justin shook his head and closed the laptop, reaching for her until the smooth silk of her slip brushed against his fingers. He pulled her onto his lap.

"You must be exhausted. How long did you guys work today?"

He shrugged his shoulders. He was tired as hell, honestly, but a guy had to have priorities, right? "It's still early in L.A."

She smiled, then cuddled up against him. "I missed you."

He kissed the soft spot on the side of her head. "Me too," he admitted, and he meant it. As cool as this filming experience was, he'd still thought about her every day. Justin sucked at talking on the phone when he was filming, and their lives were so different right then that it didn't seem like they had all that much to discuss anyway. But this—her curled up against his body, her chest rising and falling against him with each gentle breath she took—this, he missed. He hadn't even realized how much he'd missed it until just now, when she was back right where she belonged. He inhaled the scent of her hair then brushed it away from her eyes with his finger.

"It is early in L.A. still," she finally agreed. "But I got up at four this morning for my flight."

He cringed, realizing he'd booked that flight. "Sorry. I just thought you'd want to get here early so you could see us film some."

"I'm glad. I loved watching you work." She traced her ring finger across his bare chest, sending chills up his spine. "You're really good at your job. And you seem to enjoy it too."

"Yeah, I do."

"It's funny, because I'm sure Brad and Julie are talented actors too, but they don't seem to handle the other aspects of the job as well as you do."

"What other aspects?"

"Oh, the fans. Have they ever signed autographs or anything?"

"I don't know. It's hard for them. They went from being no-names to huge celebrities overnight. They can't leave their house without bodyguards or they get surrounded by so many fans that they literally can't move."

"Aha! So they are living together. The rumors are true!"

He laughed. "I do like the fans, though. It's crazy thinking all these people are willing to wait around for an autograph or even just to see me wave at them." Justin turned to face Courtney, but noticed she was staring at something on the table beside him. He followed her gaze, then picked up the jeweled sunglasses she was eying. "Andi left them here," he explained.

"I figured they weren't yours." She cleared her throat awkwardly.

Suddenly, Justin remembered her comment at dinner, something about all the other women who visited him. Was Courtney actually jealous? "You didn't really think there were a lot of other people coming up here to visit me, did you?"

Courtney swung her legs around so she was facing him. "You mean like Keith?" she joked.

He smiled, but he wished she'd just say whatever she was thinking. "I haven't had other girls visiting, you know?"

She glanced down. "It's none of my business."

"Sure it is. You're acting like I think of you as a fangirl or something, and it's not like that." He shook his head. "Wait, have you been dating a bunch of guys while I've been gone?"

Now Courtney smiled. "Yeah, in between all-day bar exam review classes and six-hour-long evening study sessions, I've been quite the player."

He frowned, assuming that meant no. "Most evenings I just hang out with the rest of the cast. We've been playing a lot of poker. And Marshall was trying to teach me to play guitar. Andi's room is right over there, though, so she comes by a lot." He nodded towards the bar, at the small built-in door to Andi's room.

Courtney pulled away. "You have adjoining rooms?"

Justin shrugged. "Andi has always been a good friend. She also went with me to New York a couple weekends ago. Is that a problem?"

She bit her lip. "Uh, no. I just didn't realize you and Andi..." her voice trailed off.

He grabbed her hand. "We're just friends, always have been."

Courtney nodded skeptically, the look in her blue eyes unequivocally indicating she didn't believe him but didn't have the interest, or maybe the confidence, to press the issue.

"You've never had a good friend who was a guy?"

Courtney shook her head. "Every time there is a guy that I think I'm friends with, he eventually asks me out. Or hits on me. There are guys I've hung out with in a group of people that I guess I'd call friends, but never that I'd go out with alone."

Justin laughed, then decided to change the subject. There was clearly no winning this discussion. "What if we head back to bed now and you can tell me more about this new job you've got lined up," he suggested.

She snorted, but stood, his eyes immediately drawn to the crest at the top of her thighs where the lacy edge of her slip barely reached. "You mean the job I have assuming I pass the test at the end of the month," she clarified. But then he never had a chance to respond, because they had reached the bed, and he'd already busied himself with more interesting endeavors.

Justin's alarm went off at eight the next morning so he could meet Ryan at the gym, but, miraculously, the obnoxious beeping didn't awaken Courtney. Justin watched her silently, noticing her eyelids fluttering as she sighed in her sleep. He carefully slid out of the bed, ordered breakfast, then made his way to the bathroom before returning and kissing her on the forehead.

"What time is it in L.A.?" she groaned sleepily.

"Early," he replied, uncertain of the actual time difference.

She rubbed her eyes before focusing in on him. "You're going to the gym," she deduced.

He nodded. "I'll be back by 11. Order whatever you want for breakfast. And go back to sleep for a while. I just didn't want you to wake up and wonder where I'd gone."

She nodded, yawned, and her eyes drooped closed again.

Ryan was already at the small gym off of the hotel lobby when Justin arrived. Justin nodded, moderately irked that there were two other guys in the gym.

"I didn't think you'd be here this morning," Ryan said with a grin.

Justin glared. "I said I would be, didn't I?"

Ryan laughed and tossed him a towel from the bin. "You're up. I just did my first set."

Justin nodded and stretched out over the bench. Ryan switched over the weight plates and spotted him. This was why Justin liked working out with Ryan—the guy didn't waste time. It was no wonder, though. With a wife and three kids at home, plus multiple TV and screen roles, Ryan didn't have a hell of a lot of spare time. Justin was stronger and younger, but he definitely could learn a thing or two from Ryan's workout style.

"Did Courtney enjoy yesterday?"

"You mean watching us shoot or last night?" Justin laughed.

"Hey, you had separate rooms, right?" Ryan teased, warily eying the two other guys still on the treadmill.

Justin followed his gaze, but honestly, it didn't seem like those dudes had a clue who they were, let alone cared enough to eavesdrop. "I don't know, man. What did you think about her?"

Ryan laughed. "You're asking my opinion about your girlfriend?"

Justin finished the set, grunted, and sat up as soon as Ryan placed the weights back on the rack. They switched places. "You're married. That kind of makes you an expert."

"Well, as the expert, I'd say the only thing that matters is what you think of her. But she seemed pretty perfect to me."

Justin sighed. "I just can't read her. It drives me crazy. I think she likes me, but she won't give me a straight answer about anything having to do with us. She said she didn't want a relationship, but that was a year ago and she's still hanging around."

Ryan frowned, his reps slowing down as he reached the end of the set. "You think she's using you or something?"

"No. I don't think she gives a shit about my money or the fame. That's maybe the problem. I just don't know if she takes me seriously." As he spoke, Justin realized Courtney would probably like him even more, or at least be less freaked out by the prospect of any commitment to him, if he were some broke no-name.

Ryan wiped down the bench and they both walked over to the free weights. "I can't help you with that," he muttered.

"Well, how did you know when you were ready to settle down and stop seeing other people?"

Ryan dropped his weights. "You're still dating other people and you're worried she's not taking you seriously?"

Justin shrugged sheepishly, trying to wipe a trickle of sweat off his eyebrow without setting down the weight. "I wouldn't say

I'm dating other people ..." he didn't finish the sentence, knowing how trashy it sounded. "For all I know she could be dating other guys, too."

"Then either come right out and tell her you don't want to see other people or do something big and show her."

They lifted quietly for a few minutes before Justin spoke again. "You never answered my question. How'd you know you were ready to settle down with Audrey?"

Ryan hesitated, then stepped closer and lowered his voice. "She was pregnant."

"I thought you were engaged before."

Ryan shook his head. "You keep that to yourself, though."

Justin nodded, and slowly finished his set.

On Courtney's last full day in Toronto, Justin served as her official tour guide and dragged her to all of his favorite spots around town. As soon as they returned to the hotel, Justin collapsed onto the couch, kicking his shoes off before stretching his feet onto the coffee table. "So what do you want to do now? Watch a movie?"

Courtney laughed, tossing her purse onto the bar and following him to the couch. She plopped down beside him and he pulled her legs up and stretched them out over his lap. "No."

"Well, what else is there to do?" he asked with a sly grin.

Courtney raised her eyebrows before leaning in to kiss him. He kissed her back, for a moment, but was tentative, then pulled away.

"Your test is at the end of the month, right?"

She nodded, irritated that he'd now reminded her of the single most stressful event in her life, which she'd spent all day trying to forget.

"We should finish up here in two weeks, and then I've got to be in New York for a couple of days, but I'll probably be back right around the time you finish your test. What do you have planned for August?"

"Well, I'll probably take off a couple weeks before I start working. And I need to go visit my parents, I guess. Why?"

He grinned. "Perfect."

"What is?"

"I spoke to my mom after Ryan and I finished up at the gym, and she wants me to visit sometime in August too. I think you should come with me."

Courtney frowned, sure she wasn't understanding. "You want me to meet your mom?"

"Why not? It's only a couple of hours from your parents, right? We'll go to one, then the other."

"You mean, like fly to Indiana together, and then both of us go to see your mom and then both of us go to see my parents? Wouldn't it make more sense for me to go to my parents while you visit your mom, and then we can spend half as long in Indiana?"

"You always say you miss Indiana."

"Not August in Indiana. I miss autumn, I miss snow, I miss spring. I don't miss humidity."

"My mom's cool. I think you'd like her."

Courtney turned to face him, her finger still absentmindedly tracing the ridge of the ring on his middle finger. His bright blue eyes were gazing back expectantly. She looked away quickly, before he could flash those dimples and convince her to do anything he wanted.

"I can't."

"Why not?"

Courtney hesitated. She couldn't very well tell the truth, that she couldn't meet his mother because then this whole thing with him and her—this whole arrangement that was supposed to be casual—would start to feel a little too real, and then she knew she'd get hurt.

Justin squeezed her hand. "Please? You might even get to meet some of my brothers."

Courtney felt herself nodding, slowly, and then his mouth was on hers before she could process what she'd just agreed to.

As Courtney relaxed into her comfy first class seat the next day, she was more confused than ever. She couldn't deny that she had feelings for Justin, that it wasn't just about the sex. In all honesty, Courtney knew she'd never felt this way about anyone else. But she also couldn't say for sure if Justin felt the same way.

There were signs that he did, sure. He wouldn't invite her to visit him in Toronto if he didn't miss her, and he certainly wouldn't want to travel to Indiana with her if he didn't feel something for her. And while the proportional cost of a new BMW to him was probably the same as a Starbucks latte for her these days, Courtney was fairly confident that he wasn't out buying cars for tons of women. She wanted to believe that he was falling for her, that he would spend the next month alone in his hotel room, missing her as much as she hated to admit she'd be missing him, but it was hard.

For one thing, there were magazines everywhere. There were innocent enough comments that she could easily dismiss as meaningless, like his interview with a magazine for teenage girls where he said he was single. Surely there was no point in disappointing his young female fans prematurely, right? It wasn't like he was married or anything. Other things she read, like the online gossip column claiming Justin was seen apartment shopping in New York with Andi were equally easy to ignore, since Courtney knew that wasn't actually happening. But an interview with Justin's ex, Kinzie, where she mentioned a recent trip to Toronto— that seemed a little suspicious.

As the date of the bar exam approached, the calls and texts from Justin became less frequent, and whenever Courtney went online, she'd stumble across some photo of Justin out at a night-club. She read "reports" that he and Kinzie had rekindled their romance, and that Justin was seen very early one morning leaving the apartment of that model Jasmine.

Her instincts told her to ignore it, to just block it all out until after the exam was over, and then she could deal with the mess that her social life had apparently become. And that worked, to some extent, until she caught a glimpse of a gossip magazine the day before the exam.

She'd spotted the magazine as she was leaving the bookstore where she had been studying. On the cover, in the corner, was a picture of Justin. A good photo, really, where he was wearing jeans that clung to him in all the right places, a sleeveless ribbed white undershirt that showed off his arms and chest, and gold-rimmed sunglasses. He was looking off in the distance, the slightest hint of a smile on his face. As soon as she saw the photo, Courtney's heart began racing. Without thinking, she bought the magazine, waiting until she reached her car to let herself really stare at this hunky man that she could actually see and touch and kiss in less than a week.

Once Courtney was alone, she glanced down at the maga-zine, smiling when the picture was just as perfect as before. But then, she read the caption: "Don't hate the player."

Courtney frowned, and quickly flipped to the article. There it was, a two-page spread containing the photos which confirmed all of the rumors Courtney had tried to dismiss over the past few weeks. Justin with Kinzie, Justin with Andi, Justin with Jasmine, and Justin posing at the awards show from just days before with some cute younger blonde who, according to the caption, was named Lacey Duvall. Courtney's eyes zoomed in on the corner of the photo, where Justin's hand rested inches above Lacey's perky butt. She skimmed over the captions, indifferent to the technicalities of when and where Justin went with all these other women, but couldn't ignore the last one, reading: "Despite reportedly rekindling the romance with longtime on-again off-again girlfriend MacKinzie Maddox, Justin Erikson still likes the ladies."

A sick feeling immediately washed over Courtney, and she quickly fumbled to switch on the ignition, desperate to blast the air conditioning. Courtney squeezed her eyes shut, breathing in the icy cool air and counted to ten before opening her eyes and reading the other captions and brief notes that comprised the article. By the time she reached the end, the ink had blurred the words past the point of being legible and it took her a moment to realize her own tears had been dripping onto the page.

Courtney closed her eyes again, wiping them on the back of her hand, and reminded herself that this wasn't a surprise, that she had known all along that this day was going to come, sooner or later. With steady resolve and a wobbly hand, Courtney climbed out of the car, threw the magazine into the nearest trash can, and drove home. What she needed was sleep before the biggest day of her life. She could feel sorry for herself in two days, when the test was over, but for now, she needed to focus on what was important.

9

Courtney answered on the second ring. It was so refreshing hearing her voice that Justin realized how long it had been since he'd actually spoken with her. He'd called each of the last three days, but he'd gotten her voice mail. She had her big test, so he hadn't been too concerned when she didn't call back.

"Hey, I'm glad I finally got a hold of you."

"Why?" she replied dryly.

He winced at her tone, but didn't take the bait. "I wanted to tell you I booked the flight to Indy. A week from Saturday. So are we still going out to celebrate tonight?"

He heard her sigh before quietly replying. "No. And I can't come with you to Indiana."

Justin had never heard her sound this depressed. "Court, what happened?"

"Nothing. I just don't think it's a good idea."

"You sound terrible."

"I'm pretty tired."

"Did the test not go well?"

"I don't know. I was a little distracted, to say the least, but I think I passed. I hope so, anyway. I won't know for sure for two months."

Justin hesitated. His least favorite thing about women was their uncanny ability to be so passive aggressive. He hated trying to read women, especially when they were clearly pissed off or upset about something. But Courtney had never been that way. With Courtney, the only games she played were in the bedroom, where they belonged.

"Courtney, you sound like something is bothering you. Why don't you come over tonight?" Justin knew if they spoke in person, he could figure out what the problem was, or, if not, he could just take off his shirt and distract her.

"I can't," she replied, and he was almost positive she was crying. "Why don't you call someone else?"

"Who else would I call? I want to talk to you."

She sniffled. "What about Andi? Or Lacey? Or Jasmine? Or Kinzie?"

Fuck. With the exception of Andi, Justin knew precisely what that list of girls had in common. "Can you just tell me what I did, Courtney?"

There was a long pause. Finally, she spoke. "You said you were filming out of town. You said you got back into town last night, or today or whatever, but according to the press, you were in town and on a date." She paused and he heard a sniffle. "Which is surprising seeing as how you and Kinzie are..."

He interrupted her. "I was filming out of town. And I said I was busy until today, which I was. I called you when I got back. You didn't answer."

"You're right," she finally snapped, in a tone that suggested she didn't really think he was right. "I guess you didn't do anything wrong. I just feel like an idiot and need some space."

"Space from what?"

"You."

Justin ambled into his kitchen to look for a drink. Keith, who'd apparently been eavesdropping on the call, handed him the bottle of whiskey. Justin nodded his gratitude and pulled a glass out of the cabinet.

"Courtney?" Keith asked.

Justin nodded.

"Alright, can you just tell me why? I honestly don't know what you're talking about."

She sighed. "I knew we weren't going to see a lot of each other this summer. I knew you were filming in Toronto and I was going to be here studying, but I hadn't realized..." her voice trailed off.

Just then, Keith scooted a stack of papers from Justin's publicist in front of him. They'd arrived a day or two before, but he hadn't looked at them. Justin glanced down at the page Keith had set in front of him. It was a printout from an internet article titled, "Justin's New Romance." He quickly scanned the page, then turned, to find multiple pictures of him with Andi; them laughing together, eating together, and one with his arm around her. And of course, it mentioned the fact that they were seen looking at apartments together.

"Fuck," he grumbled. Then, quickly realizing Courtney just heard him say that, he explained. "I think I just saw what you're pissed about. The article about me and Andi?"

She was silent.

"Look, Courtney, I'm not sleeping with Andi. We're not even dating. Never have."

"What about the others?"

Justin wasn't sure what "others" she meant. He flipped through the rest of the stack of papers to find a huge photo of him with his arm around Lacey Duvall, standing on the red carpet before the awards show on Tuesday. "Lacey?"

She sighed. "Justin, you're a free man. You can do what you

want. I just, well, right before my exam, I saw the nice photo of you and your date for the awards show."

"We have the same publicist," he explained. "She set us up as a publicity thing. It wasn't even a real date."

"And what about the interview, where you denied dating Andrea and said you were still, what were your words, 'single as ever,' with 'no one special' in your life?"

Justin groaned. This was precisely why he should stay single. Women always ended up being too needy, even those who initially acted like they weren't. "I'm not married, Courtney. I am single. My publicist would kill me if I said otherwise."

"Yeah, I guess so," she mumbled. She sniffled quietly. "We never said we were exclusive or even that we were dating. And I know I promised I wouldn't get jealous or attached to you. But I really like you. I can't keep doing this if I'm going to get my feelings hurt every time I see you with another girl. Especially the night before the most important day of my life, when I need to be focused. I'm sorry. I'm mad at myself, not at you."

She paused, but not long enough for him to get a word in. "I'm not usually that girl that gets all crazy and possessive about a guy, and I thought I'd be okay with that whole friends with benefits thing, but apparently I'm not. You were upfront with me from the start and I thought I could handle it, but I just can't. I need more and you can't give that to me now."

"Friends with benefits?" he repeated, a knot in his stomach. "That's how you think of me?"

"I don't know, Justin, how would you define it when we hang out when we can, and we have amazing sex, but you're still screwing other women?" She sniffled again. "You should have told me if you were with Kinzie again."

"I'm not seeing Kinzie," he insisted. "The last time I was with Kinzie..." Justin cut himself off when he realized the last time he'd fooled around with Kinzie was, in a technical sense, after he'd met Courtney. He was running out of explanations and patience. "Courtney, I'm sorry I hurt your feelings," he finally mumbled. Keith made a gagging gesture, so he stood up and went onto the back patio.

"What do you want me to do?" Justin asked once he was safely outside.

"Nothing," she replied. "I just need some space."

"How much space?"

"A lot."

"So you don't want to see me anymore."

"I guess so," she replied. She sounded reluctant, but resolved.

Justin sighed. He didn't have time for this crap. He'd give her a few days to calm down, and they'd either work everything out or move on. "Alright," he finally said.

"Sorry," she mumbled, then hung up.

He finished his drink on the patio before heading back inside. He refilled his glass, chugged it, then grabbed the car keys. "I'm going out. Wanna come?"

Keith hesitated. "Dude, you just pounded three shots of whiskey. You're going to be too drunk to see straight by the time you hit the freeway."

Justin licked his lips. "I feel fine now."

Keith glared back at him.

"Fine, then you drive," Justin insisted, tossing him the keys.

"You're wearing that? Where are we going?"

Justin glanced down and sighed. He hurried upstairs and changed into his khaki and blue pinstriped pants, a fitted navy blue tee shirt, and a grey hat. He slid a thick silver band on his middle finger, sprayed on some cologne, then returned to find Keith at his laptop. "Let's go," he urged.

Keith skeptically followed him and drove to a nearby sports bar. Since it was a Wednesday night with no decent games on, the place wasn't too crowded, which initially irritated Justin. But, as he tried to pull out his chair, he realized Keith was right. He was drunk. And so what if the place wasn't bopping? He just needed to let off some steam.

He groaned. *Friends with benefits?* Had she really said that? Had he actually fallen for a girl who'd just been using him for sex?

A waitress came by to take their order. When she returned with their drinks she paused, and leaned closer. "Oh my God, are you that—are you Justin Erikson?" she asked in a thick southern drawl.

"Why yes I am, ma'am. Pleasure to make your acquaintance," he replied, mimicking her twang.

The woman stood there, staring, for a moment, then smiled and scurried away.

Justin rolled his eyes. "Women."

Keith was eying him strangely, but not saying anything.

Justin tried to ignore it, but the silence was killing him. "Why don't you just tell me what you're thinking?"

Keith slowly lifted the bottle to his lips and sipped. He set it down with a sigh. "I'm thinking you're gonna regret this," he finally said.

"I've been hungover before. I'll live."

Keith shook his head. "Not the drinking. Courtney."

"What about Courtney?"

"You broke up, didn't you?"

Justin motioned for the waitress to bring him another beer. "There was nothing to break. We were never a couple. Apparently, we were just friends with benefits."

"Oh come on, Justin, that's bullshit and you know it. She's the only girl you've really even gone out with since Kinzie." He laughed. "She's the best girlfriend you've had since Kara Gooden in ninth grade."

"Not true. Since Kinzie, there've been at least four women, according to Courtney." He snorted. "Apparently, I'm back together with Kinzie. Anyone with internet access could tell you that."

"Where did anyone get that idea about you and Kinzie? Have you even talked to her lately?"

Justin shook his head. He had no fucking clue where the paparazzi came up with half the bullshit they printed about him.

"That's not what I meant anyway. You like Courtney."

Justin leaned back in his chair. "Doesn't matter now."

"What was she pissed about? Just the articles? Or did you actually do something shitty?"

Justin flashed his best smile at the waitress in gratitude for the beer before turning back to Keith. "She thinks I'm fucking Andi."

"So tell her you're not."

Justin shook his head. "If she wants to be all possessive, that's her issue, not mine."

Keith frowned. "But you're not sleeping with Andi."

Justin hesitated.

"Fuck!" Keith exclaimed. "You're sleeping with Andi?"

Justin slammed his bottle down a little louder than he'd intended. "No, Keith. God." He sighed, disgusted. "But I did hook up with Amber one weekend over the summer when I was in New York."

This didn't seem to shock Keith. "Is Amber the one from the perfume commercial?"

Justin nodded. "Yeah, the model that Jasmine introduced me to a while back."

"Does Courtney know about that?"

"No, and that's the whole point, Keith. I don't think I should have to be accountable to someone. Especially when I'm not even in the same country as her twenty-six weeks out of the year."

"Do you hear yourself, Justin? I get that you like playing the field, and if you wanna keep that up, fine. But I've seen you with Courtney, and I don't think you mean any of what you're saying. You're not going to find another girl who puts up with your shit and treats you as good as she does. And if you think *she* nags you..." he simply shook his head in lieu of finishing the sentence.

Justin glanced at his phone, uncertain of what he was hoping to see. "You know Keith, you were the one telling me I shouldn't be exclusive with Courtney, that it would fuck up my career. Now you're telling me the opposite?"

"I said you shouldn't get so involved with her to start with, but you did get serious about her, and it's a little late for you to decide you didn't really intend to have a girlfriend."

Two women approached their table. Justin turned and raised his eyebrows. "Evening ladies. Can we buy you a drink?"

The women immediately sat and began gushing about how much they loved *Days End*. One of them had a fat wedding ring on her finger, so Justin devoted his attention to the other, a Carrie or maybe Katie. Keith excused himself to make a phone call, probably to Tara, and Justin found himself tuning out. These women were boring. He wished he were talking to Courtney instead, and the fact that he'd even think that pissed him off. When Keith returned to the table, Justin turned to Katie.

"We've got to get going. Care to come with?" Justin caught a glimpse of Keith's irritated face as soon as the words left his mouth. Keith grabbed his arm and pulled him a few feet away.

"I am not driving you home with some girl you just picked up because you're pissed off at Courtney," he insisted, his voice serious. "Get her fucking number, and you can call her tomorrow if you still think it's a good idea."

Justin glared back. "It's my goddamned car, we'll take whoever I like."

"Not when I'm driving. Trust me, you'll thank me later."

Justin wasn't even sure what to say to that, and he didn't have long to consider it. Keith dropped a wad of cash on the table and started out the door.

"I'll be in the car," Keith called over his shoulder. "Meet me there alone in the next five minutes or I'm leaving without you."

Justin rolled his eyes again, but turned to the girl and shook his head. "Guess I have to go," he mumbled, angrily following Keith.

He didn't remember the ride back to the house, or really anything from that point on, but when Justin awoke the next morning, he was sprawled out on the couch in his boxers, his pants draped across a chair. He rubbed his eyes, aching from the harsh light pouring in the windows, and sat slowly, immediately regretting moving. Justin heard a loud noise in the kitchen and turned, just in time to see Cathy approaching him.

"Good morning Mr. Erikson," she said, her expression clear that he'd disgraced himself somehow. She forced a mug into his hands. "Coffee," she said. "Omelet is cooking now."

He winced at the mention of eggs and she shook her head frantically.

"If you're going to be sick again, you go to the bathroom this time," she ordered, gesturing to the rug across the room. "I already cleaned this once."

Justin stood slowly and crept up the stairs at a snail's pace, desperate to avoid jarring his head. As he showered, pieces of the night filtered back to him. He remembered his talk with Courtney, and he remembered heading out drinking with Keith. And then he remembered the girls. What had happened there?

He didn't remember leaving the bar, or anything after. Justin pulled on his gym shorts and hurried downstairs, finding Cathy in the kitchen with his omelet.

"Hey, when you got here this morning, was I alone? I mean, were there any girls in the house?"

Justin caught her rolling her eyes, but then she shook her head. He thanked her for the omelet, carrying it with him as he searched for Keith. He found him on the patio, on the phone. Justin tried to wait patiently, but Keith took the hint and hung up.

"I was talking to Marty," he told Justin.

"Yeah, quick question though. What happened last night, after the bar?"

Keith laughed. "You mean after you were a colossal dickhead?"

Justin sat beside him. "I don't remember any of it, but I know I was in a shitty mood, so if I took it out on you, sorry." He paused. "There was a girl. Did I...?"

Keith shook his head. "No, you didn't touch her. Thanks to me. You're welcome!"

"Thanks," Justin mumbled as he returned to his room without asking Keith what his trusty agent was calling about. He knew he had to fix things with Courtney, and he thought he had figured out how. He closed his door and quickly dialed Andi's number.

COURTNEY HAD JUST FINISHED DRYING her hair when the doorbell rang. She peered out the peephole, not expecting anyone and not too eager to face a stranger before she had her makeup on. It was a small-framed woman, probably about her age, wearing dark sunglasses and a hat. A black town car was idling in the drive in front of the apartment. Courtney opened the door tentatively, gasping when she saw who it was.

"Hi," Andi said. "Can I come in?"

Courtney nodded, completely perplexed.

Andi glanced around the room, then pulled off her sunglasses and took off the hat, revealing long wavy hair, a little wilder than in press photos she'd seen, but still undeniably gorgeous. She looked totally different than when Courtney had seen her in Toronto.

"Do you want anything to drink?" Courtney offered.

Andi shook her head. "Look, I suppose you're wondering why I'm here."

"I have a good guess."

The actress smiled. "Justin wanted me to come and tell you we never slept together."

Courtney frowned. "He already told me that."

"Justin didn't think you believed him. And I owed him a favor anyway." She paused. "Wait, did you believe him?"

Courtney stared down at her feet, her eyes honing in on the chipped Passion Purple nail polish on her toenails. "I try not to think about it one way or the other, honestly."

"Well, really, we've never been more than friends. Seriously." Andi fidgeted with her bag awkwardly. "You don't believe me either, do you?"

Courtney swallowed hard. "You're an actor, he's an actor. That's what you guys do, say things in a convincing way, whether or not it's true."

"Really it's not that much different from lawyers, though, right?" Andi snickered at her own joke. "Honestly, Justin's not that good of an actor. If he sounds sincere, he's telling the truth. And he's not my type."

Courtney couldn't imagine Justin not being anybody's type. "Oh? What is your type then?"

"I like musicians. Quiet, moody types. The artsy ones, not the gym rats. No offense," she added.

"None taken." Courtney made her way over to the couch and motioned for Andi to follow. "It's not like it matters anyway."

"How can you say that? Of course it matters." Andi paused, and giggled. "I mean, I've seen him in his underwear, but so has the rest of the world. And the only times we've ever kissed have been on-camera, with dozens of people surrounding us watching and talking."

Courtney turned, trying to hide her nausea at the thought of Andi's flawless, porcelain skin pressed up against Justin's stubble, her perfectly toned, thin legs wrapped around his.

"Look, I feel terrible if it's my fault you guys broke up," Andi insisted.

"We didn't break up. We were never a couple." She paused. "And it wasn't just you. He didn't even bother to tell me that he's apparently still been seeing his ex this whole time."

Andi looked surprised. "I don't think he is. He hasn't mentioned her for like a year, since that whole thing with...well, you know she cheated on him with Jackson Malloy, right? I can't imagine he'd forgive her for that."

Courtney shrugged. She wasn't about to admit that she'd read the entire saga of his relationship with Kinzie in a series of tabloid articles.

Andi sighed, clearly flustered. "Justin's a good guy. And he really likes you."

Courtney and Andi ended up ordering food and spending the better part of the afternoon together. Andi was funny and, while not exactly down-to-earth, she was easy to talk to. And apparently, persuasive.

By the time Andi left, Courtney agreed to travel to Indiana with Justin. She relayed her decision to him via text, adding that she refused to sleep with him until they were back in California. That way, she'd know their relationship wasn't purely physical.

Courtney couldn't sleep that night. She was nervous about seeing Justin again. She didn't know what he was going to do or how he'd act around her, and, even worse, she didn't know what she was going to do or how she would act around him. She got up early, pulled her hair back, and dressed in a low-cut grey tee shirt and navy velour sweatpants. They were super comfy and looked casual, but also accented her butt perfectly.

As soon as she saw the Escalade, Courtney opened the door, bending to pick up her own bags before Justin got to the step. He grinned when he saw her, and she couldn't resist smiling back. He was in his dark wash jeans, the ones that always made her want to grab his ass, and an olive green shirt that did nothing to conceal the muscles rippling beneath it. He left his sunglasses on as he stepped inside.

"This is everything," she said, motioning to her bags. "We can go."

He scooted past her and shut the door behind him. "We have a few minutes. I thought you'd want to talk first."

She tried to ignore the pounding in her chest that started up whenever she heard his deep voice after being away from him. "No, it's fine. We'll have plenty of time later."

He nodded, his dimples appearing as he smiled. "Am I allowed to kiss you?"

Before she'd made up her mind, his lips were on hers and his hands pressed into the small of her back. The feeling of his flesh against her was so comforting, almost like hopping into a hot bath after playing in the snow. Courtney could taste coffee on his tongue and smelled the crisp mint of his aftershave. She wondered how she was going to stay angry at him with all of her senses urging her to just focus on the good times they'd shared.

A honk came from outside and Courtney grimaced, certain Erica was now awake.

"Asshole," Justin muttered in response to the honk, picking up her bags.

Justin pulled off his sunglasses as they drove, but as soon as Keith pulled up to the airport, he slid the glasses back over his eyes and reached into the front seat to grab a burgundy baseball cap to pull over his hair. He stuck in his earbuds, then hopped out of the car quickly.

Courtney understood the routine by now. With the earbuds, some people were discouraged from approaching him, if they even recognized him under the hat and sunglasses, and if people did call out to him, he could at least pretend he couldn't hear them over his music.

Justin walked around and opened her door as Keith pulled their bags out of the trunk. He grabbed all the larger bags, leaving Courtney with just her purse. He walked quickly, facing straight ahead, and a moment later, she heard someone calling out his name. "Smile," he mumbled to Courtney, without pausing or turning his head. He paused by the baggage check area, where there was a line, and then bypassed it.

They went straight to the security gate, Justin speaking with one of the guards there and leaving the bags they sought to check with him. They were ushered through an unopened security gate, with Courtney setting off the alarm because she forgot about her cell phone in her back pocket. She glanced at Justin, wondering if he would be pissed that she'd just drawn more attention to them, but he was laughing. Once they'd passed security and collected their bags from the conveyer belt, Justin grabbed her hand firmly and they proceeded to the gate.

They boarded the plane last, only moments before takeoff. Justin took the seat by the window, and he was so quiet that

Courtney started to wonder if he had turned on his earbuds. Just then, a quiet voice came up behind her, whispering "excuse me."

Courtney turned, and a girl, maybe eleven or twelve was standing beside her. "Can I get your autograph please?" The girl spoke so quietly, her voice shaking uncontrollably, that Courtney was sure Justin hadn't heard her. But, to her surprise, he turned and held out his hand, taking the small notebook and hot pink pen the girl handed him.

"Excuse me, Miss, you'll have to take your seat. We're taking off now." a stern flight attendant announced, forcefully ushering the girl to her seat two rows back. Courtney watched as the girl returned to her mother. She looked like she was about to cry.

Justin rolled his eyes as the flight attendant made her way back to the front of the plane. He scribbled something on the girl's notepad, then unfastened his belt. He began climbing over Courtney before she realized he was leaving, and she turned as made his way into the aisle. She saw him speak to the little girl for a moment before jotting something else on her notepad and then handing it back to her.

Courtney smiled, having forgotten how sweet he could be. "So she gets an autograph but I don't?" she teased Justin as he climbed back into his seat.

He grinned and took her hand. "I gave you one eventually. Didn't you save it?"

Actually, she had, but she wasn't about to tell him that. "Sorry about the security thing," she said instead.

He laughed. "I don't mind. I just didn't want to deal with reporters." He paused. "I'm pretty sure they got your photo, though. I'll check with Jamie later."

She sighed, snuggling up against his shoulder. "Did Andi tell you all about our chat?"

"Some," he replied, already flipping through Sky Mall.

"She's pretty nice."

"Yeah," he agreed. "Does that mean you're not mad anymore?"

Courtney sighed. She wasn't sure how to explain it. She wasn't so much mad as hurt, and torn. "I just don't know if we're good for each other," she began, but he shushed her.

"We shouldn't talk about it here," he whispered, kissing her on the forehead. "Later."

Courtney nodded, then closed her eyes and leaned back, anxious about the visits that were about to transpire.

10

The drive from the Indianapolis airport up to South Bend, where Justin's family lived, was long and boring. But instead of talking about the real issues, they both talked about work, making small talk about the last few weeks that they'd been apart. When they arrived at Justin's, Courtney was pleasantly surprised. It was a normal midwestern house—nothing like she'd expected. Susan, his mom, seemed similarly average, in a good way. After a brief chat with Susan, though, Courtney realized she was losing the war against jet lag. She had no idea how Justin flew all around the world without any apparent effect to his energy levels or sleep cycles.

"Want a tour of the neighborhood? I could show you some of my old childhood hangouts," Justin offered.

"Actually, I'm really tired. Would it be okay if I took a little nap while you caught up with your mom?"

Susan smiled and answered for him. "Of course. I've got Justin's old room all set up for you two." She stood and led the way upstairs.

Courtney followed her, then paused at the doorway. In Justin's room stood a single, full-sized bed. She didn't want to be rude, and she really was tired. It would be fine for a nap, and then she could talk with Justin later about her maybe going to a hotel. Courtney knew she couldn't share a room with Justin and not have sex with him, and, at this point, sex would only complicate things.

"What's wrong?" Susan asked, interrupting Courtney's thoughts.

Justin appeared behind them, chuckling. "She won't sleep in here with me," he explained, surprising Courtney at the casualness with which he said that to his mother.

Susan seemed surprised but smiled. She turned to her son. "Well, you don't need to give the girl a hard time about that. There's nothing wrong with being old-fashioned."

"She's not old-fashioned," he insisted. "She's pissed at me."

"You watch your mouth, Justin," his mother snapped, bringing an instant smile to Courtney's face. Then she turned to Courtney. "You go ahead and sleep here. He can stay in one of his brothers' rooms."

Courtney smirked at Justin, closing the door behind her.

The rest of the evening was uneventful. Courtney genuinely liked Susan. She knew she was being more reserved than normal, but she couldn't stand the thought of putting herself out there even more just to be hurt again. True to her word, she slept in a separate room from him that night.

The next morning, she went for a jog, eager to clear her mind. Justin invited himself along, failing to take the hint when she popped in her headphones and sped up.

"Hey, Court, slow down. Can we just talk?"

For a second, she considered pretending she hadn't heard, but then she stopped abruptly, turning to face him.

"Justin, we can't have a serious discussion while we're running, and I don't really feel like hashing it out in front of your mom, either. Maybe we can go someplace alone later, like a coffee shop?"

Justin kicked at the gravel beneath his foot and wiped a trickle of sweat off his brow. "Yeah, I don't think a coffee shop would be very private."

"Right, sorry. Well, maybe later." She cranked up her music and took off, finishing the run in record speed. She hopped in the shower before Justin returned, and by the time she was dried off and dressed, he had begun to shower.

Courtney wandered downstairs and sat at the kitchen table, absentmindedly flipping through one of Susan's cookbooks. The house was quiet, aside from the shower upstairs, so she assumed no one else was home. She startled when she heard footsteps behind her.

Susan plopped down beside her. "Do you cook?"

Courtney nodded. "I try. With so many farmers markets around L.A., it seems wasteful to not even attempt to make something."

Susan pushed a different book in front of her. "This one always was my favorite before I had kids." She paused. "Of course, the boys would never eat the things I liked to cook until they grew up. Now they eat that sort of food all the time, but when they come here, they just want me to cook the same things they remember eating as children."

Courtney chuckled and began browsing through that cookbook.

"You know, you're the sort of girl I always pictured Justin would end up with if he had stayed around here."

"He must have told you I'm from Indiana."

Susan shook her head. "No, I just think you suit him well." She sighed. "That last one was horrible. I think Justin knew it too. He never bothered to bring her by. Even when I was in town I never met her."

Courtney assumed she was referring to Kinzie but didn't dare ask.

"He always told me not to believe everything I read about her, but you know, it all seemed pretty darn consistent. I think Justin just felt sorry for her, was all."

Courtney tried to think of a way to change the subject or leave the room. She wasn't sure how much more Kinzie-talk she could take.

"You know you're the first girlfriend he's introduced me to since he was in high school?" Susan asked suddenly.

"I don't think Justin really thinks of me as his girlfriend."

Susan laughed. "Well, that's what he called you on the phone. He just loved bragging about you, all that law school business, charity work, and so forth. How you got mixed up with him, I'll never know."

Courtney smiled at this. She wondered why he would tell his mother she was his girlfriend, while assuring the rest of the world that he was single.

"So are you going to tell me what this fight was over, or will I have to hear it from him later?"

"Oh, it's probably not my place to say," Courtney replied politely.

Justin's mother frowned. "You know, ever since Justin moved out West, but especially these last four or five years, it's been so hard for me as a mother to read the things about him in the papers. I used to try to ignore it, but my friends were always asking me about this and that detail that they read, so I ended up having to find out about it anyway." She sighed. "I guess I just figure, if it's that tough for me to have to read about it, I can't imagine how hard it is for you. Lord knows he isn't perfect, but I'm sure he doesn't do half the stuff those tabloids say he does."

"Hey, what are you ladies talking about?" Justin asked, popping into the room. He was wearing long cargo shorts with no shirt. His hair was still spiky and wet, and tiny droplets of water danced across his chest and shoulders. It took all the self-control Courtney could muster not to jump up and wrap her legs around him right then and there. He turned to her and grinned mischievously.

"We were talking about you, and all your recent escapades," Susan said, standing. "I'm going to water the flowers," she announced, leaving the room.

Justin filled a glass of water and plopped down at the table, flipping his chair around to sit backwards. "What escapades?" he asked.

Courtney shook her head. "Nothing specific." She paused. "Your mom said you called me your girlfriend."

He shrugged and gazed at his feet. "So?"

"You never call me that to anyone in L.A."

"I don't think it's anyone else's business," he insisted. "Is that what you've been mad about?"

"Have you been dating Kinzie and me at the same time?"

"No! I don't even know where that rumor about her started." He stared down at his feet.

"What?" Courtney knew he was hiding something now.

"Do you remember the day I introduced you to her? That was the last time we hooked up. I swear."

It took Courtney a moment to process this before she realized he just admitted to sleeping with his ex after they met. Since it was before they really got involved, Courtney decided that was forgivable, and the fact that he'd fessed up assured her that Kinzie wasn't the one she needed to be worried about.

She decided to try a different approach. "Justin, if I asked you to tell me everyone you've slept with in the, oh, sixteen months since we met, would you answer honestly?"

He immediately blushed, grinning to deflect the tension of

the question. "Dunno. Is there a gun to my head in this scenario?"

"Let me rephrase. Let's say you did tell me the truth. How do you think I'd react?"

"I think you'd wish you hadn't asked but you'd be fine with it because you realize sixteen months is a really long time and we hardly knew each other then." He paused and little wrinkles appeared above his eyebrows. "And you said you didn't have time for a real relationship. You said we weren't exclusive and…"

"I know what I said," Courtney interrupted, wanting to smack her past self for all the idiotic things she'd said to Justin. "I'm not saying all of this is your fault. I never asked you not to see other women, but…" she shook her head, swallowing the lump rising in her throat. "What if I just asked you about the women you've been with in the last year—do you think I'd react the same way to your answer?"

He nodded.

"Okay, so now I'm asking you about the last six months. Will you tell me the truth?"

He stared back, those bright blue eyes pleading with hers. Finally, he shook his head, the movement so slight she nearly missed it.

She looked down and sighed. That basically told her what she wanted to know. Why had she agreed to come with him on this trip?

"Hey," he said softly, reaching for her hand. "I'm sorry, alright. I don't want to lie to you."

"I appreciate that," she replied, tears welling in her eyes.

"Come on, please don't cry. My mom is going to think I was being mean to you."

She nearly laughed at that, but instead decided to try one more time to get him to see it from her perspective. "If you found out that I was sleeping with someone else three months ago, how would you have felt?"

"Pissed off, jealous," he admitted. "But you don't understand what it's like for me. It's hard when..."

"I don't want to hear your excuses, Justin," she interrupted. "Do you think it's easy for me? I have told virtually no one about us. I have friends trying to fix me up, guys I meet in classes or bars asking me out, and I have no decent reason to refuse it all."

"I thought I was protecting you by not telling anyone about us."

"Protecting me or your image?"

"Both."

"Fine, and I believe you, I do. I believe you like me, and I think you want me to remain your secret girlfriend, whatever that means, until someone else comes along. But I can't compartmentalize everything in my life like you do. I want to be with you and only you, and it's too hard for me to be with you at all when I know you don't feel the same way. When I have you, I don't need to sleep with anyone else. Why am I not enough for you?"

He was quiet for a moment. Courtney knew she was crying now and wanted to run upstairs, but couldn't find the energy. She only prayed his mom didn't come back inside now.

"You never gave me a chance to just be with you," he finally answered. "You're the one who called us friends with benefits. You're the one who said you didn't want a relationship. You're the one who is always pushing me away. I never said I don't feel the same way as you."

Courtney stared directly at him. "You don't have to say it in so many words. Sleeping with Lacey Duvall sends a pretty clear signal."

"I didn't fuck Lacey!" he shouted, right as his mom opened the back door.

They both turned, startled, and his mom quickly silently retreated back outside.

Justin laughed nervously, shaking his head. "At least she didn't box my ears for swearing," he mumbled.

Courtney smiled, despite her efforts not to.

He sighed. "Would you just tell me exactly what you want from me?"

"Nothing."

He rolled his eyes. "Don't play games, Courtney. That's not you. You want something, just tell me what so I can do it. You want my publicist to stop fixing me up on fake dates? An official public announcement that we're dating? What?"

She shook her head. "I just want you to stop sleeping with other people."

"Done," he said.

She was skeptical.

"I'm serious. Ask me about the last four months. You want an honest answer?" He didn't wait for her to reply. "One. One person one time other than you in the past four months. And you know what? I regretted it right away. It was dumb, and it sucked. I just, I don't know. I was always gone and I wasn't really sure where we stood anymore, and I was drunk, and there you have it." He shook his head. "I've been going crazy trying to keep my mind off you lately and I don't want to do that anymore."

Courtney held her breath while she pondered this. Obviously, she would've liked him to say there had been no one else in the last four months. But, if he'd said that, she might not have believed him. This way, she knew he was telling the truth. It could've been worse. And he was right, they'd never said they were exclusive. She swallowed hard.

"No one else, from this moment on. I promise." He grabbed her hand again and tried to make eye contact with her. "I won't even think about another woman."

She sighed. That was what she wanted, so why did it still feel wrong? "I don't want to make you miserable. I don't want you to have to change who you are for me."

"Courtney, don't you get it? I don't want anyone else. I haven't for a while now. The only thing making me miserable is knowing I've hurt you. Seriously." He raised her hand to his lips, kissing her knuckles gingerly. "I want you. I want to be with you and not have you constantly pushing me away. I don't want to hide you or pretend we're not together whenever we're in public. I want to make you happy and I don't want to have to act like you're not always on my mind."

Between the dimples and the sparkling in his eyes, he'd convinced her. She nodded slowly, and he leaned forward and kissed her, tentatively at first, then more eagerly. They broke apart when there was a knock on the door.

Justin laughed. "It's safe to come in now, Mom," he called.

His mother opened the door slowly and smiled, blushing. Then she shook her head. "That's a relief about that Lacey girl," she mumbled. "She didn't even look twenty-one."

Courtney and Justin both laughed. Justin reached forward and gently wiped the tears off Courtney's cheekbones.

THAT NIGHT, Justin's oldest brother Michael dropped by after dinner. Courtney chatted with them all for a while before heading upstairs to let them catch up. Later, after Michael had left, Justin went to join Courtney in his old room, but the door was locked. He considered knocking, but decided if she'd wanted him to join her, she wouldn't have locked the door.

Disappointed, he retreated to his own room, stripped down to his boxer briefs and stretched out on the twin bed, popping his earbuds in. He read through a few pages of a script, then closed his eyes to really absorb each line and get a better sense of the mood. Then he'd move on to the next few pages. During one of the points when his eyes were closed, he felt a soft tickle on his bicep, so gentle it was nearly imperceptible.

Justin cracked one eye, half expecting to find a bug crawling across his arm, but instead, there was Courtney. She was all ready for bed, wearing cut-off grey sweatpants and a fitted black tank top, her makeup washed off and her dark hair twisted into a loose knot on top of her head. She was so beautiful he caught himself just staring for a moment before smiling, pulling out his headphones, and rising to his elbows.

"Were you sleeping or working?" she asked, her voice soft.

"Working, but only because you locked me out."

She gazed down to her tanned feet and neatly polished nails. "I didn't want you to get the wrong idea."

Justin wasn't sure what she meant by that, except that she likely still wasn't going to sleep with him. Despite the fact that it had been forever since they'd been together that way, he was okay with that, as long as she forgave him.

"Did your brother leave?"

He nodded.

"Can I join you?"

Justin scooted over to let her slowly crawl into the tiny bed. They both lay on their sides, facing each other, her adorable button nose so close to his lips that he couldn't resist kissing it. "I missed you."

"Really?"

He wrinkled his brow. "Of course I did, Court. Didn't you miss me?"

"Yeah, but that's different. I didn't have," she paused, and he prayed she wasn't about to mention the other women. "So many distractions," she finally finished.

"I was busy," he agreed, "But you were the only distraction. I couldn't stop thinking about you."

Courtney scooted forward, pressing her face into his neck, filling his nostrils with the subtle scent of her vanilla lotion. He wrapped his arm around her back, his fingers stroking up and down the smooth skin along her shoulders and back. "I didn't think it would be that hard, being away from you for so long," she whined.

He considered this, trying to remember if he ever really minded being away from Kinzie for longer stretches of time when he was filming. As far as he could recall, he'd always enjoyed those times, able to essentially forget about her until he came back home. He had assumed that was how it should be, or at least how it had to be since an integral part of his job required him to travel, but it was noticeably different with Courtney. He'd failed miserably at compartmentalizing. He'd missed her when he was filming, and he'd thought about her whenever he was alone in his trailer or back at his hotel, struggling to sleep.

"I really like you, Justin, and I don't know what to do. I didn't mean to fall for you. I wanted to keep it fun and casual, but I..." she sucked in a labored breath, causing him to wonder if she was starting to cry.

"I was devastated when I saw that article and thought you didn't feel the same way. I could barely get out of bed the next morning. And I didn't just feel like an idiot for falling for someone who told me all along he wasn't looking for a girlfriend. I also felt like I'd let you down, like I'd ruined our perfect arrangement by forming real feelings for you."

Justin pressed his lips into the top of her head. "It was a stupid arrangement. I like the new one better. But Courtney," he began, and she looked up, her ocean eyes pleading with his. "There's still going to be lots of women in and out of my life. You know, costars, fans and the like."

Justin laughed as a particularly vivid memory hit him. "I had a girl mail me her panties once. I mean, I've had random women flash me, grab my ass, ask me to autograph their boobs, and I don't think all that will stop just because I have a girlfriend. I don't mean to sound cocky, but women are going to keep throwing themselves at me."

"As long as you're not catching any, they can just keep on throwing," Courtney replied with a laugh.

"And I'll still have scenes in movies where I'm with other women, even some of my ads have me with women. I don't want you feeling shitty every time I have to kiss someone else or see another girl naked."

"Gee, you make your job sound so challenging." Courtney rolled her eyes. "I'm not an idiot, you know. I realize you're an actor, and that you have to act. I've never made a big deal out of that."

He nodded. "I know. I just want to make sure it's all out there."

"Well, anything else?"

Justin thought. "Yeah, sometimes I need to travel with costars or other people in the business, socialize, network and whatnot. Making those connections is a big part of getting roles and on-screen chemistry once you get the roles."

Courtney nodded, so he pressed on.

"And one of the rumors about Andi and I was true."

Her eyes widened.

"Not that one," he quickly clarified. "We were looking at apartments together."

She raised an eyebrow.

"We both have been spending a lot of time in New York lately, either filming or for publicity stuff, and with the last two *Days End* movies, that's only going to increase in the next few years. We both hate hotels, but it's expensive to buy in New York, and we're not there at the same time that often."

"So you were going to do like a timeshare?"

He licked his lips, debating whether this confession was really necessary. "Well, sort of. I mean," he paused, "We already bought one. Whenever either of us is in New York, we'll stay there. And it's a two bedroom, so if there's ever an overlap, we'll each have our own room, just like before when they'd put us up in different rooms in the same hotel."

Fortunately, Courtney's breathing remained calm and even. "I see why you like her. She's nice. And beautiful."

"You're beautiful." He kissed her again.

She scooted up so her face was next to his again and kissed him back this time, her full lips eagerly pushing into his. They kissed the way he'd been remembering kissing her for weeks, Justin realizing even more fully how much he'd missed her. She rolled on top of him, lifting her own shirt off. Justin felt his lips tug into a grin at the familiar and soothing sensation of her bare breasts and smooth stomach against his skin. He pulled the elastic band out of her hair, eager to touch the soft waves with his fingers, the loose strands toppling out of their knot onto his face and shoulders. They kissed for longer—maybe longer than they'd ever kissed before, and then Courtney stopped, breathless.

The look in her eyes told him she'd changed her mind, that she wanted more of him, but he didn't budge until she said it.

"I missed you," she whispered. "I want you."

"You've got me," he replied, knowing exactly what she meant.

She shook her head, bit her lip in the sexy pouty way that drove him crazy, and pulled on the elastic band of his boxer briefs with her finger.

He grinned, flipped her onto her back, and removed their

remaining articles of clothing. They made love slowly, and quietly, both of them all too aware that his mother was asleep down the hall. After, they talked more, her nude body draped across his, then fell asleep facing the wall beside the teensy tiny bed, her back pressed against his chest, Justin holding on to her tightly as though he worried she was about to leave.

In the morning, a noise interrupted Justin's deep sleep, jolting him awake. He'd barely opened his eyes when Courtney squealed. Then, she frantically tugged at the sheets, unable to pull them any higher with his arm pressed against her, his hand cupping her bare breast.

Justin lifted his head, following Courtney's panicked gaze across the room, and saw his younger brother, Luke. He started to stand, helping Courtney with the sheet since she was still struggling to cover herself.

"Dude, don't you get up! I don't want to see that!" Luke shouted, shielding his eyes.

Justin glanced down, confirming he was wearing boxer shorts. "I'm not naked, you dipshit," he retorted, Luke tentatively uncovering his eyes. "Wait, so you shield your eyes for me but have no problem ogling her?" Justin gestured to Courtney, who had finally draped the sheets over herself but still looked embarrassed.

He scanned the room for her shirt and, not finding it, tossed her one of his own. She quickly tugged it over her head, briefly flashing him and his brother again when the sheet fell right before she pulled the shirt all the way down. Justin glared back at Luke, who was still staring contentedly at Courtney, and then punched his brother in the arm.

"Jerk," Luke retorted, rubbing the already-red patch on his arm.

Their mom walked by then, barely pausing as she said, "Boys, no fighting."

"But he has a topless girl in bed with him," Luke quickly tattled, grinning widely.

Justin rolled his eyes, but blushed all the same. Even if he knew his mother probably wouldn't mind now that they were all grown up, it was still embarrassing.

His mom stopped and ducked her head into the room. "Good morning, Courtney," she said pleasantly before continuing on down the hallway.

"Luke, this is Courtney, Courtney, this is Luke," Justin grumbled, adding, "The baby of the family."

"Hey, I'm twenty now. I'm legal."

"Not for beer," Justin said.

"That wasn't what I was talking about," Luke said, grinning at Courtney.

"Get out!" Justin shouted.

When Luke finally backed away and closed the door, Justin laughed, then collapsed back onto the bed with Courtney.

"That was my baby brother. I think he likes your boobs."

She laughed, her cheeks still beet red. "Awesome."

They kissed playfully, then dressed before heading downstairs.

By mid-afternoon, two of Justin's other brothers joined Luke — Chris, the brother closest in age to Justin, and Michael, the oldest, whom Courtney had met the night before. The four brothers immediately set off to the playground for a quick game of two on two, leaving Courtney alone with their mother and Chris's wife Beth.

"So what were the boys like growing up?" Courtney asked Susan. "It had to be crazy in the house with all of them."

Susan smiled. "The house was never quiet, that's for sure.

But Don, that was the boys' father, and I, we'd always wanted a big family and we really liked it. I wished they weren't all so competitive as kids, but it seems they've each found their way.

"Did you ever want a daughter?" Beth asked.

"Oh sure, but I don't think the boys would've fared too well with a sister. Although for the past three years now, I've been getting one new daughter a year!"

"I think that means it's Justin's turn next," Beth giggled.

Courtney quickly shook her head. "I thought there was still one older brother who hasn't married yet."

"Josh is our second oldest, but he just finished medical school and has been too busy to meet someone yet."

Beth glanced at Courtney. "You two would make some beautiful babies, with bright blue eyes for sure."

Courtney blushed, and Susan, still smiling, stood to start making dinner. Claiming she preferred to work alone, she shooed the girls off to cheer along the guys in their game. As they walked, Courtney asked Beth how long she'd been married, and learned she was four months pregnant, although she certainly didn't look pregnant yet.

"It's a fun family to join into," Beth admitted. "Do you think you and Justin will eventually get married?"

"I don't think he's the marrying type."

"Really? That surprises me. I mean, I know he's all Hollywood, but gosh, if you watch him with his niece and nephew, well, you'll see for yourself later."

"Does he come visit here a lot?"

Beth shrugged. "I'm not sure. The first time I met him was when Chris and I were engaged, and then I didn't see him again until our wedding six months later. He was in town a few months ago, too, I know, but I didn't see him then." She paused, then giggled. "Chris and I had met in high school, but we didn't start dating until college, and by the time we were going steady, Justin had already moved to Los Angeles. I didn't even realize he was famous until Chris warned me before I met him."

Beth shook her head. "And boy oh boy, when I first met him, I was so nervous I couldn't speak. I mean, I'd seen his movies, I just didn't know he was about to be my brother-in-law. But, once I got to know him, he seemed more like just a regular guy."

Courtney smiled. "Yeah, it's easier to see that about him out here than it is in L.A., though. His whole life there is still so surreal."

"You know Chris told me that when Justin got his first big paycheck from the *Days End* movie, the first thing he did was pay off their mama's mortgage. I thought that was so sweet. I guess their folks had paid it off at one time but then had to take out a new one to get money to pay for Don's chemo and what-not. I kept thinking what I'd do with a bunch of money like that, you know cars or fancy trips or a beach house, and here the first thing he thought of was his mom."

"I didn't know that," Courtney replied. "But it doesn't surprise me."

Beth asked her about when she first met Justin, and they managed to gossip the rest of the way to the park.

By the time the game was over, dinner was ready and Michael's wife Lynette had arrived, along with their two kids, a three-year-old girl and six-month-old baby boy. Courtney was quiet, observing Justin interacting with his brothers, their wives, his mom, and the kids. She wished his other brothers could've made it, but it might have been hectic to meet the whole huge family at once. She couldn't imagine not having come with him on this trip. She'd already known his family was a big part of his life, but seeing them together, Courtney really understood how much of an impact his big family and modest Midwest upbringing had had on him.

The next morning, they left Justin's house to spend time with Courtney's family before flying back.

"You really don't have to visit my parents," Courtney repeated nervously, despite the fact that they'd nearly arrived. She wished again that her brothers were going to be there, but since they'd both made the pilgrimage out to L.A. for her graduation a couple months before, neither could free up their schedule for another visit so soon.

Justin reached over and squeezed her thigh. "I thought you and your parents got along."

"We do," she sighed. "It's you I'm worried about."

"Well, don't. I'm a people person. And, in case you haven't noticed, people tend to like me." He paused. "Wait, you told them I was coming, right?"

She nodded hesitantly.

"It's the next one on the left," she said, and he pulled into the driveway.

Courtney stood nervously beside the car while Justin retrieved their bags. When she glanced up, her mother was waving enthusiastically from the front door. Courtney cringed at her mother's pinstriped pantsuit but felt the slightest tug of comfort at the familiar sight.

Courtney started to the door and was already hugging her mother, then father, by the time Justin reached the steps.

"Here, let me help you with those," her father offered, straining as he lifted one of the bags into the entryway before turning to shake hands with Justin.

"Mom, Dad, this is Justin Erikson. Justin, these are my parents, Matt and Shannon."

Justin flashed his best smile. "Nice to meet you."

Her mom smiled politely. "I'd like to say we've heard so much about you, but Courtney isn't so chatty lately." She shot a pointed glare at Courtney.

Justin glanced awkwardly at Courtney, and she guessed he was trying to remember the last time someone had said they hadn't heard about him. "I've been out of town for the last two and a half months."

Her dad nodded, as though trying to shush his wife, and offered Justin and Courtney a drink. They all sat on the musty couch, tall floral glasses of nauseatingly sweet iced tea in hand. Then, there was silence. Courtney panicked, debating if it was too soon to start up a discussion on the weather.

"How was the drive?" her dad asked.

Before they could answer, her mom piped up again. "Where were you for two whole months?"

"Toronto," Courtney jumped in, likely hoping to spare Justin.

"Now what is there to do in Toronto for that long?"

"I was working," he replied quickly, a brief glance in Courtney's direction to show he could answer for himself. He patted her leg gently, probably hoping to relax her, but as Courtney watched her father's eyes widen at the sight of Justin's hand on his daughter's thigh, she felt queasy.

"Is this the friend you went to visit in Toronto over the Fourth?" her mom asked.

Courtney nodded.

"Tell me, what business are you in again?" her dad prompted.

Justin apparently couldn't help it anymore, and a tiny chuckle escaped his lips.

"He's an actor, Dad, remember?" Courtney jumped in, nudging Justin's hand away.

Courtney's mom frowned at her daughter's irritation.

"What sort of acting were you doing in Canada?" her dad asked, in a tone that implied Canada was some uncivilized place void of technology.

"We were shooting the final film in the *Days End* series,"

Justin replied calmly, as Courtney anxiously dug her fingernails into her thighs.

Her parents eyed each other warily, as though trying to gauge telepathically whether the other knew what that was.

"Is that on the Sci-Fi Channel?" her father asked.

"Have you been in anything we might have seen?" her mom chimed in.

Justin turned to Courtney, and she quickly tried to think of something he might have been in that they'd know, but she was drawing a blank to the point where even she couldn't remember anything he'd done.

"Oh!" her dad exclaimed. "Weren't you the one in that ad for those fancy orthotics?"

Justin smiled politely, but shook his head, miraculously not throwing his iced tea at her father.

This seemed to disappoint her parents. Her mother glanced out the window, apparently bored already.

"Well, you should look into the ad business. I bet commercials for those shoe inserts alone could keep a man busy enough," her dad advised.

"Honey, I'm sure those are hard to get. There's probably auditions and everything," Courtney's mom whispered loudly to her spouse.

"I've done a few commercials, but I really prefer full length films," Justin said.

Her parents both eyed him as though he just professed a hatred of animals and orphans. Courtney felt her blood pressure rising and considered faking a horrible stomach virus so they could escape and spend the next few days at a hotel.

"I bet those public service ads are easier to nab," her father said.

Courtney jumped up. "Enough already!" she screeched. "This is ridiculous!"

Her mom frowned. "We're just trying to be helpful. Everyone appreciates a little career advice."

"He doesn't need your advice, Mom."

She noticed Justin blushing as he stood, setting his drink on a wooden coaster bearing a picture of a rooster. "I'll go get the rest of the bags."

Courtney waited until Justin was out of earshot before continuing. "You are embarrassing me!"

Her mother narrowed her eyes. "You're embarrassing yourself, Courtney. We were just trying to help him out. It's hard to make a living these days."

"And what I'm trying to tell you is that he doesn't need your help. He has an agent, a publicist, and a manager who handle all that. He's not some struggling actor. He's rich, and he's really successful with his work." Courtney pulled out her phone. She went straight to the internet and typed Justin's name in the search box. Then she handed the phone to her parents and watched as her mother's eyes grew wide.

"That's not the same man," her father began, scrolling down the page.

Her mom sighed. "When you told us he was an actor, we thought you meant theater. Practically everyone in L.A. calls themselves an actor, don't they? You never said you were dating the next Brad Pitt!"

"You never said he was famous," her father said, gasping at a photo of one of Justin's billboards. "What is he wearing there?"

Courtney cringed and snatched back her phone, but not before a surprised "Oh!" escaped her mother's lips.

"He also does some modeling," she tentatively explained.

Her parents stared at each other in shock.

"Look, just treat him like any other guy I'd bring home, okay?"

"Well, that's what we were doing before you showed us that," her mother cried. "Why didn't you tell us this sooner?"

"I did tell you."

"Courtney Lynn," her mother began.

She raised her hands defensively. "Fine. I wasn't sure what to say. At first, it was just casual and then he was out of town working for so long that it seemed like a moot point." Courtney sighed. "Justin's had to work really hard to keep his private life, well, private, or as private as possible, and the fewer the people who know we're dating, the better."

Her mom rolled her eyes. "You could've asked us not to tell anyone and we would've agreed." She shook her head. "Are you really telling us you've been dating a celebrity for close to a year and a half and never thought to tell us?"

Courtney tried to think of an answer, but was saved by a hesitant Justin carrying her other bag in the door. "Nice timing," she whispered.

Her parents both stared at him like he was an alien.

"We'll go take these upstairs to my room and be back in a few minutes,"

As soon as Courtney shut the bedroom door, Justin began laughing uncontrollably. She exhaled, relieved he wasn't angry. "I'm sorry I didn't tell them more. I just knew if I did, they'd start following you in the tabloids or online and then I'd have to deal with my parents interrogating me about rumors that you're dating other girls, on steroids, gay, an alcoholic..."

"Who said I'm on steroids?" he interrupted, panicked.

Courtney rolled her eyes. "Why don't you just ask your publicist?"

He laughed and stepped closer, placing his hands on her hips before leaning in for a kiss. She closed her eyes, focusing on the softness of his lips and the warmth of his tongue, until finally, she felt her breathing return to normal.

"Better?" Justin asked as the kiss ended, his blue eyes frozen less than an inch from her own.

Courtney smiled and kissed him again before remembering that her parents were downstairs.

"Your parents seem really nice," Justin said.

"They are," she agreed. "But they're also overprotective and conservative, and they ask a ton of questions."

He hugged her, his thick, strong arms soothing her. "Then shouldn't we get back down there before they start to think I'm taking advantage of you?"

She nodded, and trudged down the stairs.

Fortunately, by then, her parents had calmed down. They all took the dog for a walk, Justin charming her parents by holding the leash and recounting the day he found his own precious Bella at an animal shelter in L.A. Later, Courtney and her mother cooked dinner while her dad watched TV and Justin caught up on some phone calls.

Conversation flowed relatively smoothly at dinner, although Courtney's dad made Justin blush more than once with odd questions about his modeling work. Then they all played board games after dinner. By the time Courtney and Justin were finally alone upstairs, she felt like a twelve year old again, especially since they were sleeping in her childhood room, which was still painted a soft lilac and decked out with identical twin beds.

DESPITE THE STRANGE START, Justin had managed to survive and even somewhat enjoy the visit with Courtney's parents. Courtney seemed a little tense, but he got the feeling that was more about her not wanting her parents to embarrass him. Other than that, he thought things between them were back to normal, especially considering that they had already made up...

boy had they ever made up. They'd made up three times in the last forty-eight hours alone.

After the first night at the house, Justin had awakened feeling refreshed. He and Courtney were sharing her old room, but thanks to the tiny twin beds, he had ended up moving to his own bed a few feet away from hers in the middle of the night. Justin liked sleeping next to Courtney, with her butt pressed against his groin, but after a while, his arm went numb and his nose would start itching from her hair tickling it, so he appreciated having an extra bed available. They both dressed and went downstairs for breakfast, but then Justin was interrupted by an "urgent" call from his agent.

When Justin finished his phone call, he returned to the table and, seeing that Courtney had disappeared, decided now was the best time to talk with her parents.

He cleared his throat awkwardly. "I, uh, just wanted to give you a little heads up," he began, then panicked, as both Courtney's parents turned to him expectantly. He prayed they weren't expecting him to announce his intent to propose or any crap like that.

"Now that Courtney and I are both in L.A., we're probably going to be spending more time together, so there's a pretty good chance the paparazzi will find out sooner or later that we've been dating." He paused, but neither Matt nor Shannon responded, so he continued. "For the most part, they tend to edit non-celebrities out of photos, but there's a possibility that you'll see something about Courtney pop up in a tabloid or maybe a picture or something. My publicist is pretty good about keeping the details of my life fairly protected, but if the reporters get interested in the relationship, you just might hear more about it. If anyone gives you any trouble, though, I can put you in touch with my publicist."

Matt frowned. Shannon turned to Courtney, who had just returned to the kitchen. "I don't understand."

"Mom, he's just saying that if the tabloids found out my name, they might try to find out more details on me or my life. More likely than not, no one would care enough to bother, but there's just that chance my photo or name might show up somewhere."

"And it's possible someone would call here to try to talk to you two," Justin added. "Especially this spring when they start really publicizing the movie's summer release."

Courtney eyed Justin warily, then spoke. "Don't worry about it, guys. If something comes up, we'll just let you know."

THAT NIGHT, Courtney's mom approached her while Justin was still finishing his workout.

"Sweetie, I wanted to talk to you alone for a minute. Your father and I have some concerns."

Courtney forced a smile. She had been expecting this. There was no way she could bring a guy home to meet her parents and not raise "concerns." Even though she was nearly twenty-six, her parents would always assume she couldn't make her own decisions without their input. Because of that, she'd stopped sharing most of the details of her private life about halfway through college, leading her parents to believe she was living the life of a nun. But now, she realized it was possible that tactic was backfiring, and that her parents might have handled the situation more calmly if they'd had more time to adjust to the notion of Courtney dating an actor.

"It's just that you're such a hard worker, and you've always been so focused on your career aspirations. I'm sure it's been nice to spend time with Justin, and he is a very charismatic person for certain, but don't you think you could find someone else a little more like you? Someone you have more in common with?"

"I have fun with Justin."

"But life can't always just be about having fun," her mother began. "At some point a person has to grow up and accept some responsibility."

Courtney knew her mother meant Justin, not her. "Justin has been handling significant responsibilities for quite some time now. He is an extremely hard worker, and he's very focused on his work. And now that he's becoming more well-known, he's on-duty 24/7. He can't do anything without considering his public image and career."

"Aren't you worried this Hollywood lifestyle might be putting too much pressure on you?"

Courtney shrugged. "Me? No, I'm not worried. But you were the one who said you had some concerns, so why don't you just tell them to me before Justin finishes his workout and wonders where I am."

Her mom sighed. "Well, that's one of them. He sure exercises a lot. Don't you think he's a little too worried about his appearance?"

Courtney laughed. "Justin is required to look that way for his job. He's a model and an actor, so yeah, he spends a ton of time exercising and making sure he looks good. He can't even leave the house in L.A. without looking camera-ready. People photograph him everywhere he goes."

Her mom frowned. "The internet said he uses steroids and might take other drugs."

"You can't believe everything you read, Mom. He doesn't use drugs."

"I've seen photos of him drinking," her mother countered. "Is that made up too?"

Courtney rolled her eyes. "No. You saw him drink at dinner! So what? He's twenty-seven."

There was a pause. "Well, just because he has to be so obsessed with his looks doesn't mean you have to, right? Are you sure you're still eating enough? You've lost some weight."

"Five pounds, maybe ten. It was all the studying, though, not Justin." She paused, trying to envision anyone successfully losing weight hanging around Justin, with all he ate. "Anything else you read about that you want to bring up?"

"Does he gamble?"

Courtney hesitated too long to simply lie in response. Still, this was a tricky one, since even she wasn't altogether comfortable with his gambling. "A little, Mom, but he's not like an addict. He and his friends just have too much money. Is that all?"

"What about him with all those other girls?"

She winced. "There are no other girls, Mom. The tabloids just like to speculate."

Her mother lowered her voice. "I hope you're being safe anyway, you know, taking precautions to protect yourself."

"Mother! I am not going to discuss safe sex with you!"

Her mother blushed, then sighed. "He does seem nice. And much more down to earth than you'd expect."

Courtney nodded in agreement, smiling, and added, "He's really close to his mom."

"I'm just worried you're going to get hurt."

She sighed. "Well, I'm sure I will eventually. Pretty much every relationship ends up that way at some point or another, right? But for right now, I'm happy, and Justin's happy. I wish you and Dad could just be supportive."

Her mother nodded hesitantly. "Should I not tell my friends?"

Courtney laughed. "You can tell whoever you want."

11

As soon as they returned to L.A., Justin decided it was time. For too long, he'd felt torn between pretending to be single to avoid pissing off his agent and publicist and wanting to treat Courtney as his girlfriend. Not a huge fan of direct confrontation, though, he'd discussed it with Keith over drinks and they'd devised a pretty safe strategy. The next day, Justin thrust his plan into action.

He went jogging with Courtney during the day, pausing in front of a large crowd before kissing her. Then, at night, they met up with one of his *Days End* costars, Jason, for dinner outside a popular restaurant. After, they walked down the street to a club, right past the paparazzi.

As soon as Justin, Courtney and Jason got closer to the cameras, blinding flashes began lighting up the otherwise dark streets. Courtney winced, turning to Justin, who pulled her even closer before waving and flashing a casual grin at the two men. Then he stopped and kissed her.

"What was that about?" she asked as they walked around the bouncer into the club.

Justin beamed proudly. "I was going to call my publicist this morning, to let her know you're my official girlfriend now and that she should back off, but this is easier."

"You think you got your point across?"

Justin flashed his mischievous grin. "I've only just begun."

By the time they got back to his place that night, Justin was feeling pretty good. He hadn't realized how much energy he was wasting trying to pretend his relationship with Courtney was purely platonic every time they were in public. He loved flirting with her in public, touching her, even kissing her, all without regard for who might be watching. For Justin, the whole night was foreplay.

Keith and Tara had settled on the couch downstairs, and Keith asked Justin if he and Courtney wanted to watch a movie with them. Justin cringed, simultaneously pitying his buddy who was doomed for a night of TV with his girl and praying that Courtney didn't agree to it.

Thankfully Courtney shook her head. "I'm pretty tired, actually. We should probably get me straight to bed," she giggled.

Justin grinned, picking her up and eliciting a loud squeal from her as he carried her up the stairs, her legs wrapping around his back. He dropped her onto the bed, falling on top of her as she pulled his head towards her. Her soft, smooth lips tasted like vodka. He kissed her hungrily, perhaps too much so, because she suddenly pushed him away. Flustered, he sat up, watching Courtney as she crossed the room and closed the door.

"Oops," he mumbled, standing.

He stepped closer to her again, but before he could kiss her, she'd unbuttoned his pants and dropped to her knees. Justin was breathless the moment she touched his skin, first with the tip of her tongue gently circling the head of his erection and then stroking up and down the entire length of it before she wrapped her lips around it, taking him into her warm, wet mouth. He felt his arms tremble as they gripped her smooth shoulders, his fingers tangled in the tips of her long hair, and he heard himself moan softly in between rushed breaths.

He pulled her up when he knew he couldn't take any more, and she smiled, clearly proud that she'd so completely tantalized him. The rest of their clothes were off almost immediately, and Justin lifted her onto the bed, his mouth reaching for the soft peak of her supple breasts.

Her hands reached for his head, her fingers pulsing against the nape of his neck while she squirmed, thrusting her nipple further into his eager mouth. Justin slid his hands between their bodies, reaching his fingers across her thigh until they reached the warm dampness between her legs, and he knew they were both ready. They made love frantically, as though it were something new.

JUSTIN LEFT for New York on Monday for a couple days of promos with other *Days Ends* actors. Courtney hated that she hadn't known until Sunday that he was leaving, but she was determined not to be the naggy type. Plus, she wasn't positive Justin even realized he had the trip scheduled. She'd started to learn that Keith was more in control of Justin's calendar than Justin himself.

Courtney was thankful for her new job. If she weren't so overwhelmingly busy at work, she might be jealous that her boyfriend was currently sharing an apartment with a gorgeous actress. Justin called every day while he was gone, and they texted back and forth, too. Several of the nights, she spent her evening watching whatever interviews he'd done that day. It was strange, watching him be interviewed, especially since he was usually seated suspiciously close to Andi or his on-screen love interest.

The only solo interview Justin was scheduled for during this trip was on a late night show. Courtney was excited, because he really didn't get to field as many of the questions when he was interviewed along with his costars. The show apparently taped in the morning, and Justin called her as she was driving home from work that evening to remind her to watch it.

The interview had started predictably enough, with the host asking about his latest project, joking about how busy he'd been, and so forth. Courtney anxiously waited for them to move on to his personal life. She wasn't expecting much, since she knew from Justin that a lot of actors would specify in advance types of questions they wouldn't answer, and that others, Justin included, would just give vague answers to interview questions.

"Hurry up, you're missing it," she shouted to Erica, who had been microwaving popcorn in their tiny kitchen.

Erica rolled her eyes unenthusiastically before plopping down on the couch by Courtney just as Justin finished describing his next project.

"So now I'm going to ask what everybody really wants to know about," the interviewer told Justin, raising an eyebrow.

Justin flashed his dimples, drawing attention away from his now blushing cheeks. "What's that?"

"The girl."

Courtney's smile broadened to the point that her cheeks hurt, watching Justin as he laughed and nodded on the screen. Erica's eyes widened and she turned to Courtney excitedly.

"There's all this speculation in the media—is he single, is he not?" The interviewer turns to the audience again. "For a while all we hear about is this MacKinzie Maddox...Justin and Kinzie dating, Justin and Kinzie split, Justin and Kinzie back together. But then we just start seeing you out there alone. I mean, it's like the whole damn country forgot that the economy sucks and we're still at war." He paused to allow for the audience's laughter. "All we want to know is this guy's dating life." He turned back to Justin, laughing right along with the audience. "Then all of a sudden all these pictures show up of you and a girl."

Justin shrugged, still grinning, and raised his hands.

"So there is a girlfriend now? You'll confirm that?"

Courtney grinned, watching as Justin nodded.

"Is this a new girlfriend?"

"No, I wouldn't say that," Justin replied.

"Alright, well, here she is," the interviewer said, gesturing to the large screen displaying a photo of Justin and Courtney holding hands, walking into a shop in Venice Beach. "In case you forgot what she looks like," he joked to Justin. The audience let out a dramatic "awww" in unison. "So is she someone you've met through work? A model? An actress?"

Justin shook his head, laughing. "No, she's a lawyer."

"A lawyer?" The audience laughed along with the interviewer. "Oh the jokes I could've come up with if you'd given me this detail in advance." He paused to let the audience chuckle again. "Now how come we're just now seeing this girl if she's not new?"

Justin hemmed and hawed, tilting his shoulders from side to side. "She's not really big on the whole paparazzi thing. She's more of a private person."

"She does know you tend to attract the public eye, right?" the interviewer whispered. He laughed louder as another picture flashed on the screen—this one a photo of Justin's underwear ad billboard. "Of course she does. It's hard not to know that when your boyfriend's butt is plastered over Sunset Boulevard." The audience whistled and cheered.

Courtney noticed Justin holding his breath until the photo left the screen.

"So for our single female viewers out there," the interviewer continued. "Should they give up on you? Is this a serious relationship? Would you say this is love?"

Justin grinned at the screen. Courtney bit her lip watching. "Yeah, I think those are fair statements."

The audience went wild. Courtney felt her heart skip a beat and tuned out the rest of the interview.

She dialed his number as soon as it ended. From the sound when he picked up, Justin was either at a club or a party. The music was so loud, she wasn't even sure how he'd known his phone was ringing. He might have said hello, but she couldn't be sure, and then there was a scuffling noise, and it was quieter.

"Did you watch the show?" he asked.

"Of course. You looked so cute I just had to call."

He laughed. "So what did you think?"

She paused. "He made you blush."

"Yeah," he admitted. "Anything else?"

She felt herself smiling. "No. You were perfect. It was sweet." She heard him whisper something to someone else in the background. "So when do you get back?"

"Tomorrow night, late. But you could still come over."

She sighed. "I've got a seven A.M. meeting Friday. I might be able to sneak away after that, though."

"I'll see you then," he promised, hanging up.

Courtney exhaled with disappointment. She had hoped he'd be alone, so they could talk longer. She had wanted him to tell her what he'd told the entire late-night viewing audience he felt about her. And she wanted to get rid of the nagging thought in the back of her mind that he was in the exact same town he was in the last time he hooked up with someone else.

~

Late Friday morning, Justin had just dabbed on cologne when there was a knock at the door. He slid across the hardwood floor in his socks, opening the door with a smile, ready to pounce. "Hey!" he shouted excitedly, his happiness evaporating as he saw his visitor.

Kinzie stood there, eying him skeptically, then pushed past him to walk in. "There's the kind of welcome I deserve."

Justin rolled his eyes, trying to decide how to get rid of her before Courtney arrived. "I was expecting someone else," he explained. "This isn't a good time."

She narrowed her eyes and smirked. He knew exactly why she was here. She had seen his interview Wednesday night, heard him talking about Courtney, and got jealous. The rules had always been clear with Kinzie—she could move on, but he should not.

Kinzie bent at the waist to set her purse down, offering him a clear view down the front of her extremely low-cut top. Then she spun around, obviously eager to show Justin that the back of the shirt was equally revealing, especially when paired with the skin tight leggings she wore. He averted his eyes, not wanting to give her even the slightest glance out of fear that she'd start taking her clothes off. Luckily, Kinzie took the hint and sat on the couch instead.

"How was New York?" she asked, dramatically flinging her hair over her shoulder.

Justin started to answer, but then heard a noise at the door. Courtney ducked her head inside, then smiled when she saw him. Justin reached his arms around her and immediately pulled her close for a kiss, stretching his hands up her back so his fingers could run through her hair. He had completely forgotten Kinzie was even there until Courtney pulled back, cleared her throat and bit her lip like she always did when she was nervous.

"Hi Kinzie," Courtney mumbled. Then she turned back to Justin. "I've got to be back at the office in an hour."

He couldn't read her expression to gauge if she was mad about Kinzie's presence. "No problem. Kinzie was just leaving." He glared pointedly at Kinzie, but she made no effort to stand. Frustrated, he turned back to Courtney. "I can work with an hour," he assured her.

Courtney shook her head, still warily eying Kinzie.

"Sorry, Kinzie. We'll have to chat later," Justin said. He grabbed Courtney by the hand and pulled her up the stairs, knowing full well Kinzie would leave immediately, probably in a pissed off fury from not having been adequately ogled by him.

Courtney laughed when they heard the front door click shut. "Nicely done," she commented, unbuttoning his jeans.

"She just dropped by," Justin explained. "I don't even know why she was here."

Courtney nodded, apparently accepting of this explanation, so he moved on.

"An hour? Seriously?" he repeated, fumbling with the million tiny buttons along her blouse before giving up and thrusting his hands up under her shirt, pressing his palms against her warm, smooth skin, tracing over her stomach up to her breasts.

She kissed him eagerly, passionately. Justin knew he was smiling. This was the perk of their schedules. Even though it sucked that they never saw enough of each other, he couldn't beat the fact that she always missed him and wanted him—bad —when they finally did see each other. "You are so hot," he whispered, nibbling playfully on her earlobe, adding, "I missed you."

Courtney didn't answer, instead pulling off his jeans. He took the hint and dropped his boxer briefs, hoisting her skirt to her waist and yanking off her panties before lifting her up in the air.

She wrapped her long, perfect legs around his waist as he pushed her against the wall and made love to her with the same passion as their first time together. After a minute, he turned, flinging her onto the bed and climbing on top. In a relationship filled with good sex, this was definitely at the top of the list.

Courtney was breathing hard but smiling when their eyes locked. "I missed you too," she finally whispered, kissing just below his collarbone.

Justin traced his finger along her body, then stretched out on the bed, pulling her thong out from behind his back. She snuggled her head onto his chest, her breath tickling him. "It's been over three weeks," he commented as she rubbed her fingers over the sprinkling of hair across his chest, trying to remember if this was the longest he'd gone without a waxing since they'd met.

She kissed his chest, then propped her chin against him and looked up.

He smiled at the cute sparkle in her baby blue eyes.

"Did you mean what you said at the interview?" she asked. "About us? About how you feel about me?"

He lightly pressed his lips against her forehead. "Of course I did. You know that."

She shook her head. "You've never told me."

"Are you sure?" Justin asked even though he knew she was right. He sucked at that sort of discussion. He contemplated telling her right then, but decided against it, determined to find a more romantic time and place.

She groaned. "I have to go."

He didn't move the arm draped across her back, holding her to him for another minute. "Are you coming back tonight?"

"Tomorrow morning?" she suggested. That drove Justin crazy. It wasn't like she played hard to get, she just never made herself overly available.

"I've got to hit the gym tomorrow, but after," he replied.

She nodded and sat up, buttoning her top. "This sucks," she mumbled. "Even when you're in town, I never get to see enough of you."

"Why don't you move in here?" Justin suggested, shocked to hear the words come out of his mouth.

Courtney laughed. "We'd never get any sleep."

Justin grinned at the thought. "I'm okay with that!"

She rolled her eyes and snatched her panties from him. "Not what I meant. It's just, I always have to be at work early, and you're always up late."

He sighed, enjoying watching her dress and knowing the smudges in her makeup, wrinkles in her blouse, and unruliness of her hair was all because of him.

"Plus you're not here that often," she reminded him.

Justin pulled his jeans back up to walk her out. She lingered at the door as they kissed, then ran to her car.

He closed the door behind her and turned to see Keith standing there with a can of soda, laughing.

"Dude, did you seriously just ask her to move in here? What the fuck has happened to you?"

Justin locked the door. "How much were you listening to?"

Keith laughed harder. "Don't worry, I just caught the discussion at the end. If you'd shut your door all the way, this wouldn't be an issue."

He rolled his eyes, trying to figure out how neither he or Courtney had noticed leaving the door open. "Well, she said no anyway."

12

———

The following weekend was the annual fundraiser for the shelter that Courtney worked for. It was a formal event where all the employees attended with guests along with all the major donors from the community. Justin was eager to show Courtney he could adapt on her turf just as well as she had on his.

The night of the benefit, Justin arrived at Courtney's right on time, barely stepping out of the Audi before she reached the curb. She wore a floor length emerald green gown with her long hair elegantly falling across her shoulders in thick curls. Justin whistled as she approached. She smiled, twirling to reveal the back of her dress which dipped dangerously low for an attorney. He squeezed her as he kissed her, lifting her feet off the ground.

"You're pretty handsome yourself. I'm surprised that suit still fits," she added.

Justin turned to her. "Really? You remember this one?"

Courtney raised her eyebrows. "Oh yeah. You wore this suit to those music awards right after we first met. I spent so much time drooling over the photo of you grinning at the cameras in this." She ran her fingers across the smooth, silky material, pausing naughtily on his upper thigh.

He cleared his throat. "Courtney, there are going to be some important people there tonight. You better behave," he teased, worried more that, between that slinky dress and Courtney's wandering hand, he'd be too distracted to even pretend to understand what all the lawyers were talking about.

When they arrived, Justin paused, momentarily confused by the lack of cameras at the entrance. Then he laughed softly at his gaff and loosely wrapped his arm around Courtney's waist. Actually nervous for once, Justin was relieved when he spotted the bar. He ordered a white wine for Courtney and a double shot of whiskey on ice for himself, over-tipping the bartender since he had no small bills in his wallet.

For the next half hour, Justin followed Courtney around like a well-trained dog, politely smiling and shaking hands with the people she introduced him to, unsure of whether to feel relieved or offended that no one seemed to recognize him. Dinner was supposed to start at 8, but he was already feeling antsy. He turned to Courtney, about to say he needed to make a phone call, but she spoke first.

"You're doing great," she whispered, in a voice that didn't sound as condescending as it probably should have. "But you look like a caged rat. Why don't you meet up with me when the dinner starts? We're at Table 12."

He nodded, relieved, finishing the last drops of his drink and dashing outside. It was a nice night, so instead of escaping to his car to listen to music, he just stepped around the corner, and started messing with his phone, catching up on emails and social media. A voice mail from his publicist instructed him to call her urgently, so he did. He wasn't worried though, since everything was urgent to Jamie.

"Jamie? It's Justin. I don't have long. What's up?"

He heard her sigh and wondered what he'd done this time to irritate her.

"Justin, it's your life and you can do what you want, but if you want me to handle your PR, you need to keep me in the loop, even about your personal life."

Justin stepped further away, spotting another guy on his phone near the entrance of the building. "Is this about Courtney?" he quietly asked.

"Yes," Jamie snapped. "Were you planning on telling me you broke up?"

He frowned. "We didn't. I'm with her now."

There was a pause. "Can you get away for a minute? I need to talk with you where she can't hear."

"I'm outside now. Just tell me what's up."

"When did you start seeing Kinzie again?"

Justin nearly laughed at this. "I didn't. Send me the photos you've got and I'll date them for you. They've all got to be old." He didn't understand why the tabloids kept trying to pretend they were together again, but he was getting tired of it.

"Justin, it's not photos. It's an interview." Jamie's voice sounded hesitant. "Kinzie said that you two talked in person last week and worked everything out."

He froze, struggling to swallow the hard lump in his throat.

He heard Jamie sigh again. "Look, Justin, like I said. I want you to live your life, but I just need you to keep me in the loop. I pass no judgment, but some of your female fans might not approve of you openly dating two women at once. We need to meet tomorrow so we can decide how to spin this."

Now Justin was irate. "There's no spin. I'm not dating Kinzie!"

"So you didn't meet with her last week?"

"No!" he shouted, then paused. "Well, I mean, she came by

the house, but we barely even talked, let alone rekindled any romance."

"Are you sure? Did anything happen that Kinzie might have interpreted to mean you were interested in her?"

The condescension in her voice irritated him even more. There was a time in his life when he might have led someone on, but he wouldn't now, and his publicist had no business assuming he was fucking around behind his girlfriend's back. "No. I'm with Courtney and I didn't fuck Kinzie, if that's what you're asking. She came by my house, then Courtney showed up, and she left."

"Was anyone else there?"

"Like a witness? No."

There was another pause. "So you're telling me that it isn't true?"

"I'm telling you she's a lying bitch." Justin startled, realizing Courtney had appeared by his side as the words left his mouth. She looked confused, but not angry.

"Any ideas why she would do that?"

Justin glanced at Courtney. "Yeah, I've got a pretty good idea." He swallowed hard, then reached for Courtney's hand. "I've got to go now, but I'll talk to her in the morning and straighten it out, and then I'll call you back." He hung up before Jamie could protest.

He turned to Courtney again and kissed her quickly on the forehead. "Sorry, babe. That was Jamie. I need to make another quick call, and then I'll be in, okay?"

Courtney frowned. "Everything okay?"

Justin nodded, wishing he believed that. He watched her head inside before calling Keith.

When he hung up with Keith, he took a deep breath, and dialed Kinzie, depressed that he still had her number memorized even after deleting it from his phone over a year ago. She answered immediately, her voice sweet as syrup.

"Why hello there, stranger. How are you doing?"

"What the fuck are you thinking, Kinzie? I just got off the phone with my publicist, and I don't know what you're thinking with this recent stunt of yours, but I'm not going along with it."

She was quiet for a moment, and then responded. "Sweetheart, I don't really know what you mean, but if your publicist is upset over something I said, I'm sure it was just taken out of context."

"Bullshit!" he caught his breath and tried to control his temper. "Do you think your precious Jackson is going to react well to hearing you tell people you're back with your old boyfriend?"

Kinzie sighed. "Look, Justin, I'm awfully sorry if something I said was misconstrued, but I certainly didn't do anything on purpose. And I don't see why you're so upset anyway. Even if people did think we were back together, I'm sure that would just help your reputation."

Justin pursed his lips and clenched his teeth together to keep from screaming at her.

"Oh," she continued, her obnoxiously sweet voice now adding a mock hint of concern, "You're not worried that girlfriend of yours will believe what she reads in the papers, are you?"

"Kinzie, I don't know why you can't get this through your fucking skull, but we are through. If you ever mess with me again, you will regret it." He punched the "end" button on his phone so hard that the phone nearly flew out of his hand. He shoved it in his pocket, took a couple of deep breaths, and paced.

When he finally made his way back in, Justin remembered the check in his pocket that he'd brought to donate. Justin had no idea what the standard or appropriate amount was to donate at these sorts of events, so he'd just done ten grand. He dropped the check off with one of the ladies standing at the table near the entrance where they'd gotten their table assignments on the way in, then made his way back to Courtney, already seated at the table.

"I ordered you another drink," she whispered, gesturing to it, apparently not irritated that he'd been gone way longer than anticipated.

He squeezed her hand, determined to forget about Kinzie until morning. Small talk filled the table and Justin managed to stay blissfully uninvolved, smiling and nodding when it seemed appropriate, subtly checking his phone for sports scores under the table. And then the woman seated to his right spoke to him.

"Are you an attorney also?"

He looked up quickly and flashed an easy smile. "No, ma'am. I'm afraid I wouldn't do too well in law school. Too much writing for me."

The woman smiled knowingly. "I agree. So what do you do then?"

The table turned to him expectantly and Justin nearly laughed at the bemused grin on Courtney's face. He knew most of these people worked with her, and while she'd told him she didn't discuss her personal life at work, he was surprised she hadn't even mentioned him.

"I'm an actor," he replied.

This elicited a variety of responses from the table, with some people seeming impressed, and others looking at him pathetically.

"Now, tell me, in this economy, is it near impossible to get work?" a man across the table asked.

Justin shrugged and licked his lips to keep from laughing. "I've managed to keep busy," he replied.

"You do look pretty familiar," the woman beside him

commented now staring unabashedly. She lifted a finger, saying, "Now wait, don't tell me. I'm sure I saw you in something." She frowned, then leaned across Justin to face Courtney, her face desperately searching for a clue.

"He does some modeling, too," Courtney said.

And then a woman across the table gasped. "You're on the billboard!"

He nodded, blushing, and Courtney giggled.

"*Days End*. That's it, right?" The woman beside announced proudly, as though she'd just solved a game of Clue.

Justin nodded again, and then answered questions about his costars and his career until the main presentation started.

By the end of the evening, he had posed for pictures with about a dozen different people, danced to four separate songs with Courtney, and drunk enough whiskey to let Courtney drive his car home. He felt like an actual grown up for once, having survived his first real business social function.

And for a moment, he even convinced himself he could handle Kinzie.

Courtney spent the night at Justin's. There was definitely something relaxing about waking up beside him, having her coffee on the deck by the pool, then sneaking back inside for some mid-morning sex before getting dressed for the day. Justin seemed a little frazzled and had some work to do with Keith, but he promised they'd go out to lunch before he drove her back to her place.

When the doorbell rang a little before noon, Justin was on the phone in the kitchen, so Courtney opened the door. She didn't bother to check who it was, but then froze, startled to see Jackson Malloy standing in front of her.

"Hi," he said, his voice deeper than any other she'd ever heard. "Is Justin here?"

"Who is it, babe?" Justin called from the other room, pacing with his phone pressed tightly to his ear.

"Uh," she started to respond, but Justin thankfully glanced over and saw for himself. He waved at Jackson, as though the two weren't supposed enemies. Courtney frowned, wondering if she'd been wrong about the man's identity. Surely Justin wouldn't be politely greeting the man that slept with his ex before they had actually broken up.

"I'm gonna have to call you back," Justin interrupted the caller.

He shook Jackson's hand, then spoke, "What can I do for you, man?"

Jackson leaned forward and replied, almost in a whisper, "Kinzie's in the car, in the driveway. She wanted to speak with you."

Justin's polite smile disappeared. "Why is she in the fucking car?"

"She didn't want to risk the paparazzi seeing her come in here," Jackson said, blushing enough to show he clearly saw the ridiculousness of this sentiment.

Justin didn't move.

"Look, she didn't tell me what it was about either, but she said it was important, and honestly, I need to be somewhere in an hour, so if you could just..." Jackson's voice trailed off as Justin stormed out the door.

Courtney was left standing next to Jackson, who was more than a little intimidating since he looked like a well-muscled serial killer. She could see why he was always cast to play a hardened criminal. He was decidedly creepy, but in a somewhat sexy way.

"You can sit," she mumbled, gesturing to the couch as she sat back in a chair.

He obeyed, giving her a thorough once-over. "So you're Justin's new girl?"

"Not so new," she replied.

"Are you a model?" He asked this as though it was a grotesque and unlikely possibility, and he just couldn't think of any other reason Justin would be with her.

She shook her head. "Lawyer."

He frowned, then laughed a little too hard. "Seriously?"

Courtney nodded. An awkward silence ensued. "You really have no idea what they're talking about?"

He shrugged indifferently. "You know Kinzie. There's always some drama."

"I really don't know Kinzie," Courtney said.

"Yeah, who does," he mumbled in response.

Courtney had no idea what to say to this. She wondered if all celebrities were this awkward, or if they were just so accustomed to everyone else begging to hear the details of their lives that they didn't know how to engage in normal conversation. Or maybe he was just shy. Was it even possible for an actor to be shy?

Courtney noticed him gawking at her chest. Since she'd been lounging by the pool reading all morning, she was still in her bikini top and shorts. In retrospect, she probably should make a habit of putting on a shirt before answering the door. She shifted, trying unsuccessfully to casually cover her cleavage with her arms.

Jackson smiled in response. Courtney could see the attraction now. The deep voice was sexy and he didn't really look forty. Plus he had a nice face and a warm smile. He was also big, but Courtney suspected not quite as toned as Justin. Of course, he was quickly losing points for every second he didn't at least pretend he wasn't staring at her breasts.

"Do you just represent celebrities, or do you do something else too?" he asked, interrupting her thoughts.

She frowned, confused.

"In your job."

"Oh, no. I mean, I just started, actually, but I represent a coalition of women's shelters in the L.A. area. We do a variety of legal things for them, from helping collect child support and alimony to working out some criminal matters."

"Like a battered woman's shelter?"

She nodded.

He frowned. "That's ironic."

"How so?"

"Never mind."

Courtney let it drop. "Where did you have to be after this?" she asked, hoping it was someplace interesting.

"Lunch reservations."

"Oh, I thought Kinzie didn't eat anything," she joked, forgetting for a minute that she was talking with Kinzie's boyfriend.

The joke didn't seem to offend Jackson. "Oh, she's not coming. I'm dropping her off at the Sun Center on my way."

Courtney racked her brain to remember where she'd heard of that place before. At first she thought it was a spa, but then her eyes widened as she realized. "Kinzie's going to rehab?"

He nodded nonchalantly, glancing again at her breasts.

This time, Courtney crossed both hands over her chest. "For what?"

He shrugged, clearly trying not to laugh at her futile attempts to cover herself. "Who knows?"

Courtney would've dwelled a little longer on this oddity—of Jackson seemingly not caring why his girlfriend of, what was it now, nearly two years, was going to rehab, but Justin stormed back in then.

"She's all yours, man," he said to Jackson. Then he turned to Courtney before stomping up the stairs. "I'm taking a nap."

She and Jackson exchanged a wary look before he stood to go. "Nice talking with you," he said, leering at her one last time before showing himself out.

Courtney, deciding to give Justin some time to cool off, checked messages on her phone, then went out and read the paper by the pool for about a half hour before deciding she might as well go home. She tiptoed upstairs and glanced in Justin's room, half expecting him to be napping as he had said. Instead, he was lounged out on the bed, watching an early cut of a film he had done years before.

"Hey," she began, stepping inside the room and closing the door behind her. "I'm gonna head back over to my place so you can have some time to yourself."

Justin continued facing the TV, making Courtney wonder if he'd even heard her, and then he turned, pausing the film. "You don't have a car here," he reminded her. Then he laughed sardonically. "You are nothing like Kinzie. If I told her I wanted time alone, she'd nag me and refuse to leave my sight."

Courtney frowned, not sure where he was going with this.

"You know that first night we met? The only reason I invited you back to my hotel room was because you were so different from her. Polar opposite."

"I thought it was because I'm irresistibly attractive and you wanted to have sex with me," Courtney replied with a smile, sitting on the bed beside him.

He shrugged. "That too, but mostly I just wanted someone to talk to. Someone nice. Someone who wasn't so annoying and shallow and self-obsessed."

"Oh, well, the reason I went with you was because you are

literally the hottest man alive, and I was dying to see the only part of you that isn't readily viewable on the internet," Courtney joked.

"I love you," Justin said, looking into her eyes.

Courtney froze, feeling her heart pound uncontrollably, his timing having caught her entirely off guard. She stretched out beside Justin and kissed him softly on the lips. He returned the kiss, but then spoke after a minute.

"Aren't you supposed to say it back?" he inquired with a squirrelly grin.

Courtney shook her head. "You know how I feel about you," she said, repeating his own words from weeks earlier back to him.

"Touché. How was your chat with Jackson?"

"Awkward," she admitted. "He kept staring at my boobs."

Justin glanced at her chest. "Who can blame him?"

"Well, apparently our talk went better than your chat with Kinzie."

"Aren't you curious what Kinzie wanted to talk to me about?"

Courtney was dying to know but would never tell him that. "It's not my business. If you want to tell me, you will."

Justin located something on his phone, then handed it to Courtney. She skimmed the brief interview of Kinzie, unable to get past the part where she indicated she and Justin were back together.

"Jamie told me about this last night," he explained. "And then I called Kinzie and yelled at her."

Courtney nodded, now understanding why he'd acted so strange after disappearing for so long at the dinner. She'd assumed he just didn't feel comfortable with her crowd.

"It's not true," he quickly added, a look of panic in his eyes.

She handed the phone back to him.

"I thought she was maybe coming by to apologize today, but

no. She said she just wanted to get some things off her chest before she goes to rehab. She wanted me to know she forgives me for everything I did to her."

"What does that mean? What did you ever do to her?"

"She said I used her to get famous and then dumped her when I didn't need her anymore."

"Hmm. And her sleeping with Jackson had nothing to do with your breakup?"

He laughed. "Yeah, but she wasn't totally off base with the rest. When we met on the set, I thought she was attractive but knew she wasn't my type. I only went out with her because she was exactly who I thought I should go out with. Well, and because my publicist said it would help get my name out there."

"I don't think it's your fault she's going to rehab," Courtney assured him.

"I know that!"

"Jackson didn't seem to know or care why she was going to rehab. That seemed weird."

"I think they broke up," Justin said. "Or maybe he's just moved on and Kinzie doesn't want to admit it yet. I can't imagine he'd stick around after she told reporters she's back with me." He snorted. "That's probably why she's going to rehab, the breakup. She doesn't have a drug or alcohol problem that I know about."

He sighed, then kissed Courtney's head. "Anyway, I don't want to talk about Kinzie. Let's get back to that part about how you think I'm the hottest man alive. What exactly was it you wanted to do to me?"

Courtney giggled, then let him flip her onto her back. She closed her eyes and remembered the first time they made out, how excited and anxious she was at the sensation of his lips pressing into her skin or his fingers sliding across her collarbone and down to her breasts. Now his touch was familiar, almost predictable even, but still caused her heart to race and made her breath come in short, fast spurts. And within minutes of kissing him, Courtney still felt that familiar ache, a burning desire to have him.

He loves me, she told herself, tuning out all the other thoughts sprinting through her mind. She repeated the mantra over and over in her head, as his hands pulled off his own shirt, then lifted her up to remove her bikini top. She heard herself moan as his teeth raked across her nipples, his fingers pushing down past the waistband of her shorts, and stroking her most sensitive parts. Courtney arched her back, thrusting her breasts more fully into his warm mouth, then relaxed, raising her hips and tugging her shorts down. She pulled at Justin's pants, but he ducked away, his mouth moving lower and lower on her body until finally, his tongue reached the peak of her desire, darting in and out, tracing back and forth along her until the burning grew so intense she nearly cried out.

She saw him grin proudly as he quickly pulled off his own shorts. Courtney pulled him into her, squeezing his butt until his hips were flush against hers, then lifting her own hips to meet his, and groaning with ecstasy. They repeated their familiar dance over and over, their mouths searching for each other in between gasps and moans, their hands exploring each other's body as though they didn't already have the territory memorized. Courtney pressed her mouth into his shoulder, her teeth digging at his bare flesh as the burning became too intense and she felt herself explode into him right as his own moaning intensified and climaxed with him sucking on the side of her neck.

"Wow," Courtney gasped as he finally rolled off of her. "You're amazing."

"You're amazing," he repeated back to her.

They lay quietly, side by side, for several more minutes.

Finally, Justin spoke again. "Have you ever thought about having a baby?"

Courtney sat up, startled. "On the pill," she replied, over-enunciating each word.

"I don't mean now," he clarified. "But someday."

"I don't see how kids would fit into your current lifestyle."

"That's not what I asked."

"Well, yeah. I always assumed I'd have a baby someday."

He narrowed his eyes. "But not with me."

"I didn't say that," she insisted, seeing the hurt in his eyes. "I just think it's strange of you to ask about this now."

"I could be a good dad."

"I'm sure you'd be great, Justin. I only meant that the way your current life is, it clearly isn't the right time. If you had kids, you'd do a lot less working, traveling, partying," she paused, "fucking."

"Hey, that's not true," he protested.

She laughed. "Babies are cute and fun, but nothing about them is an aphrodisiac. If you think spending time with something that cries and poops and wipes snot on you is going to make you into more of a sex god, you're delusional."

"Then how do you explain people having more than one kid? What about Ryan? He has three kids, and he's still acting, traveling, and at least when he conceived kid number two and three he was still doing it. And there is such a thing as a nanny."

Courtney laughed.

"You know I can change I diaper," he added.

"I did not know that," she replied. "Good for you, I guess."

He still looked offended. "Seriously, Courtney, do you ever think about a future with me?"

Courtney suddenly felt very naked. Only an underwear model could comfortably have the most serious discussion of a relationship in the nude and not feel totally vulnerable. "Of course I do, Justin."

"When we were in Indiana, I heard you tell your mom you didn't think we were going to last."

Courtney grimaced, generally remembering the conversation but not positive that was exactly what she'd said. "I was just trying to reassure her that I was happy, that I wanted to be with you now, regardless of what may or may not happen down the road."

He sighed. "Can I tell you what's worrying me?"

She nodded.

"Every other girl I've been with since moving to L.A. seemed to really relish the whole fame thing. I mean, most of them were either already somewhat famous or trying to become famous, but either way, they liked that people knew who I was and all the attention that came with it." He paused. "You don't really seem to care, though. Sometimes I think you'd like me better if I was an unemployed loser."

Courtney frowned. "Justin, I like you because you're you, not because you're famous or rich or plastered above every highway in America in your skivvies. How is that a bad thing?"

"It's not. But if you don't really enjoy the perks of fame, you're more bound to get fed up with the drawbacks, like the travel and the constant press." He paused. "If people didn't know who I was, then you wouldn't have to worry about the whole country thinking I've reunited with my ex. I just want to know if you're going to get sick of it."

She bit her lip. She wanted to tell him the truth, but she wasn't sure exactly what that was. To some extent, he was right. If he'd been some no-name actor, she probably wouldn't have worked so hard over the past year trying not to get attached. But now, well, all of that was in the past anyway. "Justin, I love that you have an awesome house with a gorgeous pool. I love that you can afford to take me to cool restaurants and clubs. And I do think it's cool that everyone knows who you are and that you work with tons of talented people. I also really admire how well you handle it all, and I see how great you are at your job."

Courtney glanced down. "But I'd also like to be able to go online or read a trashy magazine without seeing something that might affect me personally. I'd love to go to a regular movie with you in a normal theater or just have an ordinary date with you in public. I want to go to an amusement park with you to play the games and ride the rides without being hassled by random people wanting your attention as much as I do."

She paused again, feeling like she was performing a monologue. "I can't predict how I'll feel in the future, Justin, but if you're asking me as of right now, it's worth it. If I haven't spent a ton of time imagining our future together, it's not because I don't want that. It's just because I'm so happy with you now and I don't want to detract from that."

He appeared to consider this for a moment, then pressed his lips into her hand. He turned to her, smiling, and said, "I think we'd make pretty cute babies."

She laughed. "I'm sure we would." Courtney sat up and reached for her bikini top.

"Hey, what are you doing?"

"Getting dressed."

"What about round two?"

Courtney rolled her eyes. "No offense, but all this baby talk hasn't exactly gotten me in the mood."

"I bet I could change that."

She shook her head, knowing full well he could, but not wanting to let herself get distracted again. After that conversation, she needed to think, not to lose her head all over again.

He snatched her suit and tossed it across the room. "Look, we've got to at least have makeup sex," he insisted.

"That wasn't a fight."

Justin climbed over her, pinning her legs to the bed as he kneeled over her lap. "Too bad. Looks like you're stuck. You just stay there and I'll do all the work" he mumbled, leaning in to kiss her neck. Courtney resisted for a moment, refusing to cooperate, until he reached his arms out and began caressing her breasts, his lips still burrowing into her neck.

She finally relented and kissed him back, finding his kisses rougher and more aggressive than before. Her body tingled at the thought of this being different, more exciting. His hand rifled through her hair, matting it, then pulling harder, just enough to tilt her head back and expose the soft area of her neck again. His teeth scraped along the side of her earlobe and he traced her collarbone with his tongue. Then he leaned back, lifting her on top of him, his hands firmly pressed into her back as though he thought she would even dream of pulling away from him now.

Courtney pressed her lips into his neck, working her way around his stubbly chin. Then she moved her hands and mouth down his body, dancing her tongue around his nipples before moving lower, licking and rubbing his hard length before sucking the tip into her mouth. His hands wandered through her hair then fell limp at his side as he groaned softly. She increased the pressure, moving her hands in sync with her mouth, and he groaned again, this time pressing his fingers into her shoulders. She giggled playfully, glancing up at him, and caught his eye. His bright aqua eyes widened, and he nudged her off of him, and delicately flipped her to her stomach.

Courtney lifted up onto her knees and arched back into him, wanting his body to join hers as much now as earlier, needing him to fill the void left by their words. Justin's hands first fondled her breasts, already tingling with yearning from rubbing against the sheets of the bed each time Courtney rocked forward. Then he worked his hands down her body until they reached her hips, where they guided her into the movement, bringing her back and forth as their bodies fell more in line, moving faster and faster. Justin came first this time, his chest pressing flush against her back and his arms wrapping so tightly around Courtney that her elbows lifted off the bed, sending her into a whirlwind of passion, the sudden intensity of the heat burning through her like a fire.

They collapsed onto the bed, again, winded. Justin casually kissed her shoulder, then spoke. "I'm starving."

Courtney laughed.

13

The next day, they went shopping together. Courtney laughed at the suggestion, claiming she'd never before gone clothes shopping with a boyfriend. Justin hoped she wasn't insulted. In all honesty, he did want her input on his buys, and it was always a turn on to watch his girl try on clothes. Mostly, though, he just wanted to pay for her, and he knew she'd refuse if he just offered her the cash. It wasn't that he thought she was completely broke, but ever since she'd confessed her salary, Justin had been doing the math and realized between her rent and other bills, she couldn't possibly have anything left for the dozens of new outfits his publicist had encouraged her to buy.

With three new movies coming out in the next year, Justin knew the press around him was about to pick up, and he just wanted Courtney to be prepared. He couldn't stand seeing her become a casualty of the paparazzi, especially after it was his idea to propel their relationship into the spotlight.

They'd stopped at three stores and were debating another as they strolled down Rodeo Drive, hand in hand. It was one of those idyllic L.A. days, where the sun was shining and the breeze was like a cool whisper blowing past his cheeks. A perfect day for a cookout on the beach, Justin thought. He turned to Courtney, catching her eye and winking. She smiled back, and he stroked her hand with his fingers.

As they walked past the next block, two reporters with cameras hopped out beside them. Justin tuned out their voices as they called to him, instead offering a simple, dignified smile. Courtney, as instructed by Justin's publicist, stared straight ahead, a nervous smile plastered to her face, her fingers anxiously digging into his hand. Justin squeezed her hand again to relax her, then paused, offering one last shot for the cameras.

As he started up again, one of the reporters' questions caught his attention.

"Do you have any comment on reports of MacKinzie Maddox checking into rehab?" she shouted over the growing commotion.

Justin shook his head politely, praying they didn't ask about him supposedly hooking up with Kinzie again, especially since he could no longer claim he hadn't spoken to her in a while. So instead, he gave the generic response.

"Kinzie's a great person. I wish her nothing but the best," he replied, hoping the cameras couldn't tell he was gritting his teeth through the lie.

"Then what is your response to her allegations of abuse? Her assertion that you hit her during your relationship?" the reporter asked.

Justin froze, shocked. For a brief second, he forgot that he needed to maintain his composure, letting his forced smile slide away for a mere moment. It was long enough. A knot formed in his stomach, and Justin knew as soon as he turned that they'd already gotten what they wanted—a photo of him looking like the crazed angry man Kinzie had apparently portrayed him to be.

He considered responding, denying it on the spot, but then he heard Courtney gasp and realized she was even more shocked and panicked than he was. He turned to Courtney just as a camera man crouched down to snap another shot and bumped into her leg. She stepped to the side to try to dodge him, but another reporter swung around and suddenly, Justin felt Courtney's hand pulling away.

It felt like slow motion, watching Courtney tumble to the ground. Justin tried to keep her up by holding firmly to her hand, but instead she simply tilted as she fell, smacking her face and other hand on the ground. Justin immediately crouched to the ground, lifting her up. Courtney was clearly dazed and scared, with blood already trickling from her lip, but she let him stand her upright.

"No more questions!" he barked, feeling his blood boil. Justin turned to the camera man who had bumped into Courtney and shouted, "Back off or I'm calling the police." He wrapped his arm around Courtney, trying to scurry her along more quickly, but he felt her knees buckle, so he picked her up and carried her instead.

"Hang on, I'll get you inside," he whispered to her while glancing around for the best place to go. He couldn't look behind him, wasn't sure if the reporters were still following, and didn't let himself think of the shitstorm that had apparently already begun. He spotted a lingerie store. He struggled at the door, then ducked inside, certain the cameras wouldn't be allowed to follow him into the store.

He marched past the intrigued associate and two browsing customers, straight to the dressing rooms, delicately setting Courtney on the leather bench. "I'll be right back," he promised, kissing her on the forehead before pulling the curtain shut behind him.

Justin turned to the two associates now staring wide-eyed at him and removed his sunglasses, in case they didn't recognize him. "Sorry to barge in here, but we're having a problem with the paparazzi. Can you call security please?"

One nodded and immediately moved to the phone. The other one stared back at him in awe. "Can I get you anything?" she finally asked, still gawking. "Is she okay?"

"I think so," he replied, answering the second question first. "Some water and a bandage if you've got one."

He returned to Courtney, still sitting on the bench, surrounded by all of their bags, now pushing her middle finger against her lip.

"I'm bleeding, aren't I?"

Justin exhaled with relief at the normalcy in her voice. Her bone-pale face told him she was still shaken up, but she at least sounded like herself. "Yeah, just a little."

The saleslady came up and handed him some tissues and a bottle of water. "We're still looking for a bandage," she explained nervously.

"Thank you," Justin replied at the same time as Courtney. He knelt in front of her, pulling her finger away from her wound and dabbed at her lip with a tissue.

Courtney wiped her finger on another tissue, then released a nervous laugh. "There are going to be photos floating around of me falling on my face on Rodeo Drive, aren't there?"

Justin rose and sat on the bench beside her, pulling her into his arms. He kissed the back of her head as her body slowly relaxed against his chest. He didn't want to answer that, didn't even want to consider what might or might not happen. He held her tight as he pulled his phone out of his pocket, quickly dialing Keith.

"Hey, we had some issues with the paparazzi and Courtney got hurt." He began, pausing as Keith asked if Courtney was okay. "No, she's fine. But we need a ride. My car is blocks away." He told Keith where they were, then hung up.

Justin glanced up, noticing the sales lady still standing there. He wished she'd go away, but then realized she was actually just keeping the other customers out of the dressing area so they could have some privacy.

"Do you have a bathroom I could use?" Courtney asked.

The woman nodded. "I'll show you."

Justin helped Courtney up, then sat back down on the bench until she returned. Sighing, he dialed Jamie, his publicist. Her assistant said she was in a meeting, and Justin really didn't feel up to dealing with her yet, so he left a message for her to call, offering the gist of what had happened. After hearing the recap, her assistant quickly offered to interrupt the meeting, but Justin declined, saying he had to go. As he hung up, he heard male voices. He stood, ready to confront whoever had followed them in, but it was two uniformed officers.

He spoke with them briefly, certain that nothing would ever come of it since they hadn't exactly knocked Courtney over on purpose, but also knowing he might need proof of his side of the story at some point. When Courtney emerged from the bathroom, she spoke with them as well, and then they left.

Justin checked his watch, wondering how long it would take Keith to arrive. Courtney had started browsing the store, a sign that she at least was feeling better. He grinned as she held up some particularly raunchy items, shaking his head as she started to collect more.

"Hey, the least we can do for barging in here is buy some stuff," she insisted, smiling. Justin laughed and handed her his credit card.

The associate had just finished wrapping her items when the store door opened again, and a vaguely familiar man walked in.

He immediately turned to Justin. "Keith is in front with the car. He sent me in to get you and the girl."

Justin smiled. Keith always had been a smart one. It hadn't even occurred to him that they might get smashed all over again by the paparazzi if they just walked out unprotected. "Have we met before?" he asked.

The man nodded. "I'm Craig. I've been covering Brad."

Justin nodded knowingly. After the second *Days End* movie had hit theaters, the press around Brad and Julie had exploded. Lately, Brad always seemed to have a whole throng of bodyguards.

"I'll take the girl out first," Craig offered.

"Courtney," Justin nodded, snatching the bag from her.

Craig wrapped his large arm around Courtney, nearly enveloping her small frame in his jacket. "Keep your head down and just get into the car," he instructed.

Justin watched them climb into the car, then grabbed the rest of the bags, and headed out as soon as Craig returned.

COURTNEY HADN'T SPOKEN during the car ride back, instead just curling into the safe spot under Justin's arm, tuning out while he recapped the incident in greater detail for Keith. When they arrived back at Justin's, it was dark. Courtney realized her stomach was growling, and that it was getting late.

"I should get home," she mumbled as they climbed out of the car. "I've got to work tomorrow."

Justin followed her upstairs as she went to retrieve the bag she'd left in his room, closing the door behind him.

"Give me a call when you hear anything," she asked.

He nodded. "You sure you're okay?

There was a knock on the door. "Justin, Jamie is on the phone," Keith yelled.

"I'll be there in a minute," Justin replied.

Courtney attempted a smile. "I'm fine, just a little shaken up, I guess."

"Your lip looks better."

She didn't believe him. It certainly didn't feel better, and from what little she knew of injuries, she was anticipating a swollen purple phase before it healed.

He sighed, frowning. "I want you to know, Courtney, that it isn't true. I never hit Kinzie."

Courtney turned to face him, reaching her hand to his cheek, caught off guard by the obviousness of his statement. "I know that, Justin."

He kissed her, gently, and she grimaced, the corner of her lip stinging.

"I'm going to have Keith and Craig follow you home in case you have any trouble."

She shook her head. "Not necessary, really."

"It'll make me feel better," he insisted, adding, "They need to go pick up my car, anyway."

When she got home, Courtney told the whole story to Erica while icing her lip. It was after midnight when she got to bed, but she still hadn't heard any update from Justin. She had to be at work by seven-thirty, though, so she crawled under the covers, leaving her cell phone on in case he called.

At work the next day, Courtney did her best to ignore the suspicious glances people shot her after she explained, again and again, that she busted her lip falling. By lunchtime, she finally got the nerve to look online. She typed Justin's name into the search engine, and the second hit on the results immediately caught her eye. She clicked on it, holding her breath as she read:

News flash—Hollywood's very own MacKinzie Maddox just

checked into rehab for stress-related trauma. Even bigger news—Maddox points the finger at former beau Justin Erikson, claiming he was violent and regularly abused her during their lengthy on-and-off again relationship. Since their breakup, Maddox has been seeing actor Jackson Malloy, while Erikson has heated things up with attorney Courtney Robbins. When asked about the allegations, both Erikson and his new girlfriend declined to comment. Sources close to the couple report that both Erikson and Robbins state that her injuries in the photo here resulted from 'a fall.'

Courtney groaned, seeing the photo of Justin glaring at a photographer, looking all the part of the overly aggressive bully, while her hand was raised to her bloodied lip. Super.

She called Justin on her way home, and he sounded worse than she expected, insisting he'd call her when he left his publicist's office the next morning.

He didn't call, though, and when she called him just after lunch, Keith answered their home phone and said Justin had blown off the meeting with Jamie and was still asleep, exhausted after a night of video games and drinking. She asked him to have Justin call her, and then hung up, more worried than before.

Courtney drove straight to Justin's after work. When Keith answered the door, Courtney saw a man and a woman seated in the living room, in the middle of what appeared to be a meeting.

"Oh, sorry!" she exclaimed, stepping back towards the door. "I didn't mean to interrupt."

The man stood to approach her. "Hi, I'm Marty Weiss, this is Jamie Bloomberg. You must be Courtney?" he phrased it like a question, but seemed pretty confident he was correct.

"Justin's agent and publicist," Keith explained.

She nodded, then glanced around the room for Justin.

"He's upstairs. He won't come down."

"Have you spoken to anyone about the incident Sunday?" Jamie asked her.

Courtney shook her head. "No. Oh, except my roommate." She paused. "Well, and some people at work asked about my lip. I just said I fell. I didn't give them any details."

"Okay, well, don't," Marty quickly instructed. "Can you convince him to get down here? We need to talk to him."

She inhaled slowly, carefully choosing her words. "I'll let him know you're here, but maybe it would be better if you just went over everything with Keith and then he caught Justin up later."

Marty rolled his eyes. "Oh, that's just fucking great."

Courtney resisted the urge to snap back at him, to remind him that they worked for Justin, not the other way around. Instead, she turned to Keith, awaiting instruction.

Keith nodded for Courtney to go on upstairs. She opened Justin's door slowly, unsure of whether he'd even be awake. He wasn't sleeping, but instead was lying on his back on top of his comforter, tossing a soccer ball towards the ceiling and then catching it. A sizable collection of beer bottles and empty shot glasses adorned his nightstand.

"Can I come in?" she asked, although she was already technically in the room. He nodded, so she shut the door behind her. "You know your agent and publicist are downstairs and want to talk to you."

"They can talk to Keith."

"Yeah, that's what I told them." Courtney forced her bottom lip into a pout. "I hate seeing you so depressed."

"How am I supposed to act? The entire country now thinks I'm the biggest fucking jerk alive." He tossed the ball into the air again and caught it, right before Courtney grabbed it and placed it on the bed beside him.

She swung a leg over his waist, straddling him, and leaned forward until the ends of her long brown hair were pooling against his shirt. She paused, waiting until his bright blue eyes peered back at her before speaking. "I realize this all seems horrible now, but people will figure out the truth eventually. You're an amazing, nice guy, and everyone will see that sooner or later."

He sighed, reaching around her to see if any of the bottles still held any beer. "No one cares what the truth is. This makes a better story, and no one wants to hear anything else." He turned his gaze up to the ceiling, avoiding her eyes. "I spend so much of my fucking time and energy trying to look and act the way everybody expects me to, and in the end, it doesn't even matter anyway because they all just believe what they want to believe."

Courtney didn't have a response to that, so instead, she tilted his face back towards hers. "Justin, I love you."

As soon as the words were out of her mouth, his lips curved into a slight smile. She continued before he could answer.

"I love the way your hands are always so soft even though you're this big manly man, and I love how you're still self-conscious even though every guy wants to look like you and every girl wants to sleep with you, and I love how nervous you get around new people even though you're hilarious and always know the right thing to say. I especially love that you are so close to your mom and your brothers."

She paused, gently placing a finger over his lips so he wouldn't interrupt. "I love that I can still see the man you were before you became famous. I love that you've always been so accepting of me even though I'm just a regular old girl. And I love your adorable dimples, that sultry smile of yours and those killer hips of yours that are always getting me in trouble."

He grinned wider. "And I love that you know exactly how to cheer me up."

Courtney laughed. "Oh, I haven't even begun trying to cheer you up yet," she teased, pulling off her shirt. Justin smiled and sat up to kiss her. She tried to ignore the taste of beer on his tongue and the way he delicately avoided the swollen part of her lip, pretending instead that everything was fine. They made love tenderly, as though they were each afraid of hurting the other. After, Courtney curled up against his shoulder and waited for his breathing to even out before speaking.

"You know they're probably still down there, waiting on you," she said quietly.

He laughed. "Yeah, I guess it's not fair to jerk them around when it's Kinzie I'm pissed at."

She started to sit up, but he held her tight. Then he got a strange look on his face and rolled onto his side, facing her.

"What?" she asked, his curious grin making her nervous.

"Marry me," he blurted out, still smiling.

She rolled her eyes and avoided looking at him, acutely aware that her pulse had reflexively shot through the roof at his words. She knew he was just messing with her, but regardless, it was her first proposal since Billy Porter in fourth grade, and this was considerably closer to the real thing than that was.

"Hey, what kind of a response is that?" he teased.

Courtney sighed. "Justin, you can't be serious."

"What if I am?"

She smiled. "You're not."

"How do you know that?" Justin sat up, a cute pouty expression on his face now.

"Because a sincere proposal doesn't usually come in the moments after sex."

He paused, still pouting.

"Real proposals usually involve some advance thought and a ring," she added.

"I bought you a car. Now you need a ring too?" His tone was indignant.

"That's not what I said, Justin. I just meant if you were serious about your proposal, you'd probably have a ring."

Courtney sat up and began to smooth her hair. The conversation was making her uncomfortable. She knew he wasn't really asking her to marry him, but she also didn't want to discuss it because then she'd probably start thinking about what she'd do if he was serious, and she just couldn't handle that kind of curiosity right now.

He stood, then picked up her left hand and inspected it, his perfectly sculpted naked body frozen inches from her face like a statue. He dropped her hand, her fingers still tingling from his touch. "What kind of ring?" he inquired, retrieving his jeans and heading into the bathroom.

"Justin, it's not polite to tease a girl about engagements. It's a touchy subject, you know."

He laughed and ducked his head around the corner. "You're the one who says I'm not serious. *I* think *you* are the tease."

Courtney held her breath, but Justin dropped the subject. He emerged from the bathroom in his jeans, planted a quick kiss on her head, and started down the stairs while still putting on his shirt.

Courtney covered her face with a pillow and shrieked with frustration. She had no idea what to make of Justin lately. She suspected the only reason he was even considering marriage was because it was one of the few things he could do to distract the media from his current debacle. Still, between that and the talk of having a baby, she was beyond confused.

THE NEXT FEW days weren't any better. Justin's talk with Jamie and Marty completely ruined the effort Courtney had made to cheer him up, especially since they had no good news and frankly, no actual plan. What Justin needed was to fix this mess. He wanted to sue Kinzie, or at least confront her. Actually, what he really wanted was to kill her, but he figured that wouldn't help his reputation much.

Jamie forbid him from speaking with Kinzie, based on the lack of success he'd had the last time he confronted her about her lies to the tabloids. She also promised to "monitor" the situation, whatever that meant, and to get in touch with Kinzie's people to encourage her to retract the statement. If that didn't work, then they'd consider a lawsuit. But a lawsuit would take years to clear his name, whereas the damage from Kinzie's lies would be done in weeks. On the bright side, he wasn't hurting for work lately, since he'd already booked the next year or so with movies he'd be filming. While the production studios could back out of working with him, they'd owe him enough money under the contract that Marty was fairly confident none of them would do so, especially based solely on unsupported allegations.

Keith and Jamie insisted Justin keep Craig as bodyguard for a while, at least until the situation calmed down, but Justin hated the idea. He felt like a wuss for needing an armed guy to follow him around, essentially protecting him from nothing but herds of swooning preteens. And it wasn't that Craig was a wimp, but Justin was pretty sure he could bench a lot more than Craig, so he wasn't too eager to fork over money to pay this guy to "protect" him.

"It's just to keep the paparazzi off you for a while," Keith insisted the next morning, as Justin hemmed and hawed about taking Craig with him to the gym. "If the gym gets robbed, you and Ryan can still beat the perps off with your bare hands, but at least Craig can be there when you walk in and out to keep a good perimeter around you so the tabloids don't photograph it all."

"How is that going to look to my fans? I don't want them to think I'm hiding."

Keith rolled his eyes. "So keep signing autographs. Do whatever the fuck you want. Just bring Craig along." He stormed out to the patio.

Justin exhaled loudly and grabbed his keys. Craig was waiting by the front door. Justin wondered if he'd overheard that entire conversation. "I'm driving," he mumbled, gesturing for Craig to get in the Audi.

He beat Ryan to the gym, so he decided to do an extra set while he waited. He considered asking Craig to spot him but quickly dismissed the idea. By the time Ryan arrived, his triceps were already burning.

"You're late," he mumbled.

"You beat women," Ryan retorted, grinning.

Justin rolled his eyes. Only Ryan could get away with that crap.

"I see you borrowed one of Brad's guys," Ryan noted, gesturing to the edge of the room where Craig waited.

Justin nodded. "I don't know how Brad stands it, having someone follow him around all the time. I was grateful when Craig came to get me and Courtney, but when it's just me..."

"So, how are you dealing?"

He shrugged. "I'd feel better about it if my fucking publicist had some sort of plan. She and my agent seem to be content to just wait it out."

Ryan frowned. "Have you tried talking to Kinzie?"

"They won't let me." Justin let the weight plate fall with a clang. "It's probably for the best, for now anyway. I think if I saw her now, I really would beat the shit out of her."

Ryan chuckled but shook his head. "You better keep that to yourself. There are ears everywhere." He finished his set and slowly sat upright. "So you didn't see this coming at all?"

Justin hesitated, sure he misunderstood. "Are you asking me if it's true?"

Ryan stood, shaking his head. "No, of course not. I know you, and," he chuckled, "More importantly, I know Kinzie. What I meant was do you know why she said it?"

"She came by a few weeks ago and wanted to talk to me, but I'd just gotten back in town and Courtney was coming over and could only stay for an hour, so I blew off Kinzie. She must have been pissed, because she leaked some story about us getting back together, and when I heard that, I might have yelled a little. Then she and Jackson came by the house a few days ago, right before she checked into rehab. I should've known she was up to something."

Justin paused, adjusting his glove. "Kinzie was always jealous. The only reason she stayed with me for so long was to keep me from dating anyone else. And then when she saw how happy I was with Courtney, that was the last straw. Well, and I got the impression it wasn't working out with Jackson."

"Shocker," Ryan mumbled.

Justin nodded. "Still, I never imagined she'd be capable of something like this."

"She always seemed like a bitch to me."

He laughed. "Yeah, but this takes it to a whole new level." He sighed. "I mean, my mom read what Kinzie said. If it's hard for me to explain it to people, how's my mom coping?"

Ryan nodded. "So, are you still coming tomorrow? Audrey might freak out if you cancel on us. She's in this homemaker entertaining phase and I don't want to irk her."

Justin frowned, trying to decipher what he meant.

"Dinner, tomorrow, remember? You wanted to bring Courtney by so you could show her how wonderfully normal your super famous friends are?"

"Oh, right. I forgot. Hey, does Audrey still keep in touch with Kinzie? Maybe she could talk with her," Justin began.

Ryan shook his head furiously. "Man, you know Audrey.

She's on your side and all, but there's no way she'll get involved and risk the wrath of Kinzie."

Justin had expected this response, but it disappointed him anyway. He considered the dinner thing and decided they didn't have anything better to do the next night. "Yeah, we'll be there tomorrow." He wiped the sweat off his forehead and reached for his gym bag.

14

When they pulled into Ryan's drive, Courtney was awestruck by the house. It was massive—much larger than Justin's, and beautiful. As they walked to the door, Justin's hand lingered soothingly on her back against the thin material of her sleeveless sundress. She tried to imagine how intimidating it had been for him when he first broke into the business, to show up at homes like this without a comforting partner at his side.

Before Courtney could daydream further, Audrey answered the door, a dish towel in one hand and a small child tugging on the other.

"Hi!" she greeted them warmly, turning immediately to Courtney with a broad smile on her face. "I'd shake your hand, but," she tilted her head down at the child.

Justin crouched down. "Hi, Stella. How are you?"

The girl blushed and raced into the other room, latching on to her father's legs as he appeared in the doorway.

"Sorry about that," Audrey mumbled. "So, you must be Courtney. We've heard so much about you. Come on in!" She gestured for them to enter the house, but Courtney remained on the step, frozen. Audrey looked exactly the same as she had ten years ago when Courtney would watch her on television every Thursday night, well, except maybe a couple years older. Her skin was the same smooth creamy porcelain Courtney remembered, and her cute blonde hair was still cropped just above the shoulders.

Justin turned to see why Courtney wasn't moving and grinned as soon as he looked at her. Courtney knew he'd probably tease her later, but she couldn't help it. She hadn't anticipated it being this cool to meet Audrey. Justin reached for her hand and pulled her inside. "You okay?" he asked softly.

She bit her lip, blushing, then giggled like she'd heard Justin's star struck fans do many a time. "I'm so sorry," she finally gushed. "I swear I'm not usually like this. I just, well, I grew up watching you on TV. I used to tape magazine pictures of you to my wall." She shook her head. "It's just so strange to see you in real life, and I half expect to see you here with Eric, not," she gestured to Ryan and then covered her face with her hands, certain she was humiliating herself.

Audrey chuckled casually. "You know, there are some days that I think I'd trade, if only Eric were real," she replied, shooting her husband a knowing smile.

Ryan stepped forward and shook Courtney's hand. "Good to see you again." He led them into a large sitting room. "Can I get you both a drink?"

Courtney hesitantly followed Justin, quickly accepting the wine Ryan handed her.

"I don't think I've ever seen Courtney impressed by someone I introduced her to," Justin announced.

"Yeah, I don't think I got any reaction out of you at all when I first met you. I'm a little insulted," Ryan joked.

"Well, don't be too offended. She hasn't watched half of my movies," Justin added, grinning at Courtney.

"I have too! I just didn't harp on it because I didn't like all of them," she said with a smile.

They all laughed and Justin flashed a fake angry face at her.

Audrey joined them in the sitting room after whispering something to an older woman Courtney presumed to be the nanny. "Personally, I think it's nice. When we first married, we had a pretty even number of fans, but since the first *Days End* movie came out, he's totally eclipsed me. He'll have hordes of teenage girls following him on the street, fan mail covered in glitter and perfume, and even a few stalkers. When Ryan and I go out together, I get about as much attention as the bodyguard."

By the time she'd started sipping her second glass of wine, Courtney felt much more relaxed. Audrey and Ryan seemed like a normal couple, and the way she and Justin casually leaned against each other on the couch, his fingers absentmindedly tapping her thigh, she easily forgot she was in a room with three famous actors. The whole conversation was surreal, especially as Courtney realized that the way they dished on different directors and costars was no different from the way she and her friends gossiped about their own coworkers and bosses.

The kids ran into the room shortly before it was time for the adults to eat. Audrey quickly stood and wrapped Stella into her arms, kissing her forehead and running her fingers through the girl's honey-colored hair.

"Courtney, this is Stella, my baby," Audrey said, quickly correcting herself, "Our baby." She smiled at Ryan. "And this is Sabrina and Sebastian."

"Nice to meet you," Courtney said to the older two.

Justin slid off the couch and immediately dropped to the floor where Sebastian was playing with matchbox cars. "Do you still have the ramp in your room?" he asked the boy, who nodded eagerly.

"Hang on a second buddy," Ryan stopped Sebastian before

he scampered out of the room. "You guys need to head up to bed before too long. Did you eat all your dinner?"

Sebastian wrinkled his brow and then nodded. Ryan released him, and he sprinted up the stairs, Justin trailing closely behind.

"It's like they're on a playdate," Ryan joked.

"Do you want to give me a hand?" Audrey asked Courtney. "I just want to check on everything in the kitchen."

Courtney nodded nervously as Audrey passed Stella off to Ryan. The kitchen was enormous, gorgeous, and well-stocked. It was everything Courtney had always imagined in a kitchen. "So you cook?"

Audrey pulled an oversized stoneware dish from the oven and placed it on the countertop, gingerly peeling back the foil. "Since the children came along, I've tried to cook more. You know, we wanted to give them more organics and home cooking, and especially after I had Stella, it just made sense. I haven't been working as much, so there's more time."

She paused, pulling a loaf of bread out of the oven. "I took classes," she confessed.

Courtney smiled, unable to think of what to say next.

"You and Justin seem to be getting along well. I don't see him very often, but you know he and Ryan work out together, and apparently Justin talks about you nonstop."

Courtney blushed, still speechless.

Audrey perched on one of the barstools next to the counter. "You know I used to work with Kinzie for a little while," she said calmly.

Courtney frowned, her hand moving to the slowly healing cut on her lip. She wondered if Audrey hadn't heard about Kinzie's latest antics, or if she just didn't realize how touchy of a subject it was. "Oh, yeah. I guess I did know that."

"Justin did a few episodes as a guest star, and that was where they met." She glanced over at Courtney, perhaps expecting some reaction or response. Instead, Courtney just sipped her wine anxiously. "He seems different with you than he did with her." Her almost accusatory tone caught Courtney off guard.

"Different how?"

Audrey shrugged. "I can't really put my finger on it. Maybe just more relaxed?"

"That's a good thing, isn't it?"

Audrey nodded, gazing up to the ceiling wistfully. "They had a lot in common. It always seemed like they matched up, you know, like they could fit into each other's lives without any real effort. But, Ryan always joked that Justin was just dating her because his publicist told him to. I don't think they ever really had any connection or spark, or at least not for Justin." She turned back to Courtney. "I certainly never saw him watch Kinzie the way he stares at you."

Courtney smiled politely.

"I'm sorry, I'm probably making you completely uncomfortable, especially in light of everything Kinzie's done lately. I didn't mean to drag you in here just to embarrass you. I honestly only wanted a hand carrying all this out. It's just so interesting for me to watch you guys together. I dated so many men before Ryan, so many, many men," she paused to giggle. "For me, though, it just never worked out with guys who weren't at least somehow involved in the entertainment industry. It was always just too complicated. It's such a different lifestyle."

"I'm starting to learn that," Courtney replied, clearing her throat.

Audrey smiled and then started out to the deck with the food, so Courtney grabbed the salad and followed. Ryan and Justin met them outside with the wine. Audrey excused herself to go say goodnight to the kids, who were on their way upstairs with the nanny.

Justin leaned in to kiss Courtney before sitting beside her. Courtney noticed Ryan look away when they kissed and wondered how often they'd had Kinzie over to dinner with Justin.

"You have such a beautiful home," Courtney said once Audrey returned.

"Thank you. We love it," Ryan said.

"Which is a good thing, really, since it sometimes feels like we're prisoners here whenever a new movie comes out," Audrey added.

Ryan shrugged. "It gets a little crazy at times. I've probably got it easier than you, though," he said to Justin. "Audrey just worries with the kids."

"Well, don't let the food get cold. Hopefully it's all edible!" Audrey laughed.

They all ate and chatted the rest of the evening. It was cooler when they left, and Justin threw his jacket over Courtney's shoulders as they walked to the car, swinging their hands back and forth.

"They seem really nice," Courtney said. "I can't believe I forgot to get her autograph though," she added with a smile.

"We could go back," Justin joked, kissing the top of her head before climbing into the Audi. "Yeah, Ryan's a really cool guy. They make it all look so easy."

Courtney paused, not oblivious to the wistful expression on his face. "That's what you wanted it to be like with Kinzie," she finally said, without even the slightest hint of bitterness.

He turned to her, startled, and frowned. Then he sighed and focused his eyes on the road again. "Yeah, I guess so. I thought it would be like that someday, but it never would have. Some things that look good on paper don't pan out in reality."

Courtney stared out the window, wondering if the inverse was equally true. She kept quiet though, instead watching the headlights of the cars whizzing past them on the freeway blur together like the flashing lights of the Midway.

"I don't think I had it all wrong," he added, interrupting her thoughts. "I mean, I still want that, someday. Just not with Kinzie."

Courtney felt his hand searching for her own, then let him squeeze her fingertips before she turned back to the window.

THE NEXT FEW days were better. Between Courtney and Keith, Justin didn't have time to himself to mope. His publicist helped him craft some comments to post on social media for his followers, and she worked fast to spread good press about him. For the most part, he'd noticed a larger outpouring from fans in the past day or two anyway. Of course, nothing had been officially resolved yet, so Justin still felt like he was walking on pins and needles whenever he left the house, and having Craig in tow wasn't helping.

Courtney issued a statement on the fly to a reporter who accosted her outside her office one day. Justin knew Marty or Jamie would've told her not to speak with anyone, but he was secretly pleased that she felt confident enough to ignore their advice. Justin was just reading the printed version of it when Courtney pulled up on Thursday:

"Kinzie is clearly having a hard time and is looking for someone to blame. I'm sure when she's recovered, she'll apologize for accusing Justin of something so completely untrue and we can all move on. In the meantime, though, I can assure you that my lip was injured when I was knocked down by paparazzi interrogating Justin about Kinzie and not as a result of anything he did. Anyone who has ever met Justin knows that he is an extremely sweet and gentle guy who could never hurt anyone."

"Did you see this?" he asked Keith, waving the paper in front of him.

Keith nodded. "Jamie sent it over this morning."

"Courtney did pretty well, huh."

"Well, aside from the part where she was supposed to say she had no comment."

Justin smiled. He had never been a "no comment" type of guy with his fans, and he didn't want to force his girl into that position either.

Courtney came through the unlocked door just as he was setting the paper down. "Hey!" he greeted her cheerily. Then he froze. Something wasn't right. Courtney's eyes were red and blotchy, and the fake smile she'd kept up around him the past few days was noticeably missing. "What's wrong?"

"I need to talk to you," she said, her voice scratchy.

Justin nodded and stepped closer. Keith followed.

"Alone," she clarified, stepping past both of them and making her way onto the back deck.

Justin followed her nervously, closing the door behind him.

He stepped up behind her, wrapping his arm around her since she was already shivering. "What's wrong? Did something happen?"

He felt her take a deep breath. "I lost my job. They fired me."

Her tone was so calm, so matter-of-factly, that he almost thought he'd misheard. But then he felt her labored breathing as her chest rose and fell again, and he realized she was struggling to hold it together.

"I don't understand. You're amazing at your job."

"My boss called me into her office this afternoon, right after she got out of a long meeting, and she said I was doing a great job, but that it just wouldn't work out. I asked her why, and she said that with all the press you'd been getting lately, it was casting a negative light on the organization."

Justin felt a lump rise in his throat. From the moment she'd said she lost her job, he sensed it was his fault, but now it was confirmed. "But that's not fair. You can't help that."

Courtney forced a fake laugh. "Oh, actually, I could, according to my boss. She said if I wanted help, that it was available, and that if I left the abusive situation, she wouldn't see any conflict with me continuing to work."

"Wait, so they said you had to dump me to keep your job? Did you tell them it's not true, that I didn't do that to you?"

She turned to face him, rolling her eyes. "Of course, Justin. But they don't believe me. Karen spends every day with women who claim to have tripped and fallen down the stairs or run into a wall. Her job is to make it easier for them to get out of the relationship even when they're in denial about the situation."

Justin felt behind him for the chair and sat, leaning forward with his elbow on his knees, raising his hands to his head. He didn't know what to say. He had never imagined this as an outcome of the whole ordeal. Courtney had always made it clear that her career mattered to her, possibly more than he did. Even if Justin couldn't find a quick fix for his Kinzie problem, he had to find a solution for Courtney.

Suddenly, it came to him. He stood up. "Tell her you broke up with me."

Courtney shook her head. "I can't just tell her that. There would have to be something public, everyone would have to know we broke up." She sighed, and he cringed, knowing she was starting to cry. "When I brought you to that charity dinner and you made that big donation, everyone found out we were dating and the organization got a lot of press because of it. Karen doesn't care about me or what's actually going on, she just doesn't want the organization to seem hypocritical."

"Then dump me in public."

She sniffled. "Justin, that's ridiculous. I love you."

He stepped forward, relieved at her response. He placed his hands over her forearms and gently pressed his lips into her forehead, lingering there until he thought up a reply. "Then we don't actually have to break up. We can just tell everyone we did."

Courtney shook her head and leaned into his chest. "Justin, if people thought I broke up with you now, they'd assume Kinzie was telling the truth about you. I'm not going to do that to you. I would never give Kinzie that satisfaction." She curled her arms onto his chest on either side of her face, and he pulled her closer, wrapping his arms around her back. "Besides, we just stopped sneaking around. I don't want to go back to that."

Justin kissed the top of her head in lieu of reminding her that at the present, they were essentially hibernating, which was even worse than sneaking around.

What had he done? He had finally found someone who cared about him more than he'd ever imagined possible and he had ruined her career in one fell swoop. All along, he'd been hesitant about falling for Courtney, certain he was no good for her, and now, just as he'd predicted, he'd hurt her. He hated himself for not protecting her from the paparazzi, for letting Kinzie get pissed off enough to pull this shit, and for even dating Kinzie in the first place.

If felt like they'd been standing there forever, clasped together silently, when Justin realized Courtney was shivering harder. "You're freezing. Come on, let's go inside."

He heard her exhale, watched her wipe her eye with her finger, and then she let him lead her back into the house.

"Why don't you go upstairs and take a bath? I can order some food, get you a drink and meet you up there in a few." Justin suggested.

"Not hungry," she mumbled, turning groggily and trudging slowly up the stairs.

Justin went into the kitchen and quickly downed two shots of bourbon. "She lost her job because of me," he explained to Keith. "It's bad press for the shelter for her to date me."

Keith cringed. "I'll call Jamie," he offered, seamlessly transitioning into his taskmaster mode. Then he motioned to a large casserole dish on the stove. "It's some chicken dish that Cathy made. It's pretty good."

Justin nodded and dumped a large serving onto a plate, realizing he was still hungry even if Courtney wasn't. Then he had an idea. "Don't call Jamie. I'm going to go see Kinzie tomorrow, in private."

"You'll only make it worse."

He shook his head. "I don't think that's possible. Don't tell Jamie, though. I don't want anyone knowing I'm going. And no Craig, either. You can drive me."

Keith clearly still didn't like the idea, but he nodded reluctantly.

Justin wolfed down the chicken casserole while making drinks and went upstairs to Courtney.

Her clothes lay neatly in a pile by the door, but she wasn't in the bath. Instead, she had curled up under the covers, forming a lump so tiny he hardly noticed her there. At first, he thought she was asleep, but then he noticed her eyes were open. He sat on the edge of the bed beside her, setting a cosmopolitan and a glass of white wine on the nightstand.

She smiled meekly.

"Come on," he urged, standing and making his way into the bathroom to the gigantic Jacuzzi tub which he really never used. Now seemed like the perfect time. He turned on the water and let it start filling up while he took off his shirt. He glanced back at Courtney, now sitting up in the bed, watching him sadly, her breasts peeking out from above the covers. Even when she was depressed, she somehow managed to look amazing. He nearly laughed, though, realizing this was probably the first time he'd been with her that he wasn't thinking about having sex with her. Now all he could think about was how fragile and defeated she seemed.

He stripped naked, cognizant that she was still watching him. He climbed into the bath, motioning for her to follow. She did, bringing both drinks with her, and as soon as she sunk into the hot water, he wrapped his arms around her, pulling her back against his chest. His mind was still racing, but the sound of the jets started to drown out his thoughts. Still, he knew he had to fix this. Talking to Kinzie tomorrow would just be a start.

He was going to be traveling a lot over the next six weeks. It was mostly short trips, doing publicity for the *Days End* movie opening on Thanksgiving, but he wouldn't be able to hang out with her all day and cheer her up. "Hey, maybe this is a good thing. Now you can come with me on the publicity tour." He paused, nervous when she slurped the cosmopolitan in lieu of replying. "You wouldn't have to come everywhere, but we could at least travel to all the cooler cities together."

"Yeah, and I'll just magically come up with the money for my rent and student loans."

"I'll pay it."

She laughed. "No, Justin. You already got me the car. That's enough. Too much."

"I only got you part of the car," he insisted, knowing that was hardly a critical distinction when his part was roughly eighty percent of the purchase price.

"I really didn't work my ass off in law school so I could meet up with a sugar daddy to pay all my bills," she retorted. "I want to work."

This shouldn't have surprised him. "Fine, then we'll find you another job you love. A better one."

She finished the cosmopolitan, the glass clinking into the

edge of the tub as she reached to place it on the ledge. "Yeah, I'm sure that will be super easy in this economy. In the meantime, Erica can just pay my part of all the bills." Her voice was thick with bitter sarcasm.

"Look, Courtney, this was my fault. I'll pay your rent until you find a new job and then you can pay me back if you want. It's not up for discussion. I already feel bad enough and it isn't going to help anything if you get evicted." He paused, realizing he didn't actually know exactly what his financial situation was, let alone hers. "What is your rent?"

"We each pay $1100 a month."

Justin nearly laughed. Her apartment wasn't great, but still, he had no idea there was stuff that cheap in LA. He was sure he could cover that without even noticing it.

They soaked in the water quietly until Justin felt his toes start to wrinkle.

Finally, Courtney spoke. "Why won't you make love to me?"

Her voice sounded so sad, so lost, that Justin wasn't sure how to respond. Well, except to do the obvious. He reached for a towel, handed it to her, then stood, grabbing another for himself. Then he picked her up, carried her into the bedroom, her hair and shoulders still damp, and made love to her.

The next morning, he and Keith left early, before Courtney was up. He left her a note saying he was going to the gym and to run some errands. He wore athletic shorts, a tee shirt and an oversized sweatshirt, throwing on a baseball cap and sunglasses. He inspected the small recorder Keith handed him, then placed it in his pocket.

"What car do you think will attract the least attention?" he asked Keith.

"The Audi or the Escalade? Either way, if reporters are there, they're going to be curious about who's coming by." Keith paused. "Even if you borrow Courtney's car, it's iffy."

"Fine, then we'll just take the Audi. I need to fill up on the way home anyway." He tossed the keys to Keith. "You drive so you can drop me off at the door and leave until I text you to come back."

"This is a terrible idea," Keith mumbled, taking the keys.

They arrived at the rehab facility before nine, a time when he figured no one would ever check in, so theoretically there wouldn't be much press. Of course Kinzie had to go to a rehab at a place that was popular with celebrities, probably because it was more spa-like than anything else, but that alone upped the risk of someone seeing them. There didn't appear to be anyone around, so Keith pulled up to the door, barely pausing while Justin flew out.

The lobby was empty, so Justin sauntered right up to the desk and asked where he could find Kinzie. A lady in a pale green uniform eyed him warily, then told him it wasn't visiting hours.

"It's really important that I speak to her in person, and I won't be in town later today," he lied, flashing his best smile.

She sighed, acquiescing to the dimples as everyone always did, and handed him a clipboard. "Sign in please."

He used a common alias, one he knew Kinzie would recognize.

"Remove your sunglasses," the woman requested.

Justin frowned. "Why?"

"Because you're indoors. If you're wearing sunglasses to hide your eyes and cover up that you're drunk or stoned, well, we don't need you visiting here."

He rolled his eyes, but complied.

The woman hesitated, clearly recognizing him, then glanced down at the paper. She cleared her throat. "Chris, that's your name?"

He nodded.

"You look a lot like someone else."

Justin forced a smile. "Just one of those faces, I guess."

She sighed wearily. "Can you confirm that you have no drugs, alcohol, or other related paraphernalia on your person?"

He nodded, adding, "This isn't necessary. Kinzie doesn't have a drug problem."

"I'm afraid I can't discuss a resident's medical status with you. Have a seat and I'll check if she's up for visitors."

Justin sat briefly, then stood and paced nervously. He wasn't sure what he'd do if Kinzie refused to see him. After what seemed like an eternity, the same woman returned, alone. The knot in his stomach tightened.

"She asked that you wait for her in the courtyard." She motioned towards a door.

Justin sighed, then headed out. He had spent the last eight days rehearsing what he wanted to say to Kinzie when he saw her next, but then last night, he'd rewritten the whole script. The tough part was going to be sticking to it. He patted his shorts nervously, praying the recorder in his pocket didn't malfunction. He and Keith had tested it earlier, ensuring that it would pick up their conversation from within his pocket.

He had his back turned when Kinzie approached.

"Hi Chris," he heard her say.

He turned quickly, and forced a smile. She wasn't wearing much makeup, and her hair was pulled back into a ponytail, but he could tell she hadn't changed. Maybe lost a little weight, but nothing significant. He offered her a polite, but distant hug, and then they sat on a bench in front of a winding man-made stream. Justin made sure she sat on the side of him nearest to the recorder, and then he scooted closer, not wanting to take any chances.

"Why are you in rehab?" he asked, focusing on keeping his

voice calm and sympathetic. "I didn't know you were having problems."

"There's a lot you don't know," she replied icily. "But I'm here for stress. I needed to detoxify my life."

"Have you been keeping up with the news?"

She shook her head. "No, I've been focusing more internally. A lot of yoga, some journaling."

"Well, do you know why I'm here?"

"I could guess."

Justin had never hit her or any other woman before, but man, the way she played games made him want to slap her more than anything else at this very moment. He thrust his hands into his pockets instead. "Kinzie, I'm sorry about the way things turned out with us."

She gasped at this, clearly not in a million years having expected him to apologize. He was grateful for her silence, and continued.

"You made such a huge difference in my life and my career when I first came out to L.A., and we really had something special for a while there." he paused, knowing he needed to give her more to get the confession he wanted. "I'd just figured you and me would be together till the end. It really hurt me when I first suspected you were involved with Jackson." He winced, desperate to seem as vulnerable as possible.

She raised her eyebrows. "Well, that's over for now."

"I'm sorry to hear that. I really do want you to be happy, and I realize now that you and I were just not meant to be."

Kinzie opened her mouth to speak, but Justin held up his hand, knowing he needed to finish before he lost the nerve and instead blabbed what he really thought about her right now. "I just wanted to tell you that I'm sorry if I hurt your feelings and I'm sorry if I made you feel used. I don't always think through my actions, and I didn't mean for those consequences to happen."

"Why are you telling me all of this?"

He sighed, and patted her bony, ice cold hand. She'd always had cold fingers, which was fitting, he thought, given her personality. "Look, Kinz, I know we've had some misunderstandings in the past, and I know you don't owe me anything, but I could really use your help at straightening something out now."

She leaned back as though she'd been expecting that.

He cleared his throat. "Somehow the tabloids got it in their heads that there was some physical abuse in our relationship and that has caused some pretty big publicity problems for me lately. I know you're over me now and you probably don't even want to be friends, but I thought you'd at least like to know."

"Oh? I hadn't heard that," she said, looking him straight in the eye.

Justin clenched his hands into fists, concentrating on keeping his face calm. "Yeah, it really surprised me. I mean, if I thought there was any chance you still had a thing for me, I would've suspected you leaked that rumor, but I know that isn't the case since you have moved on." Justin knew he was rambling, but he was desperate to get anything useful out of her. They used to talk all the time, and so easily. It seemed strange that their conversation now was so strained.

"Are you still with that girl?"

"Yeah. Courtney and I are still together. It's going really well, and that's actually sort of why I'm here."

Kinzie raised an eyebrow.

"She lost her job when the rumors popped up about you and me. And I don't think she wants that job back anyway, but I figured we should try to clear up this misunderstanding."

"And why do you think I'd be interested in helping you and your new girlfriend?"

He shrugged. "Well, I know you're over me now, and I figured you'd just want to move on and put everything that happened with us in the past." He paused and looked down, unable to face her while lying through his teeth. "And because that's just the kind of person you are."

"So what do you want from me?"

"People think I hit you. I think you could help clear up that rumor and save both of our reputations."

She chuckled. "I don't see how it hurts my reputation for people to think you hit women."

Justin was ready for that one. "If people believe these rumors, they're going to see you as this weak victim-type. I know you have way more confidence and self-respect than that."

Kinzie rolled her eyes, but he sensed she was considering his words.

"I mean, you and I both know I never hit you, right?"

She nodded, accompanied by another eye roll. He cringed, desperate for a verbal response, anything at all audible for the recorder.

Flustered, Justin reached into his pocket, pulling out the statement he had prepared, with a little help from Keith this morning.

Kinzie snatched the paper and read it slowly.

Justin read along with her, although he practically had it memorized. It said: "In the time that I have been away from home, taking a short but much needed vacation from my work, it has come to my attention that some rumors have cropped up regarding my relationship with Justin Erikson. While we, like most couples, had the occasional disagreement, there was never any physical violence in our relationship, and it is troubling to us to hear reports stating the contrary. At this point in our lives, Justin and I have both moved on to new relationships and would appreciate privacy concerning our personal lives." There was a space at the bottom for her signature.

She handed the paper back to him. "Justin, you could just say the same thing from your point of view. This really is the sort of stressor I'm supposed to be avoiding."

"You're right. Maybe I'll talk to Jackson instead. He could probably help us both out here, right? I'm sure you told him I never hit you."

"I don't think Jackson would care what you said about me."

Justin knew it was time to be blunt. "Kinzie, you never told anyone I was abusive, did you?" He stared directly at her, praying she couldn't let him down as long as his baby blue eyes were piercing into her.

"Of course not. Why would I say something like that? What possible motivation would I have?"

He shrugged, avoiding the temptation to shake her and list her possible insane motivations, like jealousy, revenge, pure hatred. He handed the paper back to her. "Just sign it and I'll leave you to your yoga. There can't possibly be anything too stressful about the truth." He paused, knowing he was losing her, then added, "I know you don't owe me anything, but if you ever really cared about me like you say you did, you'd want to help me out."

She rolled her eyes, but held the paper in her hand.

"Whatever, just keep it. If you change your mind, you can send it to me, or to my publicist. Unless you're still hung up on me, you'd want to sign it and get this all over with."

He stood, knowing there was nothing else he could do or say. If she wouldn't sign it, at least he could use the recording, or maybe just threaten to. "I better go. It was good to see you, Kinzie. I hope your, uh, recovery goes well." He started to head back to the door.

She sighed. "Good luck with what's-her-name."

"Courtney," he supplied, knowing she already knew that.

Kinzie laughed, and he turned. "Does she know we fucked after you met her?"

Justin tapped his hand against the recorder, confirming he still had it. "Yeah. I tell her everything. She's pretty amazing. I really think she might be the one." And then he walked off without turning back. He texted Keith from the lobby, then waited until he saw the Audi pull up to quickly hop in the passenger's seat.

"Did she sign?" Keith asked immediately.

Justin shook his head, flustered. He had felt like the mission had been a success, at least until Keith asked the obvious. After all, Justin had successfully talked to Kinzie, without killing her, and as far as he knew, without being recognized by anyone other than the triage nurse. "I think the tape might be helpful, though."

Keith nodded. "Should we take it to Jamie?"

They drove immediately to her office and dropped it off there, not waiting around to talk with her since they both knew she'd be furious with Justin for even talking with Kinzie. Justin prayed Jamie could do something with it at least.

15

On Sunday evening, Courtney returned to her apartment for the first time since Friday morning. As soon as she walked in, Erica popped up from the couch.

"Where have you been?"

"Justin's," Courtney replied.

"What happened to your phone? Is it broken? Lost?"

"It's in my purse. I didn't really feel like talking to anyone." Courtney started towards her room, hoping Erica would catch the hint that she still didn't want to talk to anyone.

"Courtney, I called you, I texted you, and I left you messages. You could've just texted back that you were okay. I don't know Justin's number."

"Sorry. I didn't mean to worry you. I thought you'd know where I was."

Erica stood, following her into the bedroom. "Yeah, I had sort of figured, and then Justin told me yesterday. Courtney, I heard what happened at work. I just, I don't know. I wanted to make sure you were okay."

Courtney nodded, not exactly thrilled that the news was

getting around already, and then she paused, confused. "Why did you talk to Justin?"

Erica seemed surprised. "He came by yesterday. He dropped off your rent."

"What do you mean?"

Erica laughed. "He handed me an envelope stuffed with hundred dollar bills. Twenty-two of them, to be precise."

Courtney rolled her eyes, not really surprised by Justin's actions, but a little irritated that he did it behind her back.

"And your mom called me. She has been trying to reach you, too, and she said if you didn't call her before the end of the day, she was flying out here first thing tomorrow."

"Awesome," Courtney said through clenched teeth. "Did you tell her about my job?"

Erica shook her head, frowning. "Of course not, but she was asking a lot of questions about you and Justin. I think she heard about the Kinzie stuff."

"Shit. Okay, I'll call her now," Courtney promised. She glanced up at Erica, noticing her friend really did look concerned. "I'm sorry I didn't call you back. I just, I don't know what to do, and I am not really ready to talk yet."

Erica nodded solemnly. "Justin told me that you could keep your job if you broke up with him."

"I'm not breaking up with him. He didn't do anything wrong!"

"I know, I know. I think you're making the right choice. You worked too hard in law school to waste your talent at a place that wants to manipulate your personal life. I realize I haven't always been Justin's biggest supporter, but maybe I underestimated him."

Courtney hadn't expected that from Erica. "Thanks." She smiled halfheartedly and gave Erica a quick hug before closing her door. Then she stretched out on her bed, scrolling quickly through her messages and missed calls before taking a deep breath and calling her mother.

"Where have you been? I've been calling and calling..." her mother began, bypassing any normal greeting.

"Mom, I'm fine. Stop lecturing me or I'll hang up." She paused, and her mom was quiet. "I'm sorry I didn't call you sooner. I had some issues with my phone. So how have you and Dad been?"

"Courtney Lynn, you know why I've been calling. I'm worried about you. We've been hearing some things about that Justin, and I..."

"Mom," Courtney interrupted, not offering her mother the opportunity to say something negative about Justin. "I know what you've heard. It's terrible, isn't it? Everyone is just shocked that Kinzie would even say something like that." She took a deep breath. "But she's going through a difficult time now, so there's no telling when she'll come out with the truth and an apology. Remember that you can't believe everything you read about Justin."

Her mother was quiet, a fact which worried Courtney even more.

"Mom?"

"I gather you're still seeing him, then?" Her mother's tone couldn't have been clearer that she was hoping her daughter would reply no to this question.

"Of course I am. It's going great. He's an incredible guy."

"What about your lip? We saw photos. Were those made up too?"

"No. I fell," Courtney replied, knowing the truth still sounded just as dumb as the last four hundred times she'd told it.

"Has he ever hit you, even on accident?"

"No, Mom, never. And I know he never hit Kinzie either. He

isn't that type of guy. He never even raises his voice. He doesn't have a bad temper."

"Courtney, I want to believe you, but I just don't think you'd tell me any differently even if…" her mother sniffled. "I know he's big stuff out there in LA, and I hear about how all those Hollywood types are, with their drugs and drinking and…"

"Mom, Justin does not do drugs. I don't even understand how you can say all this stuff. You met him. You've seen what he's like." Courtney realized she was crying now, too. "It's one thing when people who only know him from what they read in the tabloids say this stuff about him, but God, you're my mother. Don't you trust me? You have no excuse for believing this trash and I'm not going to stay on the phone with you while you criticize him."

Her mother sighed audibly. "Where were you the past few days?"

"I've been staying at Justin's. The paparazzi has been pretty bad lately, and I had a rotten week at work, so I just wanted to get away from it all." She casually omitted the part about it being her last week at that particular job.

"Courtney, I don't think it's good for you to be isolating yourself from your other friends now."

Courtney knew her mother wasn't going to let up, so she just decided to get it over with. "Well, I guess I'll have a lot more time for my friends now because I got fired over all this bullshit in the tabloids."

Her mother gasped. "You should come home for a little while."

"I already told you I'd come over Christmas."

"But you can come sooner now since you're not working."

"No, I need to be here to look for jobs."

"Courtney, be realistic. You can't afford to live there until you have a job, and now there's nothing keeping you there. You could move back, find a more affordable place here, get a terrific job, and stay away from all that Hollywood talk."

"And what about Justin, Mom?"

"You said he travels a lot anyway. He could still come visit you and it would be like nothing changed."

"That's not what I want. I'm not ready to give up on L.A., Mom, and I don't want to move away from Justin. He's a really important part of my life, and I need to be with him now."

"But sweetheart, that still doesn't mean you can't come back here for a little while. I'm not suggesting you break up with him, and you know if it's meant to be, you'll make it even if you're apart."

Courtney sighed. "Mom, look, I understand this has to be hard for you and Dad, to be so far away and to read all this stuff about Justin, but you have to trust me. I have a pretty good track record of making good choices for myself, and this is what I want, to be here in L.A., with Justin. He's a really good person and I'm happy."

Her mom was quiet long enough that Courtney started to think she had won this round. But then her mom spoke again.

"Oh, Courtney, even if he is the wonderful man you say he is, he still can't give you the life you deserve. I know it seems great now, with the expensive cars and all the fancy parties, but it's a completely different lifestyle. Constantly being in the spotlight, loving a man who travels and has to kiss all these other women and pose in his underwear, that's never going to be easy."

"It's easier than being apart from him," she replied finally. "I'll keep you posted on the job hunt. Let me know if there's specific days you want me to come in over the holidays." She hung up before her mom could argue more.

THE NEXT WEEK WAS HARD. After the initial thrashing from Jamie, she conceded that at least the recording of Kinzie would be helpful if they had to resort to litigation. But it did nothing to help Courtney's job situation. Courtney clammed up and wouldn't talk about it, giving him the generic "I'm fine" bit, and spending long hours each day reading by his pool with headphones on.

It wasn't that she didn't deserve the time to feel sorry for herself, but he was leaving town at the end of the week, doing some interviews and publicity stuff to promote *Days End* in four different cities over the next two weeks. Courtney seemed irritated when he invited her along; yet, he wasn't really sure how she'd get along with him gone. He couldn't shake the feeling that she was slipping through his fingers.

She drove him to the airport for his flight, staying in the car while he climbed out and retrieved his bags. "Hang on," he hollered to her, dropping his stuff at the curbside check-in area before returning to the car. "Don't I get a real goodbye kiss?" he asked.

Courtney smiled, and leaned closer, uncomfortably nodding towards Craig, who was standing right next to the car on high alert. Justin shook his head and motioned for her to get out. "I can't leave the car here. We're in a loading zone," she protested, but complied, hesitantly stepping out of her car.

"Then we won't leave the car," he promised, wrapping his arms around her as he leaned her back against the car door and kissed her. He could feel Craig's glaring eyes on them, but he didn't care. Justin sensed almost immediately that other people were watching too, but he didn't want to think about them either. Justin wanted to remember exactly what Courtney's lips tasted like, precisely how her tongue felt pulsing against his own, and just how his hands fit around the small of her back and the curve of her hips.

She smiled drunkenly as the kiss ended. "Have a good trip," she murmured.

He grabbed her hands and squeezed them quickly. "I love you," he said, immediately wondering if she'd say it back for once.

She did, and then she leaned forward and buried her head on his chest. "I'm going to miss you."

He smiled as he walked off, pausing to sign an autograph and grin for a photo with a thirty-something who'd gotten her daughter to hold the camera, and then pulled out his phone to call Courtney. He saw her shake her head before merging into the other lane.

"Hey you, how's the trip so far?" she asked, her chipper voice convincing him she'd be fine in his absence.

He chuckled in lieu of answering. "I'm going to miss you, too," he said before hanging up. He made a mental note to check the internet in the next few days for any amateur videos taken of him making out with Courtney, to see if he looked like as big of a schmuck as he imagined.

Justin had gotten Craig a seat in first class on the flight, right next to his. He wondered if that was the right protocol, or if he was supposed to stick him in the back, but he figured it wouldn't hurt to have someone to chat with on the flight.

"You'll make things easier on yourself if you don't pull stunts like that," Craig insisted, clearly referring to his goodbye with Courtney outside the airport.

Justin ignored him, instead stepping forward to shake hands with a woman smiling and waving enthusiastically at him.

"We should board the plane," Craig said.

"In a minute," Justin replied, pausing to pose for a photo with another woman and her small child and signing two autographs.

The flight to New York was pleasant and uneventful. Craig

proved to be a worthwhile travel companion, offering some useful, albeit unsolicited, advice on Justin's sports picks for the week. And in the baggage claim area, instead of being swarmed by fans when he wasn't exactly at his freshest, Justin sat in the corner, peacefully playing with his phone while Craig positioned himself in front of Justin, discouraging people from approaching by his mere presence.

But then, Justin heard a familiar voice.

"Is that Justin Erikson?" the female squealed.

He glanced up, prepared to pose for a photo or sign an autograph, but to his surprise, it wasn't a fan. "Andi!" he exclaimed.

She smiled at Craig, then walked around him, her own bodyguard chatting with Craig. "You're stealing Brad's guys now?" she teased.

Justin grinned. "I didn't see you on the plane."

"I flew in from Chicago," she explained. "I was finishing up a project there." She paused, then lowered her voice. "I heard about everything with, well, you know. That sucks. If there's anything I can do, let me know."

Justin hugged her and gave her a quick kiss on the cheek, immediately considering how that gesture would undoubtedly be misinterpreted by anyone witnessing it. "Thanks. I think it's all starting to blow over. I just hope it doesn't affect the movie publicity."

Andi snorted, a long lock of her hair falling out of her baseball cap. "No one believes the rumors, Justin. And I don't think anything could hurt this movie."

He nodded despite disagreeing with her words. "All I know is my publicist is panicked. She worked with me all day yesterday on my scripted responses to questions about Kinzie even though she's also made certain that all of the interviewers know they can't ask me about it."

Andi locked her arm through Justin's. "Let's share a cab," she said.

The first day of signing autographs and interviews went smoothly. No one asked Justin about Kinzie or his women-beating tendencies, but he didn't feel like himself. Normally, he was at ease with the fans, signing pictures, shaking hands, chatting comfortably, but today, he was a nervous wreck, assuming that each onlooker was thinking the worst of him.

His publicist had called twice, but he hadn't returned the call, too stressed already to field another lecture from her. Keith had called too, but Justin figured that wasn't too urgent either. They acted like he was incompetent, always calling and checking up. It wasn't like he couldn't make his own decisions when he was out of town. He didn't need his manager and publicist babysitting him.

At the end of the day, Justin was exhausted. He didn't even feel like joining the others for dinner, instead retreating to his hotel. Andi was staying at their apartment, and while at this point, he didn't think Courtney would mind if he did, too, he didn't want to risk complicating anything else now.

The hotel room was dark and quiet, aside from a flashing light on the phone indicating a message. Justin pulled his shirt off and tossed it over the phone, covering the damn light. He stepped out of his jeans, eager for a long, hot shower before he investigated the room service options. He glanced at his phone before placing it on the bathroom counter, ignoring the missed calls and voice mails, but checking his texts. The first one was from Courtney. It was short but sweet, like all of hers. "Still missing you," it read. She'd sent another one about an hour later. "Call me ASAP. Great news."

Justin paused, considering calling right after his shower, when another message popped up, this one from Keith. It read, "Kinzie signed. You're home free. Nice work!"

He pounded his fist into the counter excitedly. After a short celebratory dance, he pulled his jeans back on, grabbed a new shirt from his suitcase, and called Andi to let her know he was going to meet up with them after all. Now he was in a mood to celebrate. As he scurried down the lobby, he texted Courtney back, telling her he heard the good news, loved her, and would call later.

Justin felt his confidence soaring as he strutted to his cab. The whole drive to the restaurant, he prided himself on coming up with this plan to solve the Kinzie problem all by himself. Sure, Keith had helped some, but the initial idea was all him. If he could do that, surely he could figure out a solution for Courtney's job situation, too.

Justin decided to tackle that one in the morning. Tonight, he was celebrating.

OVER THE NEXT TWO WEEKS, Justin called way more than he normally did when traveling. Courtney could tell he was worried about her, but his constant concern was starting to make her feel even more pathetic. But the final straw was on the day before he was scheduled to return. Courtney was out to lunch with Erica when he sent her a text.

"I've got good news. Want to know now?" it read.

Never having been the patient type, she called right after their lunch. "So what's the big news?"

"I got you a job." Justin announced proudly.

She didn't even know how to respond.

"Court? You still there?"

"Um, yeah. I'm here. I don't know understand though. What do you mean?"

"Well, I...oh crap, they need me for photos. Call you later?"

He hung up before she could reply. Flustered, Courtney scrolled through her contacts, sure she had Keith's number somewhere. She quickly found an unidentified number in her list of received calls on a day where she was pretty sure Justin had called her from Keith's phone. A man answered.

"Keith?"

"Yeah. Courtney? What's up? Is Justin okay?"

She found it amusing, and a little creepy, how concerned he was about his buddy. "No, he's fine, but I was just talking to him and he mentioned something about finding a job for me, but then he had to go before he could give me the details. I was hoping you might have some idea what he was talking about."

She heard Keith sigh before he replied. "Oh, that. He gave your resume to Marty, his agent, and asked him to pass it on to the firm they use, and I guess they had an offer for you. It's some sports and entertainment law firm."

Courtney heard papers shuffling in the background. She still had no idea what to say.

"Here, I have a copy of the offer. I'll send it over to you. Are you picking him up tomorrow? He arranged for Craig to go back to work for Brad as soon as Kinzie signed the retraction."

"Um, yeah. Thanks," Courtney mumbled. Shortly after they hung up, she got Keith's email with the offer.

For once, she was glad Justin was out of town.

As SOON AS he collected his bags, Justin sent a text to Courtney so she'd meet him in the loading area. Just as he saw her car pull up, two more fans caught his attention. He quickly signed autographs and posed for a photo with a teenage girl. Then he waved eagerly to Courtney and threw his bags into the trunk. He swaggered over to the driver's side, relieved to finally be home, and eagerly awaiting Courtney's excitement over the job. She rolled down the window and he leaned in, kissing her quickly since there were still a couple people watching them.

"Scoot over, I'll drive," he offered. She complied. He sensed something wasn't right, but wondered if it was just that he'd been gone for a couple weeks.

He reached for her hand as he merged onto the highway. "Did you miss me?"

"Of course." She cleared her throat awkwardly. "But I need to talk to you about something."

She paused, but he didn't respond. "Keith sent me a copy of that job offer you mentioned, and, well, I know you were probably just trying to help, but I don't need your pity job offers, and I don't want to base my career on your connections. And it's a little insulting that you think I need you to get a job. I could get a job on my own if I was willing to settle, but I didn't go to law school just so I could spend my life working for overpaid, lazy, pretentious actors and jocks. I want to work in public interest law, and I want a job like my old one." Courtney finally stopped talking and gasped for air.

Justin felt his jaw clench shut. Not exactly the thanks he had anticipated. "Are you done?" he asked calmly.

"I guess so."

He inhaled noisily through his nose. "Well, first off, if you don't want the job, just say so."

"I don't want the job."

He laughed. "Yeah, I got that. I'll let Marty know later today." He stretched his arm up and then rubbed the back of his neck. "Second, I didn't get the job for you. I just forwarded on your resume, and you got the offer based on your own credentials."

"Justin, they didn't even interview me. Clearly, they offered me the job because of you."

"I was just trying to help." Justin tried to use a tone of finality, hoping she'd just shut up before she ruined the whole damn day.

Instead, she sighed, then continued. "I don't need your help. I worked my ass off in law school. I can get a job on my own. In fact, I did get a job, a great one. And now it's gone. So thanks for your help on that one."

Ouch. Justin clicked his tongue to his teeth. In a way, it was a relief to finally hear her blame him. Now it was out there and he knew how she really felt. It didn't seem like there was anything left to say, so he switched on the radio and cranked up the volume.

Courtney didn't speak to him the rest of the drive to his house. When they arrived, she stepped out of the car while he unloaded his bags. As he slammed the trunk, he tried to decipher Courtney's mood. She looked sad, but perhaps not so angry anymore. Why was it so hard for her to just offer a simple "thanks but no thanks" in response to the job offer? It wasn't like there was anything in it for him by finding her a job. He was just trying to be nice.

"Are you still coming to the premiere this week?" he finally asked her. "I'd hate for you to be stuck in a theater with a bunch of lazy, overpaid actors. Wait, how else did you describe us?"

"Pretentious," she supplied, smiling meekly. She slumped back against the car. "Justin, I'm sorry. You already feel bad enough about the stuff with my job. I shouldn't have made it worse."

Justin realized her eyes were starting to tear up. At least she was sincere. He stepped closer, pressing his hands behind her head, and kissed her firmly.

"I don't think you're lazy," she added when he pulled away.

He laughed. "But I am overpaid and pretentious."

She shrugged, then glanced at her car. "I guess I can't complain about your paycheck, really."

"I suppose you're allowed to be crazy sometimes, too. Lord knows I had my moments this month."

She made a face. "Can I come in?"

"Of course. I haven't properly compensated you for the round trip airport service," he joked.

Courtney only stayed for a few hours, since Justin had to meet up with David for a final fitting for the suit David had designed for him to wear to the premiere. But the next day, Courtney promised to join Justin for a jog.

16

Courtney had been a wreck since yelling at Justin the day before. She knew she overreacted about the job thing, but it still frustrated her that he didn't seem to understand why his gesture bothered her. And it didn't help that she kept hearing her mother's words about Justin in her head. It did seem that the relationship was more emotionally draining than most. Courtney hoped that a jog along the beach would help clear her mind.

They were just beyond the halfway point of their run, already headed back towards the house, when they jogged past the newsstand. Courtney slowed when a photo of Justin caught her eye, straining to read the caption on the cover: "Not an abuser; just a player" it read. Determined not to draw attention to them, Courtney started jogging again. She didn't need to read the article or even see the photos. She knew what she would find—photos of Justin with several other women, and she knew she couldn't stomach that today.

She heard him call her name, but kept running, trying to focus on the music on her headphones. She felt her breath picking up and mentally repeated the mantra over and over "one foot, other foot, one foot, other foot," praying she could draw her attention in to her steps. She startled as she felt his hand on her arm.

"Court, stop," he pleaded.

She glanced at Justin. He had already pulled out his earbuds. She could tell from his face that he had seen the magazine, too. He reached for her hand, and she shook her head.

"Let's just get home. I don't want to have this talk here," she said. But she complied hesitantly, and as soon as the pounding of her feet against the warm pavement had died down, Courtney felt the tears begin to well up in her eyes.

Justin reached for her hand again, this time gripping it firmly, and he led her off the path and closer to the water. Her shoes sunk into the fluffy sand, and she felt a trickle of sweat forming on the back of her neck.

"I can't do this anymore," she admitted, forcing the words out just before a tear escaped her eye.

"Can't do what?" he asked. He had turned to face her, still holding her hand in his.

"This. You. All of it." She shook her head before wiping her eye with her free hand. "You were right. It's all too much for me. I mean, the job, everything with Kinzie, I know none of it is your fault, but I just can't let it go. Not when I constantly have to see all that crap, too. Not when I'm always reading about all your other girlfriends."

"There are no other girlfriends, Courtney. You know that."

"Do I?" She sniffled. "Because maybe I'm just an idiot. Maybe since I'm not with you all the time, I should trust your little stalker paparazzi crew a little more. The photos can't all be fabricated, can they?"

"Courtney, come on. You know me. All those photos—the

stories, it's not what it seems. It's publicity stunts and costars and it's all a lot of made up crap. You know that." He stared at her as though expecting her to concede this point. When she said nothing, he frowned. "You do know that, right?"

She shrugged.

He flung his hands in the air. "I told you there was no one else. If you can't believe me, if you really think I'm that kind of guy, why are you even with me?"

Courtney shook her head and wiped her nose on the back of her hand, praying no one caught that on photograph. "I don't know Justin. I guess that's what I'm saying. I want to believe you, but I just don't know if you take this relationship seriously, and I'm starting to get some serious feelings and I can't keep setting myself up to get hurt."

"I don't take this seriously?" he repeated with disbelief. "Courtney, I asked you to marry me. That's pretty fucking serious."

"You didn't mean it, Justin. It was just something you said." She sighed, tasting a tear as it dripped down to her lip. "And why would I agree to marry you when you're still showing up all over the place with different women? I just..." She stopped mid-sentence as Justin turned and jogged back to the newsstand. She watched, confused, and he returned a moment later, magazine in hand.

"Did you just steal that?" Courtney asked, as he began to leaf through it.

He snorted. "No!"

"Well, I don't want to look at it," she insisted, knowing it wouldn't make her feel any better to hear his strained explanations.

Justin shook his head. "It's going to bug you until you do." He plopped down in the sand, a few feet from the water, and patted the spot next to him. Courtney hesitantly sat, wary of getting sand stuck to her sweaty thighs.

He pointed to the first picture. It was him with Kinzie, looking happy. He looked younger and less muscled in the photo. "This is old," he explained, pointing to it. The next couple of photos were him with Andi, generally with his arm around her, but one where they were holding hands and another where he was kissing her on the cheek. He pointed to each picture as he spoke, "Here we were just hanging out, here we were hanging out on set and she was cold. That is actually a still from a film and that one was after she won an award. This last one is recent, from the airport in New York. We were talking about you and all the Kinzie crap."

Courtney nodded, calmly. So far, this all made sense. She believed him about these photos, but she still felt overwhelmed.

He moved on to two more photos of him with his arm around an actress. "They're both costars. Nothing romantic there, ever. And that one is a still of actual footage from the film," he added, pointing to another photo of him making out with yet another actress.

Courtney frowned and tapped the last photo, one where his hair was messed and his eyes seemed glazed over. His hand was firmly planted on the blonde's ass in the photo, and they were both looking up, apparently having been interrupted in the middle of heavy kissing.

"That's an ad," he calmly replied.

"What's her name?"

Justin grimaced, and gazed upwards as though trying to remember. "Jocelyn," he finally replied.

"And you've never slept with her? Ever?"

He wrinkled his nose. "She is soooo not my type. I think she was stoned during the shoot, anyway.

"What's it an ad for anyway? Her ass?"

Justin laughed. "Her dress."

Courtney squinted. "The tiny little dress? It looks like it's about to come off!"

He laughed again. "In the commercial, it does."

She gagged. Courtney didn't want to admit it, but it still bothered her. He was telling the truth, but she still didn't feel better. She didn't want his hands on some anorexic blonde bimbo, even if it was strictly for work. Those hands belonged on her.

Justin sighed. "Look, I'm not asking you to wear blinders all the time. You're going to see stuff about me, but just ask me about it before you freak out. There's probably a logical explanation for everything."

She wiped her eyes again. "Okay, but even if I know that, no one else does. How do I explain it to my mother? To Erica? Or even to all the hundreds of random people who think I'm the biggest schmuck out there?"

Justin pulled off his sunglasses and folded them over the top of his tee shirt. His bright blue eyes pierced hers. "You don't have to explain it to anyone. You just have to believe me, and decide that it doesn't matter what anyone else thinks."

Courtney bit her lip, feeling another tear trickle down her cheek. "It's not that easy."

He laughed without smiling. "You don't have to tell me that. I'm constantly bombarded with all this shit people say and even when it's not true, it's still hard. It always bugs me that somebody out there might believe it, but there's nothing I can do about them. I can only control me and how I react. I have to keep on living my life."

He rubbed his forehead tensely. "Look, Courtney, I want to protect you from all this, and I know I've done a crappy job so far, but I am trying. Every day I'm learning, and I can make you happy if you give me a chance."

His words hit home. She knew he was right, but she still didn't feel right about it all. Courtney stood slowly, brushing the sand off her legs. He followed her cue and rose to his feet abruptly, as though he expected her to sprint off and wanted to be ready for the chase.

"Justin, everything you're saying makes perfect sense, but this just isn't me. I don't shop on Rodeo Drive or go to movie premieres or show up in magazines. I'm a lawyer, and I've always been a low-key, confident person. Now I'm a total spaz. I yelled at you yesterday when you'd tried to do something nice for me and today I'm freaking out over crap you can't control. I should be with someone who brings out the best in me, not someone who turns me into a jealous nut just by doing his job."

She paused. "And if I'm being completely honest, I don't like sharing you, even with costars. I know it's stupid, but I don't like you kissing other women in movies."

He sighed, taking his time to answer. "Keith told me I could never have a serious relationship with any non-actor for that exact reason, because you'd just never understand what it's like to film that shit unless you've been through it."

Courtney shrugged. "Keith's a smart guy."

"No, he isn't. Keith's a tool. Think of it this way, Courtney. Whether or not you're dating me, I'm going to be acting with other women, touching them, kissing them, whatever, during the day, but if you don't screw this up, then I'll still get to come home to you at night. Even if we're not together, you're going to see me with other women, but if you stick with me, you don't have to share me with anyone when I'm off duty."

She had to appreciate his logic. "That's not exactly ideal," she pointed out.

He wiped the tear off her face and took both of her hands in his. "Courtney, I'm sorry you have to deal with all that because of me. I realize it's asking a lot for you to just ignore it, but I think it'll be worth it. We are worth it."

Courtney shifted her feet in the sand uncomfortably, turning slightly to see that more people nearby were watching now. No one seemed eager to interrupt, but they were definitely accruing an audience. "You shouldn't have taken off your sunglasses," she mumbled. "Let's just go."

But Justin stood firm. "I don't care if people are watching, Courtney, I just want you to hear what I'm saying. I love you, Courtney, and only you. I don't want to be with anyone else, and I'm not going to." He kissed her forehead gently. As soon as his eyes broke away from hers, she dropped her head.

"Look at me, Courtney. Just focus on me, on us."

She complied, feeling a deep ache in her chest at the saddened expression on his face. "I already have such strong feelings for you, and that's only going to grow. It's not going to get any easier down the road, Justin."

"That's not true. It is going to get easier because we're both in the same town now. We're not hiding anymore. The more we're together, the less speculation there will be and the press will just give up on the rumor mill."

"And what about when you're away shooting?"

"You can come with me."

She snorted. "Oh, right, since I'm unemployed."

"Courtney," he began.

"No, Justin. It's not just Keith betting against us. This sort of relationship never works out. It's a fact. We're just prolonging the inevitable."

"It does too work out. We will," he insisted, his tone serious.

"You don't know that," she murmured, letting her forehead press against his.

"I do, Courtney. Because it's what we both want, and you and

I are the only ones who have any say in this." He paused. "Just be with me Courtney. Please."

She tried to think of another argument, another way to at least make him understand how hard she knew it was going to be, but she couldn't find the words. She knew she couldn't fight him and realized she never had any intention of leaving him, or at least that she never could have followed through with it.

Courtney felt herself focusing on his fingers, still entwined with hers, his damp forehead pressing against her own, and his breath falling evenly against the base of her throat. She felt more tears building in her eyes, but before she could wipe them away, Justin's lips were pressed gently first against one eyelid, then the next.

"I love you," she breathed.

"I love you too." Justin squeezed her hands tighter and kissed her, soft and slowly.

Courtney kissed him back, losing herself in the warmth of his lips.

When the kiss ended, Justin squeezed her hands again. She glanced up at him, immediately smiling at the boldness of his eyes.

"We have an audience," he whispered, and Courtney froze, now acutely self-conscious. She'd never had any complaints about her kissing skills, but she'd also never actually seen herself do it, and now, apparently, dozens of random people, many with cameras, had watched her in the act.

"I don't think I can run now," she mumbled, her legs still wobbly from the kiss.

He laughed. "Then don't. We'll walk," he said, flipping his dark glasses back over his eyes and wrapping his arm around her, slowly guiding her back onto the boardwalk and towards the house.

LATER THAT NIGHT, they were hanging out by the pool, drinking wine and flipping through a stack of scripts Marty had sent over, when Courtney casually apologized for freaking out on the beach earlier.

Justin shrugged, not really wanting to get into it with Keith sitting right with them. "You're a chick. That sort of behavior is expected."

She swatted his bicep and glared playfully as she sipped her wine. "Seriously, though," she began after she swallowed, "you don't think Jamie will be mad?"

Keith set down the paper he was reading and turned to Justin, his eyes conveying a certain level of annoyance. "What exactly happened on the beach today?"

"I stole a magazine," Justin quickly replied, not wanting to throw Courtney under the bus.

"No, he didn't. I saw a magazine with some iffy photos and got sort of upset."

"It was just a little spat," Justin clarified.

"So you were arguing on a public beach? Jesus, tell me you didn't hit her," Keith said.

"Not cool, dude," Justin replied quickly.

"It wasn't really that type of a fight," Courtney clarified. "It was more me crying and then us making out."

Keith massaged the corners of his eyebrows the way he always did when stressed. "I'm getting more wine," he mumbled, heading inside.

Justin watched Keith, then turned to Courtney. "Hey, so you had fun hanging out with Andi a while back, right?"

Courtney nodded. "You mean when you forced her to come explain to me that you weren't sleeping with her?"

Justin nodded. "I thought you might want to go shopping

with her for the premiere and awards show. She'd asked me a while back if you might be interested, but I didn't know if you'd feel comfortable. It seems like it might be a good idea, though, you know, for you to have more friends who are in the public eye."

Courtney smiled. "So you want Andi to talk some sense into me?"

He shrugged, tracing his finger across the delicate skin along her collar bone. "I'd hate for you to get starstruck at the awards show and leave me for Leonardo DiCaprio."

Her eyes widened. "You think we'll see Leo?"

Justin contemplated throwing her in the pool, but instead settled for a playful swat, followed by a kiss.

She sighed. "Am I supposed to call Andi?"

He nodded, then tapped away on his phone. "Here, I just asked her to call you."

"I still think you're more likely than I am to be starstruck at the awards show," she said, smiling.

He laughed, then considered her words and agreed. "Why is that? How do you not think it is the coolest thing ever to get to meet all these people?"

She glanced down at her bare feet, her freshly polished toes wiggling in the sunlight, enjoying the fresh air of the oddly warm winter day. "They're just people," she reminded him.

He stood to go inside. "Yeah, people who have been in awesome movies with the greatest directors and producers ever and who've done killer stunts."

Courtney laughed, shaking her head. "Your enthusiasm for the job is nauseating. Now let me have some space before my forced playdate with Andi."

Justin was psyched the day of the premiere. *Days End* had a huge fan base, the type of fans that go way overboard, pitching tents and camping outside the theater where the premiere was scheduled. Most of the wackiest, truly overzealous fans gravitated more towards Brad and Julie, but Justin had his fair share of stalker-types that he expected to see at the premiere. Courtney arrived early in the day, her hair and nails already done, and as soon as she stepped into the long turquoise dress, Justin knew she was going to be a hit that night.

To Justin's relief, Courtney seemed excited, not nervous. As soon as they arrived at the theater, he and Andi spent about an hour posing for photos, signing autographs, and conducting interviews. Courtney stood off to the side, politely smiling whenever anyone looked her direction, and talking with the other cast members and their dates when there was time.

One photographer requested a shot of Justin with Courtney, and he practically had to drag her onto the red carpet to pose. As soon as that photographer had gotten his shot, Justin pulled her in for a kiss, then realized several more cameras were snapping away. He grinned, picturing Courtney's cute panicked expression when she figured out they'd been captured on camera. The rest of the night was a blast, from the movie, to the after party, to the private after-after party Justin and Courtney held in the pool once they got home, even though it was already the middle of the night.

Shivering from the cold air as she stepped out of the water, Courtney curled up in Justin's arms, letting him drape a towel around them both. They made their way into the house, quietly, and changed into warmer clothes. Still buzzing from all the excitement, they settled on the couch together instead of heading up to bed. Justin decided now was a good a time as any to share his news.

"I have a surprise," he announced.

Courtney smiled sleepily. "I think I've already had enough excitement for one day."

"Well, that's fine. Because we wouldn't leave today. I figured we'd go in two or three weeks."

"Go where?"

"I don't know. Maybe St. Thomas?"

"You're going to St. Thomas in a few weeks?"

"No, sleepy. You and I are going to St. Thomas together. Unless you'd prefer a different island."

Courtney stared back skeptically than grinned. "Um, no I'm fine with that. What's the occasion?"

He shrugged. "Vacation." Another purpose for the trip had casually crossed his mind, but for now, that was honest enough. "Let me know what dates work for you and I'll book it."

She laughed. "I'm pretty much free whenever given the current job situation."

"You don't know, that might all change by then," he replied mysteriously.

Courtney sat abruptly and turned to face him. "What did I do to deserve you?"

Justin frowned. "You mean, like specifically? Because I can think of a few tricks you do that make you pretty deserving, like that one move with your tongue..." His voice trailed off as she playfully punched his arm.

"You're getting soft," she teased, squeezing his muscle. She was right, actually, he had lost about five pounds of muscle since he'd stopped training like crazy and returned to his normal, non-filming workout routine.

"Seriously, though," she continued. "Movie premieres, midnight swims in your private pools, a BMW, and now this. You spoil me! And you could have any girl you want. You are so out of my league. Why do you like me?"

Justin gently traced his thumb along her jaw bone. "Courtney, from the moment I met you I've known you were the one out of my league. You're always thinking about other people, you're smart, you're confident, and you aren't obsessed with what people think about you. You like sports, you're laid back and you have a sense of humor. Not to mention you are the most beautiful woman ever to set foot in L.A."

Courtney smiled and snuggled closer to him. "I love you," she mumbled, her eyelids fluttering and then closing.

17

After another week of frustrating and unsuccessful job hunting, Courtney was ready for the weekend. Justin was taking her on some surprise date Friday morning. He wouldn't tell her where they were going, but he said to dress casually. She was pretty sure he couldn't top the last weekend, especially with the Monday night premiere capping it off, but he certainly seemed determined to try.

She watched for him to arrive, knowing he wouldn't want to get out of the car if he could avoid it, and hurried out to meet him. He stepped out, glancing around himself, and opened her door, kissing her briefly on the cheek.

"Am I dressed appropriately?" she asked. She had ultimately decided on jeans and a thin baby blue sweater.

He quickly scanned her and then nodded. "And you look gorgeous, as always." He shut her door after her and then climbed into the Audi. "The sweater really brings out the blue in your eyes," he commented, smiling.

Courtney narrowed her eyes, still trying to guess what he might have planned for her. His clothes didn't really give anything away. He had on dark jeans with a thick brown belt, a long sleeved cream-colored shirt, a thin pale brown leather jacket she'd never seen before, and a grey hat. He definitely looked trendy, but that could just mean they were going somewhere public. She glanced down and noticed there were two Starbucks cups in the drink holder.

"Thanks," she said sweetly, taking a sip of one.

"Don't spill," he teased. "I'm still enjoying that new car smell."

She laughed, glancing in the backseat. "Then you might want to store your gym bag elsewhere."

"Hey, I smell like roses when I sweat," he retorted.

"So if you won't tell me where we're going, will you at least tell me what we're doing?"

He glanced over at her, probably trying to decide whether or not to give her any hints. "We're going to be working."

Courtney hadn't expected that response. "My kind of work or yours?"

Justin's smile widened. "Neither. Manual labor."

They talked for another fifteen minutes before Justin stopped the car in an unfamiliar parking lot.

"Okay, where are we?" Courtney looked around and still had no clue.

"Our job for the day," he replied, retrieving his sunglasses from their storage case above the rearview mirror and positioning them on his face. He turned to her. "They're expecting us, so there might be cameras," he warned.

She rolled her eyes, knowing really what he meant was that they were expecting him. Still, she appreciated the warning. She followed their normal routine, with him stepping out of the car first and walking around to escort her out. Ever since the fateful day with her lip injury, Justin was overprotective.

Courtney accepted his hand as he guided her out of the car and then leaned into the crook of his shoulder as he wrapped his arm around her, kissing her on the head. "Is your jacket new?"

He nodded.

"When do you have time to do all this shopping?".

"I didn't. It's one of David's new designs."

As they stepped closer to the building, they were greeted by cameras, women, and children.

Justin paused and smiled directly at the cameras, calmly flashing his dimples like he was greeting his own grandma and not a dozen flashing lights, all the while Courtney held her breath, trying to keep smiling without passing out. Finally, Courtney felt Justin nudge her along and he waved briefly at the cameras before opening the door for her.

As soon as they entered, Courtney's lips naturally parted into a smile. Waiting for them just inside the building were maybe thirty small children, at least a dozen teens, and several adult women. The kids immediately rushed up, crowding around Justin and seeking autographs. Courtney stepped back, watching as he hugged the kids, posed for photos with them, and chatted them up while signing autographs. Courtney found herself laughing, watching the teenage girls fidget in the back of the room, knowing they were all anxiously awaiting their turn to meet the heartthrob.

She didn't recognize the place, but it appeared to be a community center or group shelter of some sort.

Courtney turned quickly as she felt a gentle tap on her shoulder. A tall, middle-aged brunette was facing her.

"You must be Courtney," the woman said. "I'm April Dunfee. I run this shelter."

Courtney smiled warmly and shook April's hand. "Nice to meet you. It looks like you've done a great job here," she replied sincerely.

April shrugged. "Well, mostly thanks to Justin."

Courtney frowned. "What do you mean?"

"Oh, you know, just that his donation really made a differ-ence, and all the publicity we got from that day where he came with his friends to paint the place and drop off all the toys. And that contest he had on Twitter. I couldn't believe how much those women were willing to pay just for a chance to go on a date with him!" April laughed, then froze, covering her mouth tentatively as though she might have offended Courtney. "Not that I don't think it would be worth it. You are definitely a lucky lady."

Courtney was now thoroughly confused. She had never heard of his contest, and, not that she read all of Justin's tweets, but this seemed like the sort of thing he might have bothered to mention to her. She jumped as she felt a hand on her back.

Justin was grinning beside her. "Want a tour?"

As soon as they were out of earshot, she began pressing him for details. "Why didn't you tell me about any of this? How long have you been involved with all this? Who did you end up dating on Twitter?"

"Actually, I'm surprised you didn't hear about that one." he said with a laugh. "A while back, I guess almost a year now, David had asked Keith and I if we could get together some other guys to help do some construction work on this place. They'd had some sort of financial issue and hadn't been able to get everything finished, but they were still supposed to be up and operating months ago. So, we thought it would be cool and we came up a few times and did some work, and then we chipped in and bought some furniture and toys and that sort of thing. They still needed a good chunk of money to get up and running, though, you know, to cover all the operating expenses, so Keith came up with this idea to set up an auction where ladies could donate money to buy raffle tickets and the winner got a dinner date with me."

Courtney couldn't stop smiling now.

"Anyway, I hope you're not mad at me, but when I told you I was going out with the guys a couple of weeks ago, I actually went on a date with a Seattle girl named Jessica."

Now Courtney was giggling. "Jessica?" she repeated.

He nodded. "Nice girl. Twenty-two years old, college student."

"I didn't sleep with her or anything. Just a peck on the cheek after dinner."

Courtney shook her head. "I wasn't worried about you sleeping with her. How much money did you raise?"

His grin widened even further now. "Close to two hundred."

Her jaw dropped. "Two hundred what? Two hundred thousand?

He nodded, beaming.

"People paid two hundred thousand dollars just to take you to dinner? But your table manners suck! And you eat like a pig!"

He laughed. "Well, technically I paid for dinner. I covered Jessica's travel expenses, too."

She still couldn't believe it. "This is amazing, Justin. You have done such a wonderful thing here."

He nodded proudly. "I had a hunch that you'd like it. I considered mentioning it before, but I wasn't sure if you'd like me supporting the competition back when you were working for..." his voice trailed off in lieu of referencing her old job, which she appreciated.

Justin gave her a quick tour of the different areas, then pulled her off to the side of the hall before they went back into the main room. "There's something else, actually."

He paused, and she sensed he was nervous. "I know you said you wanted me to butt out of your job hunt, but they are hiring, if you're interested. April has a business background and can handle the day to day management, but she needs legal counsel to help out, and the quotes they got from the large firms to keep them on retainer were ridiculous. It would be pretty comparable pay to your old job, and mostly full time, but with more flexible hours. April said you could take off as much time as you needed if you ever wanted to, say, travel with your hunky boyfriend or visit him when he's filming on location."

Courtney threw her arms around him, jumping into the hug with more enthusiasm than she had intended. He kissed her, then placed her back on the floor, still grinning.

"So you're not mad that I asked about the job even after you told me not to?"

She squeezed his hand. "How could I be mad at the sweetest, most wonderful man alive?"

He kissed her again, and then motioned to the door. "Shall we?"

She nodded, and they returned to the main room. Justin headed to the gym to play basketball with the kids, and Courtney lingered with April discussing more specifics of the job.

By the end of the day, Courtney was exhausted, but gainfully employed, and more in love with Justin than ever.

THREE WEEKS LATER, Justin scanned his room one last time for anything he forgot to pack. Their flight didn't leave for four more hours, but he was picking up Courtney first and didn't want to get stuck in traffic.

Satisfied that there was nothing else he'd need for a week in St. Thomas, Justin reached into the back of the top dresser drawer and retrieved the small box. Just touching it made him nervous, more nervous than the first time he was called in to read for a part in front of the director, producer, and several other big honchos. He opened the box slowly, his breath catching in his throat as soon as the light hit the stone. He smiled, knowing he'd made the right call. Everything about it screamed Courtney, from the platinum band to the simple but gorgeous design, and, of course, the two carat round-cut diamond. Well, okay, maybe she'd have picked a smaller center stone herself, but Justin liked this one. He didn't want anyone to be unclear about her availability.

"Dude," Keith growled, startling Justin. "How are you planning on getting that through security? You can't just pack that in your suitcase, and she's sure as shit going to notice if you try to wear it."

Justin laughed at the thought of the tiny little band fitting on even his pinkie. He had, actually, considered this dilemma. "After we check our bags, I'll have her go on through security first, so we don't attract as much attention. We've done that before."

"What if she waits for you right on the other side?"

"I'll ask her to go buy something at one of the newsstands."

"And what if news gets out about you toting a big old rock around before you actually do the deed?"

He shook his head. "No chance of it. I'll ask her tonight."

Keith sat on the bed beside Justin. "You know Tara's going to kill me. We've been together twice as long as you two."

Justin laughed, then wedged the box into the middle pocket of the bag he would strap across his chest, keeping it as close to him as possible.

"You're sure you aren't rushing into this?" Keith asked tentatively.

"I'm not going to change my mind," he finally replied. "I'm sure she's the one, so there's no point in waiting."

Keith nodded skeptically. "But then there's also no urgency, right?"

Justin shrugged, remembering the day on the beach when Courtney had freaked out about the magnitude of dating a celebrity. "So we'll have a long engagement," he replied. "I just want Courtney to know I'm serious, to know I'm in this for the long haul."

"Don't you think she knows that already?"

"No. I think she still assumes I'm eventually going to cheat on her, and so she's still holding back because she doesn't want to get hurt."

"You sure she'll say yes?"

Justin laughed and shook his head. "She didn't last time."

"Last time?"

"I sorta asked her once before."

Now Keith laughed. "Dude, that's pathetic. She seriously rejected your ass?"

"Well, she didn't really answer. I don't think she thought I was serious."

"Were you?" Keith's eyes were full of disbelief.

Justin shrugged again. "I hadn't exactly planned to ask her, but once I did it seemed like a good idea. If she'd said yes then that would've been cool."

Keith patted Justin's leg and then stood up. "Well, I think she's good for you, man. Too good, probably, but if you can convince her to say yes, you guys might actually make it. I have to admit you do pretty well together." He started out of the room, then paused. "Does this mean I'm going to be homeless soon?"

Justin frowned and shook his head. "No, dude, this is your place, too."

Keith rolled his eyes and laughed. "Yeah, well maybe you should run that by the little woman after you seal the deal."

Justin felt himself grinning at his best friend.

Later, his plan to smuggle the ring past security worked

seamlessly, Courtney clearly not suspecting anything out of the ordinary at the airport. He held her hand as they waited to board the plane, then pulled out his phone.

Justin quickly tapped out one last Tweet before the flight: "Wish me luck everybody! Here's hoping I've got some good news to share tomorrow!"

Then he turned his phone off, kissed Courtney firmly on the lips, and reached for her hand.

She smiled, her gorgeous eyes sparkling, and said, "I love you."

"I love you too," he whispered back and kissed her on the forehead.

The End

PRAISE FOR LIZA MALLOY

Reviews of *For Love and Italian:*

"A fun, lighthearted and steamy romance, *For Love and Italian* is sweet, romantic, and naughty in the best ways. I was entertained the entire time and was quite sad when it was over. Liza Malloy knows how to write addictive and satisfyingly charming romance stories that will surely give you plenty of swoons and feels...I can't wait to see what she writes next."
- Karen Jo Custodio, Book Blogger.
www.SincerelyKarenJo.com

"Perfect summer read! Great writing & great characters! Can't wait for more books from this author!"
- Amazon Customer Review

Praise for *Forbidden Ink*:
"Get comfortable, you won't be able to put the book down!"
- Amazon Customer Review

Praise for *Sixty Days for Love*:
"A perfect late-at-night after the kids are in bed escape. The heroine is fun and likeable and the hero is sexy and loveable. What more could you want?"
- Verified Amazon Review

"This was such an enjoyable read, I had a hard time putting this book down. It has the perfect blend of romance, humor, and character development!"

- Verified Amazon Review

Praise for *The Brothers' Band*:
"Liza Malloy weaves together music, great works of literature, family relationships, and romantic relationships into this page turner."
- Verified Amazon Review

"Fun romance book, I couldn't put it down! Steamy love scenes and a great back story."
- Verified Amazon Review

Praise for *Legacy: The Awakening*:
"I was surprised by how much I enjoyed this (which was immensely)! It was so easy to get lost in the story and the characters. It was hard to put it down, and I am looking forward to reading more by this author and more in this series. I would definitely recommend this book. It is a super fun read!"
- Verified Amazon Review

ACKNOWLEDGMENTS

Every time I write a book, I'm filled with gratitude for so many people. This time is no different. I owe the most appreciation to my usual team- my editor Kimberly and my cover artist JD Book Designs. This book went through many versions and I'm grateful for every round of editing. Similarly, the vision for the cover for this series changed multiple times, and I appreciate the effort it took to create so many covers from scratch.

I wrote the original draft of *Hollywood Endings* roughly a decade ago. I like to think I'm a much better writer today than I was ten years ago, and much like me, this book has also grown and improved. So many beta readers and critique partners poured over early drafts, and I am so thankful for all of the input you have all given me over the years. Stacey, you especially gave me some helpful criticism on this one!

I am also extremely grateful to my loyal readers. This has been a hard year for everyone. I know you have limitations on your money and your time and it means a lot to me when you spend both on my books. I am so flattered by every email, message, or review sharing praise or excitement about my book, but I also appreciate your honesty when you offer a less than idyllic review. YOU- the readers, bloggers, and reviewers breathe new life into my books every time you read. Thank you!

ABOUT THE AUTHOR

Liza Malloy writes contemporary romance, women's fiction, new adult romance, and fantasy. She's a sucker for alpha males, bad boys, dimples, and muscles, and she can't resist a man in uniform. Liza loves creating worlds where her heroine discovers her own strength and finds her Happily Ever After. When Liza isn't reading or writing torrid love stories, she's a practicing attorney. Her other passions include gummy bears, jelly beans, and the occasional marathon. She lives in the Midwest with her four daughters and her own Prince Charming. Hollywood Endings is her sixth published novel. Her books are available in paperback and ebook, and can be found on Amazon, iBooks, Barnes & Noble, Kobo, Google Play, and more!

Visit her website at www.LizaMalloy.com

Join her email list for access to exclusive bonus content at http://bit.ly/34FrD71

ALSO BY LIZA MALLOY

Legacy: The Awakening

Her love would undo his legacy. His dark secret could destroy her.

College student Jessica craves a stable, ordinary life. But when she meets the alluring and irresistible Aiden, her life takes a thrilling turn. Jessica knows there's something different about Aiden, but she's shocked when she learns his secret. The further Jessica delves into Aiden's world, the more consumed she becomes with him.

Heir to the throne of a secret kingdom of supernatural beings, Aiden yearns to fulfill his destiny. But from their first encounter, Jessica captivates Aiden. Aiden is certain that Jessica is his only chance at true happiness. But Aiden can't deny that his presence in Jessica's life threatens to destroy the very things he loves about Jessica—her generosity, compassion and innocence.

As Jessica finds her life filling with peril she never imagined, she must decide how much she's willing to risk for love. And Aiden must choose whether to embrace his legacy or follow his heart.

Intensely compelling and powerfully gripping, *The Awakening* is the seductive first installment to the Legacy trilogy, an unforgettable, epic love story.

Click here to purchase *Legacy: The Awakening*

***

The Brothers' Band

Two brothers, one band, one woman...what could possibly go wrong?

Lily Mitchell vowed never to date another musician, but Dylan Parker is nothing like the stereotype. Sure, he's mysterious and sexy, with a flashy car and serious bedroom skills, but he's also smart, hardworking, and humble. He shares Lily's passion for classic literature and constantly surprises her with romantic gestures. Their steamy relationship moves at whirlwind pace, and Lily has never been happier.

It's all so perfect that at first, Lily wills herself to ignore the emerging red flags. As her worries about Dylan increase, she finds friendship and comfort in his brother and bandmate, Thomas. But Lily soon discovers that as much as Thomas cares for his brother, he's also fallen hard for her.

As Dylan spirals further out of control, Lily must decide what she really wants, and whom she is willing to hurt.

Click here to purchase The Brothers' Band

* * *

Sixty Days for Love

She's on the clock to win him back!

Chelsea Craig's life is perfect, until her husband David runs off with his paralegal. During the mandatory sixty-day waiting period before the divorce is finalized, Chelsea decides to transform herself into a woman David can't resist. Revamping her life isn't easy, though, and Chelsea lands in one embarrassing predicament after another. Luckily, Nick, a smoldering local cop, happily rushes to her rescue. Convinced that a fling with Nick couldn't hurt, Chelsea embraces the sizzling chemistry they share. But when the separation period draws to a close, Chelsea begins to question whether she's been working all this time to salvage a relationship with the wrong man.

Available for purchase through Amazon, Barnes & Noble, Apple Books and Kobo.

Click here to purchase Sixty Days for Love

* * *

For Love and Italian

An education in amore? Yes, please, Professore

Undergrad Bridget is no stranger to romantic advances from men. But when she meets Owen, an instant friendship forms, even though Owen happens to be Bridget's Italian teacher. Neither of them intends to cross that line, but once they do, they can't deny the passion and chemistry between them. Aware that their tryst is taboo, they keep their relationship clandestine. But like all juicy secrets, this one doesn't stay hidden for long. And once it's out, Owen and Bridget must decide what they're willing to risk in the name of love.

Available for purchase through Amazon, Barnes & Noble, Apple Books and Kobo.

Click here to purchase For Love and Italian

* * *

Forbidden Ink

Loving the bad boy never felt so good!

Ashley Kensington has it all—affluence, status, and the perfect boyfriend. Sheltered by her exclusive southern island community and overprotective father and brothers, Ashley has never strayed from the path her parents chose for her.

Until now.

When Adam Bricker rolls into town with no money, no family, and no ambition for the future, there's no reason that Ashley Kensington should be attracted to him; yet she is. Adam doesn't mind that the locals can't see past his collection of tattoos and his New England accent. Everyone assumes Adam isn't good enough for Ashley, but he's certain he can make her happy and he's ready to fight for what he wants.

For a while, Ashley believes nothing can shatter their epic romance. But when the unexpected happens, Adam is forced to accept that maybe everyone else was right about him from the start.

Available for purchase through Amazon, Barnes & Noble, Apple Books and Kobo.

Click here to purchase Forbidden Ink

* * *

www.ingramcontent.com/pod-product-compliance
Lightning Source LLC
Chambersburg PA
CBHW051646180726

48284CB00006B/1884